Revenge

Henry Scott

ACKNOWLEDGMENTS

Published by Pretty Lake Publishing House

For any inquiries regarding this book, please email:
henryscott@henryscottauthor.com

As Always for Tracy

OTHER TITLES BY

HENRY SCOTT

THE REDEMPTION SERIES

REVENGE
REGRET
RETURN
REVEALED
RECKONING
REMEMBER

STAND ALONE NOVELS

THE MANDELA AFFECTION

MONSTYR

REVENGE

REVENGE

Prologue

His hand shook as he slipped his note and a thumb drive into Mary's lingerie drawer. They were his insurance policy if things went sideways this morning— which was a distinct possibility. A duplicate file was locked up miles away as additional protection. He'd been extremely cautious when he downloaded the video, so Dolan shouldn't suspect a thing, but he was still anxious.

He should've confessed long ago. But his wife thought he was a good man. Everyone did. They were mistaken— he was corrupt, unfaithful, and a coward. He could change that this morning. But first, he wanted one more piece of evidence against Dolan.

The dresser drawer closed with a thud.

The mass of covers shifted, but Mary did not wake. He resisted the urge to brush the lock of blonde hair from her cheek. After all these years, her beautiful face still made his heart skip a beat.

He'd tell her tonight once the kids were in bed. Together they could come up with a plan, whether it was to turn the evidence over to the police, or the mob, or to run and hide. But any plan hinged on him finding the murder weapon while the office was empty.

Thunder rumbled in the distance, shaking the house. The forecasted thunderstorm would arrive soon. He checked his watch. 7:30 am. Damn. It was later than he planned. He needed to be long gone before the office cleaning crew showed up and noted his presence. It was the little details that would get him killed.

Under a green-grey sky, he drove along the lonely two-lane road past budding fields of corn rustling in the wind.

Lost in thought, he didn't notice a large snapping turtle creep off the gravel shoulder until the last second. He jerked the steering wheel to the side, narrowly missing it. Shaken, he brought his SUV to a stop twenty yards past the creature. He'd always had a soft spot for turtles, even keeping one as a pet when he was a boy— he'd see it safely across the road.

He walked back down the highway but kept his distance, so he didn't alarm the slow-moving reptile. Long claws scrapped on the asphalt, propelling it forward inch by inch.

Before the turtle could reach the other side of the road, a large V8 engine growled in the distance, its off-road tires hummed loudly. A big black pickup truck crested the rise on the desolate road.

He waved his hands above his head to get the driver's attention.

The vehicle accelerated.

Frantically, he motioned for the truck to move to the far side of the road, but it didn't deviate from its course. The reptile crawled forward, unaware of its impending doom. He jumped out of the way at the last second. The front bumper barely missed him, but a large front tire crushed the turtle.

The cracking of the shell rang in his ear like a bell.

The turtle's long neck lay slumped on the black asphalt. A trickle of blood ran from its pointed beak. A murderous red haze threatened to consume him.

"Motherfucker!"

The driver slammed on the brakes and screeched to a stop before reversing towards him.

A man with long brown hair and a coarse goatee dropped to the ground. "You have a problem, asshole?"

"Me— I'm an asshole? You just ran over that poor turtle!" He pointed to the broken animal.

Sneering, the guy stalked forward, his chest puffed out. A deep jagged scar ran down the left side of his face, and the stench of alcohol and sour sweat hung over him like a cloud. Interesting. If Dolan were on to him, would he have sent this guy to eliminate him?

No. Dolan wouldn't.

The man wore a leather vest with motorcycle club patches across the front. He was a biker, not a professional killer. The thug cocked a fist back to deliver a giant haymaker.

He really shouldn't get pulled into a stupid fight; he didn't have the time. But this idiot needed to be taught a lesson, and he was sick of being a coward. He ducked under the punch and landed a quick jab to the biker's chin. He followed it up with a right to the nose. The man's head rocked back, and blood spilled down his face.

The biker roared in anger and let loose a desperate left hook. He easily sidestepped the punch and slammed his fist into the man's jaw. He fell to the ground hard.

Looming over him, he said, "It's over. Stay down."

"Fuck you!"

The thug tried to get back up, so he punched him in the ear. The man crashed to the asphalt, coughing up blood and mucus. There was no debate, it was over now. Hastily, he walked to his car, but an itch grew between his shoulder blades. He glanced back. The biker stumbled to his feet as he reached inside his vest for something. Shit! That couldn't be good.

He broke into a run.

"Stop, asshole!" the guy shouted.

He continued to run.

A few feet from his vehicle, a bullet whizzed by his head. His insides turned to ice. He wanted to claw open the door but knew he'd never get inside in time.

"Not so tough now, are you?" the man laughed. "Turn around."

He did as he was told, realizing he'd been terribly wrong. This man was a killer. Sweat trickled down the back of his neck. He wanted to wipe at it but kept his hands in front of him, the fingers outstretched. A droplet ran down his back and soaked into a fold in his shirt.

"You don't need to do this. I can pay you," he pleaded.

"I've already been paid. Besides, now this is personal." Sneering, the thug stumbled forward, the gun still pointed at him.

Damn it. He prayed he could somehow survive this encounter, gather up his family, and run far away.

The thug stopped in front of him while thunder boomed in the distance, and lightning scarred the sky. Short shallow breaths pushed through his lips as adrenalin poured into his bloodstream. The thug's index finger twitched on the trigger.

Shifting from foot to foot, a desperate plan came to him. He leaned subtlety towards the gun. His hand was ten inches from the barrel.

The thunder crashed again. With exaggeration, he shifted his gaze over to the lightning strike. The thug followed his misdirection. He pushed off his back foot and made a grab for the gun. But he was too slow. The biker squeezed the trigger.

The bullet slammed into his chest.

He remained standing for a second before his body toppled over like a marionette whose strings had been cut. The pain was incredible. It felt like a jackhammer had punched a hole through his heart. He tried to sit up but couldn't. He felt cold. Very cold.

He knew then, he would never see Mary again. He wouldn't see the kids grow up. It was over. The only thing he could hope for now was that his best friend, Jake, would put the puzzle pieces together and protect his family from these murderers.

Putting the gun back in its holster, the man kicked him hard in the ribs with his dirty boot, then in his face. He didn't feel it. His breathing was ragged and weak.

The smell of death and gunpowder hung in the air. The biker knelt down next to him and searched his pockets but didn't take anything— not until the thug's eyes fell on the antique watch strapped to his wrist. The biker tossed his own cheap watch into the nearby field.

The storm drew closer. Lightning ripped across the sky. A drop of rain pelted the road, followed by another and then another. His world grew dim. A low deathly rattle escaped his lips.

The last thing he saw before his soul moved on to a better place was the killer admiring the antique watch on his murderous wrist. Covering the man's arm was a skeletal tattoo— a Devil's Hand.

Chapter 1

Jake Bryant stood at Tom's grave, trying to imagine a world without his best friend. He couldn't, not for a second; he would prefer Hell. Like a blazing inferno, his anger threatened to consume him. But he held it at bay, for now.

The cemetery was empty except for Jake. Yesterday's mourners had returned to their normal lives. Mary and the kids would be home wallowing in their misery— a typical day not an option for them. Yet instead of trying to comfort them, Jake had found himself here. He didn't recall the decision or even the trip, but he knew the reason. Tom shouldn't be alone while he lay in the cold damp earth.

Dirt had replaced the open hole. Jake could picture the casket's polished surface, no longer pristine but dented by rock and clay when the backhoe filled in the void. Soon, grass would cover the cracked soil, and his friend would be nothing but a memory. Yet the person responsible for his death still walked the streets. Jake couldn't let that continue— the killer would pay for his crime. He'd made that promise to Tom, and Jake would die before he broke it.

The working theory was Tom's death was a road rage incident gone horribly wrong. At least that was what the police believed. If that was the case, they were screwed. A crime with no motive, suspect, or witnesses would be impossible to solve; Jake knew that from experience. In this small town, the investigation would go cold without his help. Besides, who else would be more motivated to get justice for Tom? No one. Certainly, not the fat lazy detective in charge of the investigation.

Closing his eyes, Jake took several deep breaths and pinched the bridge of his nose to regain control of his emotions. He replaced his evil thoughts with images of the first time he met Tom. They'd played little league baseball together. Their team was terrible, but it didn't matter. They were learning the game and having fun. Everyone understood that except Jake's alcoholic father, who screamed at Jake every time he touched the ball. It was his lame attempt at parenting. It gave Jake a stomachache before every game. The other kids pitied Jake but kept their distance for fear his dad would turn on them too. But not Tom, he did what little a kid could do. He committed stupid errors just to make Jake look good by comparison.

For the last game of the season, the coach put Jake at first base. With runners in position, Jake let an easy grounder go between his legs, and the other team took the lead. Jake's dad had lost his shit. His mother tried to calm him down, but he was too drunk, so three large dads convinced him to shut up or leave the diamond. Jake's dad decided to shut up, but Jake knew he would pay for his embarrassment tonight with a beating. He wanted to throw up.

However, in the final inning, their team rallied and got runners in scoring position. The fate of the game fell on Tom. If he could get a hit, their team would win. No problem, Tom was a decent slugger, and the opposing team's pitcher looked tired. Tom took a practice swing as he cast a glance at Jake's still angry dad. Wincing, he grabbed his right arm and sat back down, telling the coach he pulled a muscle and couldn't bat.

So with Jake on-deck, it was up to him. He nervously approached the plate, avoiding his father's stare. The first pitch came right down the middle, and Jake miraculously nailed it over the centerfielder's head to win the game. His teammates carried him off the field while the fans cheered. To celebrate, Jake's dad went to the bar, and Jake got a peaceful trip to the ice cream parlor with his team.

As they ate their cherry-dipped cones, Jake noticed Tom ate his with his injured arm without a glimmer of pain. Jake called him out on his fakery, and Tom's only response was a smile. It was that day that their life-long friendship took root. Tom could've won the big game with all its childhood glory, but he'd quickly given that up to save Jake a night of torment.

By the next summer, Jake's parents were divorced, and his dad had moved to Chicago. Their circle grew by two more friends, but Jake and Tom were always the closest. And when Jake moved to Chicago after graduation to work for his dad against everyone's advice, Tom was the one who remained in weekly contact with phone calls and the occasional visit. He'd helped Jake through the loss of his job, a divorce, and a bout of alcoholism. Tom had literally saved Jake's life more than once, and then Jake hadn't been there for Tom when he'd needed Jake the most.

A cool breeze stirred Jake from his reverie. It cut through his shirt like a knife, but he remained on the cemetery's gently sloping hills. He wanted more time with Tom. Jake tried to conjure up another memory if only to keep his friend alive for a few more minutes, when a big hand grabbed him by the collar, nearly lifting him off his feet.

A deep voice growled, "What are you doing here?"

Chapter 2

Jake fought to regain his balance. "You're an asshole!"

"Seriously, what the hell are you doing here?" Bobby Andollini asked again.

"Nothing." Jake got free of his friend's grip. "Just working through some stuff."

"Oh, yeah. How is that going?"

"Not great."

Bobby nodded. "I wouldn't think so. Come on. Let's go."

Jake adjusted his collar. "How did you find me?"

"Umm— lucky guess." Bobby shrugged. "When my spare bedroom was empty, I figured that you'd came here."

Was he that predictable? If Bobby could find him, he must be. "I was fine."

"Hey, it's times like this we need to stick together."

Exhaling, Jake said, "You're right."

"Of course, I'm right. Speaking of . . . we should check on Mary and the kids. I bet they could use the company. The day after a funeral is always the loneliest."

"Don't you have to work?"

"Nah, I'll call into the garage and tell them that I'm taking another day off."

Jake nodded and followed Bobby out of the cemetery to the parking lot. "Do you think they'll want company?"

Bobby slung an arm over Jake's shoulder. "We're not company. We're family."

They got into their cars, and Jake tailed Bobby to Tom and Mary's house. The upscale subdivision had been just a cornfield when they were kids, but it had now become yet another suburb of Detroit. Parking on the street, they made their way up to the house, but Jake stopped short of the front door.

"Can I have a minute?" He went to the porch railing and rested his palms on the painted wood surface.

Pulling at his shirt collar, Bobby made room for one of his extra chins. "Take your time."

The big man came to stand next to Jake, leaning against the handrail. It groaned under the strain. The size mismatch between the two men was almost comical. Bobby outweighed him by a hundred pounds, not that Jake was a small man. Jake and Tom had met Bobby on their high school football team, along with their other friend Rick. Rick had been the hotshot quarterback with a rocket for an arm, and Bobby was the gentle giant who protected his blindside. Jake had been the tough running back who pounded defenders like a battering ram, and Tom was the wily receiver who could always get open. Together, they'd won a league championship.

"Should we call Rick?" Jake asked.

Bobby scratched the dark stubble on his cheek. "I doubt he can get off work."

"What? It's his landscaping business. You were able to call off," Jake said, selfishly wanting all his friends together.

Perspiration beaded on Bobby's olive-skinned forehead. "I have good people, and Rick already lost two days with the funeral. The grass doesn't stop growing."

Jake sighed loudly. "I guess."

"Forget him," Bobby said. "Speaking of, I forgot to ask you, did you talk to the detective?"

Jake had visited the police station yesterday before the funeral. The conversation with Detective Noles had bothered Jake. The man's investigative experience was not impressive, yet he'd discouraged Jake from assisting in any way.

Jake pushed off the railing and paced along the long porch. "Detective Noles still believes it's a random act of road rage. He wasn't very forthcoming with details, even when I told him I'd been in law enforcement."

"That's some bullshit."

"I know." Jake paused, looking around the empty yard. "I don't like him. He's fat and lazy."

"Hey!" Bobby exclaimed, hiking up his pants.

"No offense. You're not lazy."

"I get it, jerk. I'm fat while you stayed in shape," Bobby sniffed. "Brooding little Jake can still get any girl he wants."

"That's where you're wrong. I've been single for years."

Bobby shrugged. "Because that witch of an ex-wife crushed your spirit."

Jake didn't take the bait. "I'm concerned that Noles will screw up Tom's case."

"How?"

"He's worked one homicide. A murder-suicide where a husband killed his cheating wife. A trained monkey could've solved that case."

"Really?" Bobby shifted his weight. The back of his blue work shirt pulled free of his pants and flapped in the spring breeze.

"Really."

"So what are you going to do?"

Jake rubbed the back of his neck. "What do you mean?"

"Come on, you know what I mean . . . "

"Yeah." Jake bit his lip. "I was thinking I'd poke around."

"You should." Bobby smiled. "Heck, you were the guy who caught the Silkworm Rapist"

Jake's insides twisted at the mention of that terrible case. Shaking his head, he turned back to the yard. Jake had always been jealous of this dream home, a beautiful two-story house with its welcoming wrap-around country porch. The payments on the acre-sized lot must be steep; he hoped Tom had good life insurance. Otherwise, Mary and the kids would have to rent a crappy apartment similar to Jake's to make ends meet. Mary deserved better than that. Jake's brow furrowed at that dark thought.

Bobby rested a hand on Jake's shoulder. "What are you thinking about, buddy?"

"Nothing."

"Tell me."

Jake looked down at his feet. "I was thinking about *Pulp Fiction*."

"Great movie." Bobby stepped away. "I got it on DVD. We can watch it tonight."

"Maybe," Jake agreed. "But I was thinking, if I could get my hands on Tom's killer before the police, he'd wish he was never born. I'd get medieval on his ass."

Bobby cracked his scarred knuckles. They were the strong hands of an experienced mechanic. "I'm down for that. We could get a couple of wrenches and a blow torch from my garage."

"Perfect. We'll— "

Someone touched the back of Jake's arm. He leaped a foot in the air.

Cursing under his breath, he turned to find Mary standing behind him. Jake hadn't heard the screen door open. Traces of mascara streaked her pale cheeks. The strain of the last few days was evident by the deep lines in her beautiful face.

Mary arched an eyebrow. "What are you talking about? I heard something about a wrench and a blow torch."

Chapter 3

Bobby stared at Mary slack-jawed. Jake would get no help from him, so he choked out a lame answer. "Umm— Bobby was talking about a tough job down at his garage."

"I don't believe you." Mary's eyes pinched to narrow slits.

She could always see right through Jake, but he doubled down anyway. "I'm serious."

She frowned but didn't push him for the truth, that would come later, he was sure. "Fine. So what are you two doing hanging out on my porch?"

Jake said, "We thought you and the kids could use some company."

Her eyes watered. "We could. Thank you."

Bobby stepped forward. "It was my idea."

"You guys are the best." She pulled them both in for a hug.

Squeezing them extra-tight, she nestled her head between their shoulders. Being here for her warmed Jake's heart. Bobby was right. This was doing more for Tom than hanging out in a cold cemetery. After she regained her composure, she stepped back and rubbed away her tears. Which was when Jake noticed an older gentleman in a tie and jacket waiting in the doorway.

Mary followed Jake's questioning gaze. "Oops. I forgot. Tom's boss stopped by during his lunch hour to check on us too. He was just leaving."

"Gentlemen."

Mary introduced them. "These are Tom's friends, Jake Bryant and Bobby Andollini."

"Nice to meet you. I'm Dolan Magnusson."

Bobby shook his hand, followed by Jake. The grip was firm, and he had an air of authority. Jake guessed he was in his late fifties by the crow's feet. His cropped salt and pepper hair spoke of someone with military history.

Mary gave Dolan a polite hug. "Thanks for stopping by. I appreciate your concern."

"It's the least I could do." Dolan stepped off the porch. "Please remember my offer."

"I don't think that I'm ready for that, but I will let you know when I am." Mary smiled and went inside the house; Bobby trailed after her.

Jake didn't. Instead, he chased after Dolan, stopping him in the yard. There wouldn't be a better time for Jake to start his own investigation. "Wait. Do you have a minute?"

"Only a minute. I should really get back to the office."

"Thanks. So you were Tom's boss? I don't recall seeing you at the funeral."

"Unfortunately, I was out of town on urgent business. I take it that you are very close to the family, Jake."

"Yep. Tom's best friend since grade school."

"Wow. That's a long time. I've been Tom's boss for over ten years. Hired him right out of college. He was a hell of a guy."

"Yes. Tom was," Jake agreed.

"It's terrible when a man is struck down in his prime and leaves a family behind. I've seen it before." Dolan rested a hand on Jake's shoulder and gave it a squeeze. His touch made Jake's skin crawl.

Jake stepped back. "You have?"

"Yes." Dolan frowned as his hand fell back to his side. "At least Tom had a good life insurance policy. Mary shouldn't have to worry financially."

"That's good."

As Tom's boss, Dolan should have knowledge of Tom's benefits package, but sharing that kind of information was a breach of confidentiality. However, Dolan knew Jake was a close friend who would be concerned, so Jake chalked it up to an honest mistake.

Dolan leaned in close. "Can you believe the police have no leads?"

"No. I can't," Jake lied.

"The company chipped in $10,000 on the reward for information."

"I know Mary appreciates everything you've done for her," Jake said as he tried to keep his growing dislike this man out of his voice.

Dolan smiled. "It's the least we could do."

Jake smiled back. "Since you're Tom's boss, maybe you could tell me if Tom was working on something sensitive? Anything that could've got him in trouble?"

"No. Definitely not."

"Tom's death seemed too violent to be a random act. I thought being an accountant was pretty boring, but maybe there was an unhappy customer who was carrying a grudge?"

Dolan shook his head. "We perform general accounting for traditional companies. All our customers are pleased with our services."

Jake asked, "Had you noticed anything unusual in Tom's behavior the last few weeks?"

"No."

"He hadn't acted out of character?"

Dolan groaned audibly. "No."

Jake ignored Dolan's obvious frustration with his questioning. "Did Tom have any enemies? A co-worker who was possibly jealous of his last promotion?"

Dolan pointed his finger at Jake. "Tom told me one of his friends was a detective in Chicago. It must be you. Am I right?"

Jake shrugged uncomfortably. "I'm no longer a detective, but I guess you never stop wanting answers."

"Then you're doing your own investigation?"

"Not officially."

"I would guess not." Dolan rubbed his hands together. "Do you mind me asking why you're no longer with Chicago PD?"

Jake said, "Yes. I do mind."

Dolan's brow furrowed, tangling his thick eyebrows. But he regained his composure quickly and moved towards his car. "Well, I'm sorry, but I told the real detective everything I know. I'm sure they'll find Tom's murderer or murderers soon."

"I hope, and it looks like my minute is up."

Dolan grinned. "I think it was more like five minutes, but who's counting."

Jake laughed and turned back towards the house. "Maybe you, since you're an accountant."

Chapter 4

Caleb Clarke strutted into his brother's mansion. His black biker boots echoed dully on the marble tile. Jodi, gorgeously tempting in a pink silk robe, locked the heavy oak door behind him. He scooped her up and kissed her.

"There's my baby."

Jodi ran her fingers through his long brown hair. "You're late."

"Sorry." He laughed. "No rest for the wicked."

Two pug dogs circled them, barking and nipping at his feet. He set Jodi down and snaked a hand underneath her robe. She wasn't wearing panties, so he gave her bare ass a squeeze.

"You better look out," she squealed.

"Why?"

"Because my butt belongs to Sonny."

"Right now, it belongs to me."

She giggled. "True, but do you know what he would do if he caught you here?"

"Yeah." He nibbled on her ear. Her freshly washed hair smelled like fruit and lavender.

"What?" she persisted. "What would he do?"

He bit back a sigh. Every time, it was the same thing with her. If he didn't play along, she pouted, but he was sick of the shit. And he was sick of Sonny. His jerk of a brother had been screwing him over his whole life, from sending him on risky jobs like killing the accountant to stealing Jodi from him. So was it really wrong to screw her behind Sonny's back? No, it wasn't, but he needed to keep up appearances a little longer, then he'd never have to worry about his brother again.

"Sonny would cut off my hands."

"Then what?" Her voice grew husky. She traced a finger along his jagged scar.

A groan escaped his lips. "Then, he'll feed them to those stupid little dogs of yours."

"Shut up. My babies are not stupid."

She grabbed his free hand and pushed it inside her robe, pressing it against her breast. He caressed her nipple. A moan escaped her lips. His other hand slid down her side and pulled at the tie of her robe. She pushed him away and went into her enormous kitchen. He watched the sway of her ass through the paper-thin robe as the pugs followed at her heels.

"Aren't we going upstairs?" Caleb yelled. She didn't answer him.

He found her leaning against a granite countertop, a dog tucked under each arm. She took turns kissing them on the top of their heads. Both dogs eyed him, their tails quivering nervously. Caleb rolled his eyes and sat down at the large oak table. Pulling over the ashtray, he lit up a cigarette. He inhaled deeply, filling his lungs full of sweet nicotine.

He said, "It's all bullshit."

"What is?"

"He won't cut off my hands."

"You really think he'd let you live if he catches you banging his old lady?"

"I do." He exhaled. The plume of smoke hovered above his head. "It's you that should be worried."

She brought a hand to her cheek. "I am worried. If he finds out, he might kill me."

Caleb rolled his eyes. "Sonny may toss you out on your cute ass, but he won't kill you either."

Ignoring his assessment, she went back to kissing the dogs' heads. "Who is a good boy? Who is a good boy? Remy is a good boy! And I didn't forget about you, Romy!"

The dogs nearly flipped out of her arms with excitement. Caleb grunted in disgust. She turned her back to him and set the dogs back on the floor. Her robe rode up, stopping inches short of his desires, which forced a bulge in his pants. She stood up, smoothing the material back down as he eyed her like a juicy steak. In her early thirties, Jodi was a solid eight. She'd been hotter, but the last few years were rough on her.

Looking coyly over her shoulder, she said, "Sonny hardly touches me anymore, not the way you do."

Caleb crushed his cigarette out in the ashtray. "Hard not to touch with a body as fine as yours."

She brushed her hair back over her shoulder and opened her robe to reveal breasts too round and perky to be real, a flat belly, and smooth pink skin between her legs. She asked, "Do you want to touch me now?"

"Hell, yeah."

The chair scraped on the tile when he stood up too quickly. The dog's yipping and yapping began anew. Their nails clicked on the tile as they spun in circles. Before Caleb had taken two steps, she closed the robe tight against her body. "Wait. Did you park around the corner like I asked?"

"Yes, but why start now?"

"Because I think Sonny is getting suspicious. Seriously!"

"Fine, but what good will it do? Anyone from the club will know it's my truck."

"True, but my divorced friend lives there. She'll cover for us if necessary."

"She will?"

"Yes. I supply her with high-quality pot."

"And she'll tell Sonny that I'm sleeping with her? Is she hot?"

She glared at him. "Very hot, but don't get any ideas, or I'll cut your hands off myself."

"I'd like to see you try." He rubbed his cheek.

She eyed him carefully. "Is your face bruised?"

He laughed harder than he intended. "A little. I fell out of bed the other night and hit it on the nightstand. I was too drunk to feel it, but it hurt like a bitch the next morning."

"Poor baby."

"You could kiss it, or better yet, you could sit on it."

"Maybe." She cast her eyes down and batted her eyelashes.

He glanced at the antique watch strapped to his wrist. "I only have an hour."

"That's all?"

"Sonny scheduled a meeting for me," he lied. The truth was that it was his own meeting, but the less she knew of his plan, the better.

She shook her head in disgust. "Sonny is out of town, but he still controls everything."

"He's the president."

"Whatever."

She turned and headed for the marble staircase in the foyer, stopping in the kitchen doorway. She undid the sash on the silk robe. The robe slid off her shoulders and puddled around her feet. Caleb howled like a wild animal as he chased after her. She shrieked and ran up the stairs. The dogs followed, barking furiously.

Caleb tried to kick one and missed. "Tell them to stay down here. It freaks me out when they watch."

She pointed a finger at the slobbering canines. "Remy! Romy! Stay!"

The dogs both gave a small yip in reply. Their little heads turned from side to side like pendulums. Jodi gave them a stern look, and the pugs reluctantly returned to the foyer to guard the bottom step. Remy's pink tongue hung out his mouth.

"Happy?" She leaned over the marble railing, her perky nipples pointing at him.

He stepped over the dogs. "Very."

They barked at him but remained in position. Once clear of the pugs, he took the steps two at a time. Jodi renewed her squeals and ran for the bedroom with Caleb in hot pursuit.

Chapter 5

After watching Dolan drive away, Jake entered Mary's house. In the living room, he found Bobby with the three kids— Lindsey, Emma, and Hunter. By Jake's math, Lindsey was fourteen, Emma was twelve, and Hunter was eight years old, but he wouldn't want to put money on it.

"Where's Mary?" Jake asked the group.

Bobby said, "She went to freshen up. She'll be back in a minute."

On the loveseat, Lindsey furiously tapped on her phone with two thumbs. She looked so much like Mary at that age, it was scary. In fact, both girls looked like their mother, with blonde hair, pixyish noses, and long legs. Not that Tom was a bad-looking guy, but he had outdone himself with Mary.

Across the room, Emma rocked her recliner to its limits. The springs squeaked loudly in protest. Her red-rimmed eyes made Jake's heart ache. He would've liked to give her a hug but decided against it. Instead, he dropped into the seat next to Lindsey. Hunter sat slumped on a couch, his brown hair in need of a haircut. He was engrossed in a hand-held video game. Bobby watched Hunter manipulate the controls with more amusement than Jake would have expected.

The charger for Lindsey's phone was plugged into an extension cord. It stretched across the room, a foot off the floor. Jake frowned. "Lindsey, you may want to move that cord."

"Why?"

"Umm— because someone could trip over it."

"If they do, it will be Emma's fault. She won't trade spots with me."

"I was here first," Emma hissed.

"Big deal. You still should move."

"How low is your battery?"

Lindsey said, "It's almost down to forty percent."

"I'll move when it hits ten percent," Emma said with a laugh.

"You suck."

Jake said, "Come on, guys. Would your dad want you to fight today?"

Both girls regarded Jake like he was bubble gum they'd found on the bottom of their shoe. Lindsey unplugged her charging cord and stomped up the stairs. Seconds later, a door slammed shut. Emma avoided Jake's stare and went into the kitchen. Rubbing his face, Jake exhaled slowly. The escaping air sounded like a hole in an inner tube. He should know how sensitive girls could be, his own daughter, Sam, wasn't shy about letting him know when he said the wrong thing. Jake pushed himself off the couch, wrapped up the extension cord, and set it carefully on the arm of the sofa.

Bobby gave Jake a sympathetic shrug. "You should see Hunter play this game. He's really good."

"What game are you playing, Hunter?" Jake asked.

Hunter mumbled, "*Super Smash Bros.*"

"He wins every time," Bobby said.

"That's cool." Jake inched forward in his seat. "I think I should go say something to the girls."

Bobby closed his eyes and shook his head. "Even I know that's not a good idea. How about you let Mary handle it?"

Jake nodded. "You're probably right."

"I'm always right."

"You suck."

"Boys stop fighting," Mary said as she entered the room. Her face was freshly scrubbed, and she wore loose-fitting yoga pants. She pulled at a large t-shirt, probably one of Tom's. "Hope you don't mind, but I changed into something more comfortable."

"I'm jealous," Jake said. "I wish I had worn my leggings too."

Mary smiled. "I have a pair you can borrow."

Bobby chuckled. "I'd love to see that."

Mary took the seat next to Jake, tucking a leg up underneath her. "Where are the girls?"

Jake cleared his throat. "They were arguing, and I tried to intervene, but I made it worse."

She nodded her head. "It's fine."

"Sorry. I was trying to help."

"It was bound to happen, Jake. With the funeral over, they don't have to be on their best behavior anymore."

The three of them spent the afternoon talking and catching up on each other lives, which there weren't able to do during the funeral. The conversation was easy and not forced, as happens with life-long friends. Soon enough, it was dinnertime, and everyone was starving. The girls had reappeared at some point, the argument forgotten. Bobby suggested that they order a pizza, and no one objected. Of course, Bobby knew the best place in town that would deliver to Mary's neck of the woods.

After everyone's bellies were full, they remained in the dining room. Glasses, paper plates, and pizza boxes littered the table. The kids appeared to be in no rush to get back to their devices, which warmed Jake's heart.

Emma sidled up to Bobby. "Could you tell us a story?"

"Me?"

"Yes. You tell the best stories, Uncle Bobby."

Bobby beamed at her compliment. "What story do you want to hear?"

Mary said, "Why don't you tell the one about Tom's car catching on fire? That's my favorite."

"Yeah, Uncle Bobby." Jake leaned over and slapped his arm. "No one embellishes a story like you do."

Bobby puckered out his bottom lip, doing his best to look hurt. "I don't embellish my stories."

"Liar. They're like eighty percent bullcrap. Don't get me wrong. I love them too. But I can be in one of the stories, and not even recognize myself in it."

Bobby shook his head. "You're just jealous that I know how to tell a good story, and you don't."

"Whatever," Jake said.

Bobby put two big hands on the table, heaving himself up. "All right, just for you, Emma, I'll tell the classic tale of your father's car blowing up, and how I saved his life."

Jake laughed. "See, you're already starting. His car didn't blow up. It caught on fire."

Bobby ignored him. "Two score and a year ago. Christmas time, as I recall."

"I don't think it was forty-one years ago," Mary said.

"Sorry, I never claimed to be good at math."

"Just tell the story," Emma pleaded.

"All right. The story begins with four boys going to the mall to finish their shopping lists. It took forever— the stores were crowded, hot, and sweaty. I was ready to kill somebody by the end of it. The rest of us were happy to buy the first thing we found and get out of there, but not Tom. Your dad insisted on finding the perfect Christmas gift for your grandmother.

"For the trip, Tom had borrowed his dad's car. Rick was in the front seat; Jake and I were in the back. We're on our way home when the car stalls in front of the bowling alley. Which was weird because it was a new car with all the bells and whistles. Tom tried turning the key again, and— "

Bobby slammed his fists down on the table.

"BOOM!"

Lindsey gasped, and Hunter jumped in his seat. Glasses bounced and rattled on the table.

Bobby brought his hands up in front of his face and wriggled his fingers. "Flames shot out from underneath the hood. They must have gone ten feet in the air. I jump out of the car. Run across three lanes of traffic, dodging cars like I was Barry Sanders."

Bobby jogged around the room, throwing in a few juke moves on his way. "When I get to the sidewalk, I turn around. Only to find my three idiot friends still sitting in the car, hypnotized by the flames. So I ran back through three lanes of traffic and slammed my hands on the roof of the car to wake them up."

He raised his big arms high above his head. Everyone lunged for their glasses, but Bobby chuckled and slowly brought his hands back to his side.

"Finally, they jump into action, but by this time, the flames were twenty feet in the air. All the traffic on the road had stopped to watch the spectacle. Jake and Rick ran to safety, but Tom was still mesmerized by the fire, so I opened his door and pulled him out. We were almost to the sidewalk when Tom pulled free and sprinted back to the car. I race after him and get a hold of his arm."

Bobby grabbed Jake's arm to demonstrate, pretending to strain with the effort. Jake just grinned rather than wrestle free.

"I said, 'Tom, what're you doing?' He says, 'My mom's Christmas present is in there. I need to go back and get it.' And I tell him, 'Tom, don't. You're going to get yourself killed. I'll buy her another one.' He reluctantly agrees and lets me pull him away. Just as we reached the grass, the car exploded. It skyrocketed high into the air and landed on its roof."

"BOOM!"

Bobby slammed his hands flat on the table.

Enthralled by the climax of the story, no one was prepared. Hunter jumped a second time, and Lindsey screamed again while Emma laughed with delight. A glass toppled over, but luckily it was empty. Jake set it back upright.

Bobby stopped in front of Lindsey, Emma, and Hunter. "So it was only with my quick wits and cat-like reflexes that you three kids are here today."

"Thank you, Uncle Bobby," the children said in unison.

To loud applause, Bobby struck a Heisman pose. "And no thanks to your Uncle Jake."

Jake rolled his eyes but couldn't help but smile. Tom would've enjoyed this night, his family and friends laughing together. It almost felt like Tom's spirit was there too. They shared more stories, but eventually, it was time to clean up dinner, plus the kids looked tired after their emotionally draining week. Yet, they all claimed they wouldn't be able to sleep, so Mary suggested they watch a movie before bed.

"Can we watch *The Lego Batman Movie*?" Hunter asked.

"Not again," Lindsey groaned, but one look from her mother stopped further objections.

Bobby said, "You know, I've never seen that movie."

The kids begged him to watch it with them. Bobby pretended like he didn't want to, but they sweetened their offer with popcorn, and he gladly relented. The foursome paraded towards the family room, Emma to find the movie, Lindsey and Bobby to make the popcorn, and Hunter to grab a good spot on the couch. Jake and Mary stayed in the dining room.

Once they were alone, Mary shook her finger at Jake. "I want you to tell me the truth about the blow torch."

Chapter 6

Caleb gunned his bike down a rutted gravel road, a safe twenty miles from the murder scene, pulling up in front of a weather-beaten old barn. A Harley was parked near the barn. Its rider stood nearby.

"You're late," Hysko said.

Shrugging, Caleb said, "I'm always late."

"Well, don't be. It makes me nervous."

"I'm nervous too because if we screw this up, we're as good as fertilizer."

Caleb pulled open the heavy wooden door to the barn. The rusty hinges protested loudly. He waved the other man into the building that still smelled of large animals and manure. It was obvious by the thick layer of dirt and hay covering the weathered floorboards that no one had been inside the barn in years.

Scanning the room, memories from Caleb's childhood came flooding back to him. Some of them were good, like riding and brushing down the horses. But they also included the bad ones, such as the time he got his infamous scar. With his back against a thick wood column, Caleb pointed to a rickety milking stool, and the other man sat down with a weary grunt.

Hysko, the treasurer of the Devil's Hand, had been part of the club since the beginning. His beard was mostly grey, and he had more forehead than hair on his head, but he was all lean muscle and sinew, a body built to survive tough times. Caleb would need Hysko's full support if his plan was going to work— all the members respected him. But they wouldn't if they knew Hysko's dirty secret. His predilections would get him killed in their world.

Caleb lit a cigarette and inhaled deeply. Tapping another cigarette from the pack, he offered it to Hysko. "Smoke?"

"Nope. I'm trying to quit."

"Since when?"

Hysko said, "Since yesterday."

"What? You want to live forever?"

"That's the plan."

"Maybe I'll quit too," Caleb said, taking a long drag on his cigarette.

"Why don't you start with the booze? Your face looks terrible. Did you really get that falling out of bed drunk?"

Caleb absently brought a hand to the side of his face, stroking the bruise. "Yes. How else do you think I got it?"

"If you had an old lady, I'd say she hit you with a frying pan."

"Well, I don't, so drop it. What do you think of this place? Will it work?"

Four horse stalls lined one side of the structure, with ropes strung across the openings. The other side held a workbench, scrap tires, and assorted other junk. In the corner stood a rickety ladder leading to a loft littered with forgotten hay bales. The barn was surrounded on both sides by factory farms, and the closest neighbor was senile and half-deaf.

Nodding, Hysko said, "I like the location. It's very secluded."

Caleb laughed. "That's an understatement."

Hysko got up from the stool and paced between the horse stalls. "You said it used to be your uncle's place?"

"Yeah, my Uncle Jim died twenty years ago. The farm changed hands a couple of times since then, and I was able to buy it in secret. No one in the club knows about it."

"Not even Sonny?"

"Nope. He's clueless," Caleb said.

"Great."

"Yeah, and when I retire, maybe I'll fix the house and the barn up and live here. I might even get some horses."

"Retire?" Hysko laughed. "People in our business don't get to retire, but it is a nice thought."

"True." Caleb took a drag from his cigarette. "I put things in motion, so all we need to do now is sit back and wait."

"I hope it's that easy."

Caleb took a final hit from his cigarette and threw it to the floor. He ground it out with his boot with extra vigor. "You aren't having second thoughts, are you?"

"No. Of course not. I wouldn't have agreed to your plan if you weren't the better man for this job."

"Good." Caleb suspected Hysko's endorsement had more to do with Caleb's blackmailing him than his actual skills, but he let the lie go.

Hysko stuck a hand in his pocket. "But like I said, I'm worried. Sonny's a smart man."

Caleb spat on the floor while tracking Hysko's movements. "Sonny isn't half as smart as everyone thinks he is. Trust me, he won't see this coming."

The hand remained in Hysko's pocket. "But what if he does?"

"I've got a contingency plan. It won't be ideal, but we can take Sonny out ahead of time if necessary." Caleb inched his hand towards his weapon, tucked neatly in a back holster.

Pulling out a tin-foil packet, Hysko extracted a piece of gum and popped it in his mouth. Between snaps, he asked, "How?"

Caleb smiled— not only because he didn't want to reveal his plan, but also because the older man hadn't tried to kill him to keep his orientation a secret.

Hysko nodded. "Got it. Probably better if I don't know all the details."

"Probably," Caleb agreed.

"And the Outsiders won't screw this up?"

"We don't need to worry about them. Alex is keeping it small— only two or three guys from his club know."

Hysko chomped on his gum. "Speaking of which, I think we should add one more guy. That's a lot of people for the two of us to eliminate."

"You think?"

Hysko shifted uneasily from foot to foot. "We definitely need one more gun."

Caleb walked to the far end of the barn, stopping in front of the tack room. He didn't want to add one more guy. In his gut, he knew it was a bad idea, but he had included the older man for his wisdom, so he should listen to him. Caleb came back to stand in front of Hysko. "You've seen a lot and done even more, so I'll trust your judgment. Do you have someone in mind?"

Hysko nodded. "I like Larry for the job."

"Hmmm— Larry. Are you sure he's our best option?"

"He isn't the sharpest knife in the drawer, but all we need is his trigger finger."

"Fine. Let's bring him in."

Caleb glanced down at his watch. "Right. We should get back to the club."

"Yes." Hysko draped an arm over Caleb's shoulder. "We do have to keep up appearances for a little while longer."

Caleb shrugged off Hysko's embrace and placed a board into the barn's door brackets. Hysko climbed on his bike and hit the starter. The Harley's engine roared to life. Caleb jumped on his motorcycle and did the same. The men sped away from the old barn, kicking up dried dirt and gravel under the blazing yellow sun.

Chapter 7

Stalling to answer Mary's question about the blowtorch, Jake stood up with his empty glass. "I'm thirsty. I'm going to get another Coke."

She nodded. "Go ahead. I'll wait."

"Do you need anything?" he called over his shoulder as he retreated to the kitchen.

"No. I'm good."

At the fridge, he moved slowly as he considered his options. He decided to come clean about his conversation with Bobby. He really didn't have a choice, and who better to understand his motives than Mary?

When he returned to the dining room, the setting sun cast an orange glow through the large bay window. The room was warm, but that wasn't why his shirt clung to his back. Mary sat at the head of the table, nursing a half glass of whiskey from dinner. One leg was propped on the chair next to her. The yoga pants had crept up to her knee, revealing a tanned calf. However, the pain hiding underneath the tough veneer she'd had over the last few days was obvious to him.

Jake took the seat to her left. "Are you doing okay?"

"I'm a long fucking way from okay. How about you?"

"Sorry, kind of a stupid question."

"Yes. It was," she agreed.

"Look. What I meant to say was— "

"I know what you're trying to say, Jake, but stop avoiding my question. Just tell me what stupid thing you're planning."

Jake set his glass down and opened his mouth. Without preamble, his answer spilled out like a river of raw emotion.

"Bobby and I were talking about Tom. It's stupid, but we want to get revenge for him. Tom doesn't deserve to be dead while some piece of shit is out there, walking around, doing whatever the fuck he wants. And if he gets caught, you and the kids will have to sit through a trial, hearing every gory detail. And then what, he gets a life sentence where he can find religion and sell the book rights to his redemption story? I don't think so."

She frowned. "That wouldn't happen."

Jake shook his head. "You don't know. Or worse, the killer could claim it was self-defense and be out in ten years for manslaughter."

Her frown deepened. "I didn't think about that."

"Well, I have, and the real world is not an episode of *Forensic Files*. It would be the murderer's word against a dead man's. Guess who will win?"

"Shit!"

Jake slapped his hand flat on the table. "Exactly. Which is why I can't stop thinking about killing the bastard."

She reached out and laid her hand on top of his. He turned his hand over, and their fingers intertwined. It was a gesture that spoke of their deep friendship, not romantic in the least. "Don't think like that, Jake. It isn't healthy. Besides, Tom wouldn't want that."

He shook his head. "I disagree. I think Tom would want it. He wasn't ready to die."

"Tom did deserve more time. And the kids and I deserved more time with him, but we aren't going to get it. And that really sucks, but you can't change that."

Squeezing her hand, he said, "But, wouldn't you feel better if— "

"Stop. The police will catch him, and Tom will get justice."

"No. Justice would be if the killer had an unfortunate accident on the way to the courthouse."

She pulled her hand away. "You need to knock this off. I understand you're upset. I am too, but you have a daughter to think about. How can you be a father from inside a prison cell?"

Her response hit him like cold water. He was an idiot. Cursing under his breath, he said, "You're right. It's just wishful thinking anyway. Like I'd ever be able to get my hands on that murdering son of a bitch anyway."

"Seriously, Jake. Did you forget what happened the last time you killed someone? And that one was justified."

The question sent shivers down his spine. He stared at the wall behind her until he could answer without stuttering. "I handled it."

Mary snorted and slammed back the rest of her drink. The glass clunked down on the table. "You're such a damn liar. It cost you everything— your job, your marriage, and almost your life."

"My marriage was already dead."

Her mouth twisted into a scowl. "You know what I mean."

"Yeah. I do." Staring lustfully at the whiskey bottle, he polished off his Coke. "Can I get you another drink?"

"Please."

He poured her another glass and left to get more soda from the fridge. From the other room, the television emitted a loud crash. Hunter and Emma giggled while Bobby let out a deep belly laugh. Trying to ignore their silliness, he returned to Mary. She hadn't moved.

She said, "I miss Tom already."

Jake fell into his chair. "I miss him too. Tom always protected me from myself. If only I could be half the man that he was."

"Don't sell yourself short. You're at least three quarters." She laughed a real laugh that made it up to the corner of her eyes. But all too quickly, the sadness returned to her face.

Jake said, "I don't know what I'm going to do without him."

She slammed half her drink down in one gulp. "I don't either. We were soul mates. I know everyone says that, but it's true. We were."

A single tear spilled down her cheek. He watched it trickle down the side of her chin and onto her neck. He wished there was something he could say to magically comfort her and ease her pain. But he was no therapist, so he kept his mouth shut.

She tapped the side of her glass with a fingernail. It made a hollow pinging noise. "We're both pretty pathetic, aren't we?"

"I am, but you've handled this whole thing like a pro."

"Yeah, right. I'm a hot mess."

"You're most definitely not."

With her voice barely above a whisper, she said, "I am. I can't do this alone."

Jake's heart ripped in two. He went to her and held her in his arms. Laying her head on his shoulder, she cried quietly. The warm salty tears soaked his shirt, but he didn't care. Luckily, the sounds of the movie drowned out her sorrow. Barely a minute had passed before she lifted her head up and forced a smile across her face.

Feeling awkward, he untangled himself and began pacing around the dining room. He stopped in front of a framed photograph on the wall. It showed Jake, Tom, Rick, and Bobby, their arms slung around each other, smiling from ear to ear. It was one of the last times he was truly happy. Jake choked back his own tears, which tasted bitter in his sore throat. He wished he still had his copy of the photograph, but it was lost in the fire. Shaking his head, Jake continued to circle the room. She watched him from downcast eyes.

Jake knew he shouldn't but decided to tell Mary his plan, the one based in reality. He stopped his pacing and said, "I'm going to stay in Michigan. At least until Tom's murderer is found."

"You are?"

"Yes. I'm going to help with the investigation."

She arched an eyebrow. "And what do you think you're going to do?"

He dropped into the chair across from Mary. Resting his elbows on the table, he said, "I'll go to the scene. Look for evidence. Find witnesses. Ask questions."

"Umm— hasn't the real detective already done that?"

He bit his tongue. She didn't understand the system like he did, and the lead detective, Noles, was a joke! Jake had only been a detective for six months before his incident with the suspected rapist, and he was still twice the detective Noles was. He closed his eyes and counted to ten. He didn't want to say something he'd regret later.

When he was calm, he said, "Mary, please. I need to do this."

"And you won't get in the way?"

"I'd think they'd want the extra help."

She studied him before shifting her gaze to the contents of her glass. "You better not lose your temper and do something stupid."

Tracing a finger across his heart, he said, "I won't. I promise."

"Fine. Do what you need to do."

"Thank you." He released the breath he'd been holding.

"What about your job? What about Samantha?"

"My job. I have a ton of vacation days saved up. And Sam? She's busy with her painting and studying for the SATs. She won't even know I'm gone."

A long strand of blonde hair fell across Mary's face; she tucked it back behind her ear. "Girls need their fathers."

He drummed his fingers on the table. "I know. Sam's a good kid. She'll be fine without me for a few weeks."

"If you say so."

"Besides, I only get her one night a week and every other weekend. You know Kate won't let me have any extra days," Jake assured her.

"True," Mary agreed.

"So what did Dolan offer to help you with?"

She tilted her head to the side and rolled her eyes. "Oh, he wanted to hire a company to remove Tom's things from the house, clothes and stuff like that."

The hair stood up on the back of Jake's neck. "Weird."

"I know, but his heart is in the right place. He thought it would be too painful for me to do myself."

"I guess."

A clock ticked somewhere. The room had lost its orange glow a long time ago, going from gray to black. Music blared from the other room, signaling the end of the movie. Mary stood up and smoothed out her pants.

"I should put the kids to bed," she said, leaving Jake to his warm Coke.

Cries of protest came from the family room as the television was turned off. Mary trudged through the kitchen, straining to carry Hunter's limp body. Emma, all bony knees and elbows, trailed after her mother, followed by Lindsey, whose phone cord slapped against the floor.

Bobby stopped at the threshold of the dining room. He looked as tired as Jake felt. An unspoken understanding passed between them. They went to the front door as Mary ascended the staircase, still struggling with Hunter's drooping form.

In a hushed tone, Jake said, "It's late. We're going to go."

"Thank you, guys. Thanks for everything today. Love you."

"Love you too," Jake said.

Mary smiled and herded her flock upstairs, and Jake and Bobby let themselves out. When the door was closed, Jake said, "We need to find that son of a bitch and kill him."

Bobby nodded his head in agreement.

Chapter 8

The next morning, Jake visited the scene of Tom's murder. Rick, obviously feeling guilty after missing yesterday's visit with Mary, had offered to help Jake search for evidence, though he only had an hour before he needed to check on his crew. It was an unseasonably warm spring day, and Jake struggled to focus as he meticulously combed the side of the road. Rick trailed behind him.

Using an arm covered in tribal tattoos, Rick wiped the sweat from his brow. "Man, it's going to be a hot one."

"You're a landscaper. Shouldn't you be used to the heat?" Jake asked as he kicked the tall grass for a better view.

Rick shook his head. "You never get used to it."

Jake's shoes squished with each step from the morning dew. He hated walking in wet socks, but it would be a small price to pay if he found a key piece of evidence. Yet, except for grass, dirt, and weeds, Jake's only discovery so far was a plastic water bottle. He continued his intense survey while growing annoyed with Rick's half-ass assistance.

"Do you see anything?" Jake asked.

Rick shook his head, his long hair bouncing from side to side. "What are we hoping to find?"

"I'm not sure, but I'll know it when I see it."

Jake jogged to the other side of the road to perform a second circuit of the scene. He was confident that he'd find something. There was no way the killer had committed the perfect crime. No one was that smart, and Tom's death was definitely not a professional hit. If it had been, the killer would've chosen a less public spot than one where a random witness could wander onto the scene.

Rick followed Jake, going through the motions of searching. "Don't you think the police would have found something already if it was here? I mean, it's been almost a week. Whatever we find today could be completely unrelated."

"Or the killer could return to leave new evidence to taunt the police who are too stupid to find it."

"That's true." Rick nodded. "I heard John Norman Collins did that exact same thing."

Sweat dribbled down Jake's face and collected at the collar of his polo shirt. He regretted having to wear the knit shirt and khaki pants on this hot morning. However, he needed to have a professional appearance when he questioned the surrounding residents. In contrast, Rick wore a frayed t-shirt with his company logo and a pair of brown cargo shorts. On his right hand was a gaudy silver ring in the image of a wolf's head with a snarling mouth and large fangs. Rick had worn the stupid thing since high school and never took it off. Grass-stained work boots and grey socks completed his ensemble.

Jake's pulse quickened when, at his feet, a piece of silver metal reflected in the sunlight. He pulled apart the foliage only to find a flattened beer can half-buried in the dirt. Damn it! More junk. Sighing, he stood up and continued his methodical search with Rick at his side.

"How do you think it went down?" Rick asked.

"What went down?"

"Tom dying, I mean. An average family guy is shot and killed on a Sunday morning in the middle of nowhere. It's odd."

"I agree. It doesn't make sense, but people are dumb."

Rick's mouth twisted to the side. "I guess."

"They are," Jake insisted. "How many times in the news have you heard about a road-rage shooting? Two guys stop their cars, fight, and someone dies. It must happen a couple of times a year with all the concealed carry permits in this country."

Rick shook his head. "I don't know. It sounds too simple."

Jake kicked the earth with the toe of his shoe. A clump of grass tore loose. "Then what do you think happened?"

"I'm glad you asked because I have a few theories." Rick rubbed the whiskers on his chin.

Jake couldn't wait to hear them. They'd be far-fetched for sure, knowing Rick. Hunching over, Jake scanned the small radius in front of him. "Enlighten me."

Rick said, "I bet that it was two people, and they set a trap with a pretty girl wearing a short skirt who pretends to have a flat tire. Tom stops to help her, a thug appears with a gun, and they attempt to rob him. Tom fights back, and he gets shot, so they take off, and Tom's left for dead."

Jake shook his head slowly. "That doesn't make any sense."

"Why not?" Rick snapped back.

"Tom wasn't robbed. They didn't take his wallet. The only thing missing was his watch."

"Like you said, people are stupid, and they weren't expecting a fight. The gunshot was loud, and someone noticed the commotion." Rick pointed to a house down the road. "They get scared and run before they can grab Tom's wallet."

"But there's been no witnesses."

"They're too scared to report it. They're afraid the crooks will kill them too."

"I don't buy it."

"You're just mad that you didn't think of it first."

Jake snorted. "Right, that's it. So you have more of these—theories?"

"Forget it. I'm not telling you."

"Fine."

Jake checked for cars and walked across the road for a desperate final sweep. Rick followed lazily after him as Jake's frustration grew. He was missing something. There had to be evidence of Tom's murder, but he'd missed it. Jake considered getting down on his hands and knees for a better view, but he didn't want to dirty his pants until after his interviews.

Jake passed by a dead snapping turtle. The shell was broken nearly in two. Scraps of meat hung from discolored tendons. Most of the animal was picked clean by scavengers. The fishy stench clung to Jake's nostrils, and his stomach rolled as he quickly moved past it.

Unsolicited, Rick said, "My other theory is Tom was having an affair."

Jake stopped. The thought of punching Rick in his nose crossed Jake's mind, but he knew it was just Rick. He thought everyone was a sexual deviant like himself.

"Tom? Seriously?"

"Yes. Maybe he's not the perfect guy you think he is."

"You're crazy. Tom wouldn't cheat."

Rick smiled. "Did you ever screw around on your wife?"

Jake's head dropped, and he was silent for a long moment. "—yes."

Laughing, Rick asked, "What if Tom was having an affair with somebody's wife? The guy finds out about it, and he's jealous with rage. So he stakes out Tom's house and follows him to this deserted stretch of road. He sees his opportunity to kill the asshole nailing his wife, so he flags Tom down and shoots him in cold blood."

Jake shook his head. "No way."

"Why not?" Rick mopped sweat from his brow with the hem of his shirt. "If I had a dollar for every husband that wanted to kill me, I wouldn't be running a shitty lawn cutting business."

Jake growled, "I repeat. Tom wouldn't cheat on Mary."

"All right. Fine. What if Mary was having an affair? The guy is super infatuated with her, but Mary won't leave Tom because of the kids. So the guy decides to remove Tom from the equation and get Mary all to himself."

Jake's fists clenched tight, but he forced them open and walked away. Rick trailed after him. They passed by their parked vehicles off on the shoulder of the road. Jake's beat-up red Focus sat in front of Rick's hulking black Silverado work truck. Beyond their vehicles, Jake thought he saw something in the gravel and leaned down for a better look, but it was only a funny colored rock. A swift kick sent the stone sailing into the ditch.

Rick said, "You don't like my cheating theory."

"Nope."

"Then you won't like my last one."

Jake exhaled. "What is it?"

"Somebody put a hit on Tom."

"Why would somebody put a hit on Tom?"

Rick looked down at the ground. "I don't know. I just have a feeling. Why else would somebody shoot Tom?"

Jake rolled his eyes. "Like I said. People are stupid. Tom cut him off. Or he cut Tom off. Tom gave him the bird. They argue. Tom's dead. It's that simple."

"If you're right, how do you find the killer?" Rick asked.

"I don't know." Jake poked Rick in the chest. "But I will find him."

Rick held up his hands. "Chill out."

"I am chill."

"I think you're letting your emotions and your vision of Tom being this perfect guy get in the way of your amateur investigation."

"Fuck you."

Rick shook his head. "Fuck you too."

An awkward silence fell over the pair. Jake rooted through the long brush but continued to come up empty. His shoes were soaked through to his socks, and his toes probably looked like prunes. Jake had walked the search loop twice, and the crime scene appeared clean.

With his hopes dashed, he stopped walking. What had he hoped to find? A gun? An ID with a bloody fingerprint on it? Rick was right. Jake's amateur investigation wasn't yielding any results, and Tom's case was growing colder by the minute. They'd need a miracle if they hoped to solve it.

Exasperated, Jake kicked at a thick patch of grass. Inside it, something glittered in the sunlight.

Please— please be something important.

He squatted down, using one hand to keep himself from falling over. With the other, he brushed soil away from the edges of the object, then pulled it free from the dirt and held it up. It was the bottom of a glass soda bottle.

Rick said, "That's got to be pretty old."

"Yep."

Careful not to cut himself, Jake flipped his wrist like he was tossing a Frisbee. The glass disk sailed into the adjoining field. He fought the urge to wipe his dirty fingers off on his pants. Instead, he bent down and rubbed them clean in the drying grass. "I guess I'm not going to find anything."

Rick said, "If you want to work for me today, I could pay you fifty bucks."

"Sounds tempting, but I'll pass. I want to ask a few questions at those houses." Jake pointed in the same direction Rick had moments ago.

Rick opened the door to his truck and hiked a boot up into the footwell. "Don't you think the police already did that?"

Jake leaned against the side of his car. The metal was warm. "I'm sure they did, but people can withhold information if they're not asked the right questions."

"All right, Detective." Rick pointed to the rotting turtle carcass across the road. "While you're at it, why don't you take that turtle into the lab, so they can check it for evidence?"

"Shut up, Lawnboy." Jake slammed his car door and drove off, leaving Rick and the turtle in het rearview mirror.

Chapter 9

With high hopes, Jake approached the small yellow house. It was closest to the crime scene, so he'd saved it for last. It had been years since Jake had questioned witnesses, so he'd used the previous houses to revive his techniques. However, the other homeowners hadn't been able to provide information to aid in his investigation. As he feared, things were already growing cold. Jake wished he'd started sooner; then again, he'd been tied up with the funeral.

The house looked like a stiff breeze would knock it over; no wall was at a right angle to the next. Stepping onto the porch, Jake pounded on the flimsy screen door. He heard no movement inside, so he knocked again, as forcefully as he dared. From within, the faint scuffling of feet could be heard. They came closer, and a small shape appeared in the dark interior.

The door creaked open to reveal a frail man with thick eyeglasses. Grey tufts of hair protruded from his pink head like a clown's wig. He wore a yellow cardigan sweater despite the warmer temperatures. Two cats lurked in the dimly lit hallway. A third wound itself around the man's legs, leaving white hair on his faded blue sweatpants.

Before Jake could introduce himself, the man muttered, "What do you want?"

"Hi, sir," Jake said. "I'm investigating the murder that occurred down the road from you. I'd like to ask you a few questions if you have the time."

The man said, "At my age, I have nothing but time or no time at all. It's hard to say."

Jake smiled and nodded. "Well, I'll try not to take up too much of it. May I come in?"

Considering the question, the man looked down and to his left. He must've found the answer at his feet because he stepped aside and motioned Jake into the rancid house. The smell of ammonia was overpowering. Jake tried to breathe through his mouth in small short breaths, but he still wanted to gag.

The man led Jake slowly down the hall. "You're in luck. *The Price is Right* just ended, or I wouldn't have answered the door. I love *The Price is Right* even with Bob Barker retired."

It took a considerable effort for Jake not to kick the man's heels as he shuffled into the kitchen. Faded linoleum peeled up at a seam running across the middle of the room. The man sat down at a square kitchen table. None of the chairs matched; two were folding chairs. The avocado-colored appliances told Jake the room was last furnished in the 1960s. A fourth cat jumped on the table. The man made no effort to remove the feline from the eating surface. Jake sat down hesitantly, testing the chair before he let it bear his full weight. It held, but he didn't dare lean back.

"Sir, my name is Jakob Bryant." He pulled out his notebook. "As I said, I'm helping investigate the incident that occurred last Sunday morning. Can I have your name?"

"Jones. Robert Jones."

Jake fought the urge to rub his burning nostrils. "Did you see or hear anything relating to the murder on the morning in question?"

"What?" the man asked, cupping his hand around his ear.

Jake repeated himself louder.

Mr. Jones's eyes twinkled behind his dense lenses. "Yes. I did."

Jake's pulse quickened. "Did you tell the police about it?"

"I tried to tell the detective about it, but he didn't believe me."

"Was his name Noles?"

"I think so."

"Would you mind telling me what you tried to tell him?"

"I'd love to. Maybe you'll believe me." The man scratched the small orange cat on the table. It arched its back in delight.

Jake nudged his chair forward. He took a pen from his breast pocket. With the ballpoint, he scribbled down Mr. Jones's name and the date. "So, tell me everything you can remember. No detail is too small or insignificant."

Scratching his chin, the man said, "I like you, John. I can tell you're different than that other detective. He was an asshole. Pardon my French, but he was."

"Call me Jake."

Robert Jones said, "It happened Sunday morning. I remember very specifically because the day before was Saturday, and none of my usual television shows were on— like *The Price is Right* or *Wheel of Fortune.* I had a few beers, but I wasn't drunk. I know that other police officer didn't believe me, but I was sober as a gopher."

"I believe you, Mr. Jones."

"Thank you, Jason. So, where was I? Yes, I remember. I'd fallen asleep on the couch. When I woke up, I needed to take a piss. Pardon my French again, but I had to go outside since the toilet is broke. I went to the front yard since I like to save the backyard for my number two's. I was just undoing my belt when I heard the noise."

"A noise? Was it a gunshot?"

"No. It was more like an explosion."

A new cat jumped up on the table. It circled a forgotten ketchup bottle and laid down with a soft thump.

"An explosion like an engine backfiring?" Jake asked.

"No. It was a loud boom like when one of those things comes out of hyperspace. Or whatever they do. I'm no scientist."

"Hyperspace?"

"Outerspace. Innerspace. Hyperspace. I don't know, Jasper, but I know it wasn't of this world. It was triangular shaped and bigger than a football field, smooth black metal with strobing blue lights. It didn't make a sound except for when it entered our atmosphere."

Jake clenched and unclenched his fist under the table. The crazy old man was talking about a UFO instead of Tom's murder. Fighting to keep his composure, Jake inhaled deeply through his mouth and regretted it instantly. He coughed and spit for a full thirty seconds. Mr. Jones appeared unfazed by Jake's reaction.

When his blood pressure dropped to a normal level, Jake asked, "Are you saying that you saw a UFO on Sunday morning?"

"Of course not. It was Sunday night. The UFOs never come out during the day. People would get pictures, and then the NWO couldn't deny they have a pact with the Greys. Am I right, Jim?"

Through gritted teeth, Jake said, "You're absolutely right. The New World Order couldn't allow undeniable photographic evidence to be taken."

Mr. Jones leaned conspiratorially forward, his elbows resting on the tabletop. He put a hand to the side of his mouth and whispered, "The Greys visit me all the time. I think they're trying to abduct me, but I'm smarter than them. I have a secret weapon."

The empty notebook stared back at Jake. He wanted to scream, but he'd expose his lungs to more damage. However, he couldn't resist asking. "Secret weapon?"

A stupid smile crossed Mr. Jones's face. "It's the cats. The Greys are scared of cats."

"They are?"

"Yes. It's because they can't use their mind control on them like they can on people. Why do you think I have so many?"

"Well, thank you for your time, Mr. Jones."

Jake stood up and nearly sprinted for the front door. The old man chased after him; a cat yowled as Mr. Jones stepped on its tail. It scurried off to join its friends as Jake reached the door. A clean breeze trickled through the dirty screen, tasting like forbidden chocolate to a dieter.

"Wait!" Mr. Jones pleaded. "What are you going to do about the UFOs?"

Deciding to humor the crazy old man, Jake turned around. "You're in luck. I'm with a special Anti-Grey unit of the government."

"You are!"

"Yes, and I plan to file a formal request to make the air space over your home a no-fly zone."

"You will?"

"Yes. My superiors take unapproved encounters with the Greys very seriously."

Mr. Jones looked at Jake with complete adoration. "What branch of the government did you say you were from?"

"I didn't, but if you must know I'm with the— "

"Yes?"

The smell in the place gave Jake some much-needed inspiration. "I'm with NOSES."

"NOSES?"

"The National Organization of Secret Extra-terrestrial Secrets."

"I've never heard of them, and I visit the alien chat rooms all the time when I'm not watching my television. Tell me, do you report to the Illuminati?"

Jake exited the odorous dwelling. "No. The Bilderberg Group."

"Wow! They're the most important cabal on this planet."

"I know. Though to be safe, I'd add a few more cats to your defenses in case the Greys ignore our demands."

"Thank you, Jonas."

"You're welcome." The rusty door slapped shut behind Jake. The sunlight and the fresh air overwhelmed his senses, halting his retreat.

A dim outline was still visible through the screen. Mr. Jones said, "I usually don't see the Greys since they fly over after my bedtime. I just hear them in my sleep. They put words in my head when my tin foil hat falls off, but Sunday was different."

"Different how?"

"I got to see the Grey's ship on account of getting woke up by the motorcycle. The bastard messed up my usual sleep schedule."

Jake paused on the step. He couldn't allow himself to get excited over the possibility of some real information. "A motorcycle?"

"Yes, it stopped in the same spot that guy was killed. A loud one. Like a Harley. Not one of those whiny sounding rock crockets."

"Crotch rockets?"

"Right, and a guy searched on the side of the road with a flashlight. Must have been there for ten minutes looking in the tall grass. Do you think he saw the Grey's ship too and was looking for any space junk that fell off of it?"

"It's possible." Jake pulled out his notepad. "Did you tell the other detective any of this?"

"Nope. Like I said, Jeb, he didn't want to hear my story."

"Could you describe the man in the field?"

"Tall. Big. Long hair. I think he was wearing a leather jacket, but it was hard to tell. The moon was only half full."

"Anything else?" Jake asked, scribbling down the details.

Mr. Jones shook his head. "I don't think so."

Jake scribbled down his phone number and ripped off the page. "Here's my cell. Do you have a phone, Mr. Jones?"

"Of course." Mr. Jones opened the door and took the paper from Jake's outstretched hand. A ginger cat took the opportunity to bolt into the yard.

"Good. Call me if you remember anything else about the man or the motorcycle."

"I will, and if I see another UFO?"

Sighing, Jake said, "You can call me when that happens too."

Chapter 10

Two nights later, Caleb entered a nondescript bar across town. The faint hum of traffic exiting Detroit could be heard through the tavern's brick walls. He took a seat at the bar. The leather of the old stool creaked underneath him. Caleb was late for this meeting, thanks to Jodi again, but his tardiness had been well worth it.

The mirror behind the bar was broken, a jagged piece missing from its center. The shattered reflection displayed a nearly empty room behind him. One table was occupied by a pair of hipsters who must've discovered the place last week. Three barflies sat at the opposite end of the bar, not talking to each other as they stared into their beer mugs. The trio of old men had probably sat in those same stools since before the hipsters were born.

Turning back to his image, Caleb noticed pink lipstick on the corner of his mouth. He wiped it off with the back of his hand. He wished he could rub away the mark on his cheek, but it was starting to fade. A few more days, and it would be unnoticeable. He would have to be more cautious next time since he was sick of making excuses for the bruise.

Caleb coughed loudly, and the bar's proprietor materialized from behind a swinging door. Dale was a bald man with a huge belly that pulled at a white button-up shirt. Without making eye contact, Dale slid a thick envelope across the bar. Caleb smiled as he deposited the payment into his pocket. With their monthly business settled, Dale filled a frozen mug and set the ice-cold beer down in front of Caleb. Caleb took a big sip and smacked his lips with approval.

Dale wiped at the spotless bar top with a wet rag and mumbled, "I have a problem."

"A problem?" Caleb feigned surprise.

Nodding, Dale said, "You know me. I never complain, even with the increase you just hit me with."

Caleb shrugged. "It's this damn economy. We all need to make sacrifices."

"Sure, the economy." Dale half-rolled his eyes but stopped himself. "Look. The only reason I bring it up is that it affects your club too."

"It does?"

Dale pointed at the mirror. "Last night, the Outsiders paid me a visit. They informed me their club was taking over the block, and future payments would be made to them."

"The Outsiders? Are you sure?"

"I'm sure. I know all the local colors. It was the Outsiders."

"How many?"

"Two big guys were the muscle— not as big as Aces, but big." Dale brought his hands up to a distance twice as wide as his own shoulders but winced and dropped them down to his side. "The one doing all the talking had a President patch."

"I don't believe you."

"It's true. They came in through the back door after closing and scared the hell out of me. I told them to get lost because I have an arrangement with the Devil's Hand."

"And?"

"And they busted up the mirror and some chairs, then one of the big guys punched me in the stomach."

"At least they hit you in a place where you have a lot of padding."

Dale frowned as he wrung out the wet cloth. "I think they broke a couple of ribs. They said they'd be back next week to collect their first payment. What are we going to do?"

"You have nothing to worry about." Caleb took another big pull from his mug, nearly finishing the beer. "I'll take care of it personally. You'll never see them again."

"I won't?"

Caleb nodded. "You have my word. Sucks about the ribs, those take a long time to heal."

With a meaty hand, Dale mopped the sweat from his brow. "Thank you. The Devil's Hand has always done right by me. I haven't had trouble in all the years I've paid for protection— not so much as a stick-up."

"That's the way it should be. The petty criminals know you're with us and stay away. However, turf wars do break out from time to time. This is the first we've heard of the Outsiders making a push into our territories. But don't worry, we'll send them back to the east side with their tails between their legs."

"Great."

Caleb reached into his jacket and extracted a hundred-dollar bill from the envelope. "Here. Take this for your pain and suffering."

Dale palmed the bill like a magician, and it swiftly disappeared into his pocket. Beaming, Dale said, "Can I get you another beer?"

"Yeah, and I could go for some of your famous fried pickle chips too."

"Absolutely," Dale replied.

He pulled out a fresh mug from the freezer under the bar. A thin layer of frost formed on the glass as Dale filled it expertly to the top. Grabbing a new napkin, he set the beer down in front of Caleb and removed the old one before running to the kitchen.

Caleb took a sip of the beer and relished the taste; nothing beat an ice-cold draft. Still holding the mug, he rotated the stool away from the bar and surveyed the room. He could see the spot where the missing table and chairs would go. The corners of his mouth turned up in a grin until Caleb noticed the hipsters studying him like an exotic animal in the zoo. The sight of them with their goofy knit hats and their distressed clothes turned Caleb's stomach. They each nursed a bottle of cheap beer to add to the charade.

"What are you looking at?" Caleb growled.

"Umm— nothing," one of the pair mumbled.

They hastily found somewhere else to look at in the opposite corner of the room. Caleb watched them for a full minute, but neither one would meet his stare.

"That's what I thought." Caleb spun back around to wait for his food.

Chapter 11

The next afternoon, Caleb took a seat at the front of the meeting room of the Devil's Hand clubhouse. A dozen full members sat around the polished oak table littered with ashtrays and mugs of beer. The men were a grizzly bunch capable of scaring even the most hardened felon. A wooden gavel lay next to Caleb's right hand. Instead of using it, Caleb cleared his throat and said, "All right. Let's call this meeting to order."

A member entered the room, slamming the door behind him. A one-way mirror facing the main room of the clubhouse rattled in its frame. Its view showed a few naive back-warmers sitting at a table waiting for the meeting to end. One woman had boobs so big they could be mistaken for missiles. A bartender bounced around behind the bar like an eager puppy as he prepared drinks for the beautiful girls.

The late-comer, Ian, grabbed an empty chair as he did a double-take at Caleb sitting at the head of the table. Ian asked, "We're having church without Sonny?"

Caleb's stare penetrated Ian's pock-marked face. "If you had been here on time, you would know that Sonny and Aces aren't back yet from their run, but he didn't want this issue with the Outsiders to wait."

"I didn't know," Ian said.

"Well, now you do. Got any more fucking questions, or can I get started?"

Ian sneered, doing his best to maintain some dignity. Everyone else remained silent as Hysko nodded in approval. Caleb waited to make sure he had everyone's attention. "Some of you probably heard, but if you haven't, the Outsiders are trying to muscle into our territory."

Wild Bill flipped his long black ponytail over his shoulder. "No way."

Caleb nodded. "They've hit one of our businesses and told the owner to start making payments to them."

"That's bullshit," Sal shouted. He was a younger member with a shaved head covered in tattoos.

"We'll cut out their God damn hearts," Ian said.

Without warning, the door swung open. The bartender, a hanger-on who didn't have what it took to be a club member, came to the front of the table and rested a hand on Caleb's shoulder. "Do you guys need anything?"

"In fact, I do need something." Caleb leered devilishly at the man as he picked up the gavel.

The man got a big smile on his simple face. "What do you need?"

"Your hand."

"My hand?" The bartender looked around the room nervously. The club members ignored his pleading eyes.

"Put it flat on the table," Caleb ordered, his voice low.

"All right."

He placed his hand on the table in front of Caleb.

"Phil? It's Phil, right?" Caleb asked.

Phil nodded his head; his hand twitched nervously on the table.

"Was the door closed?"

"Yes."

"Which means we're having an important club meeting to discuss private club business. And you barged in without knocking. You know better than that, don't you, Phil?"

Phil squeaked, "I do."

"What if you heard something you shouldn't? That would be bad."

"But I didn't," Phil pleaded.

"Still. We can't have that."

"It won't ever happen again. I swear." Phil shook his head from side to side.

"I'm sure it won't." Caleb brought his hand high above his head.

The gavel fell like a hammer, striking the back of Phil's hand. Bones cracked, and a meaty wet sound echoed off the walls. Phil yowled and pulled his hand back to cradle it in his other arm. He fought back the tears as he danced from foot to foot.

A small grin crept across Caleb's face as he set the gavel back on the table. He looked around the room. Some met his stare. Others found somewhere else to look. The only two people who would dare call Caleb out for being an asshole were absent from the room. And soon enough, he wouldn't have to worry about them.

"You can go now," he said.

"Thank you." Phil scurried for the exit. The door slammed shut behind him.

After lighting a cigarette, Caleb asked, "Now, where was I before that dumbass barged in?"

"The Outsiders," Hysko answered.

"That's right." Caleb smiled. "I talked to Sonny this morning. He wants us to hit them and hit them hard."

Curses were muttered, and fists thudded the table.

Caleb continued, "We're going to firebomb the shit out of their clubhouse. Sonny wants you to head that up, Wild Bill."

Wild Bill nodded his head with solemn approval. "I'll need some help."

Five hands shot up.

Ian said, "We can't expect to kill all those fuckers with a couple of Molotov cocktails."

"No shit," Caleb said. "But we're sending a message, and if we can kill one or two of them, then all the better."

Hearty cheers erupted around the table.

Hysko said, "The Outsiders ain't going to sit around with their thumbs up their asses. I bet they'll hit more of our businesses tonight to make us look weak, and they're doing a pretty fucking good job of it already."

"You're one step ahead of me, old friend," Caleb said with a grin. "Sonny wants us to also protect the places they haven't hit yet. The ones under our protection. So, the plan is for the prospects to stay here and guard our clubhouse. The rest of you not going with Bill, you'll split up to watch the remaining businesses."

"Sounds like a plan," Ian said.

Caleb said, "Hysko, Larry, and I'll take Mitch's Bar since I think that's where they'll hit next. They've been under our protection forever, and it'd be a real black eye for us if the Outsiders showed their face in there."

Hysko groused mockingly, "Can't I get teamed with someone else?"

Caleb ground out his cigarette. "Fuck off, you're stuck with me. Any other questions?"

"Nope," Wild Bill said. The rest of the members agreed.

"Good."

"Then get the hell out of here, and I expect to see an Outsider's cut hanging on the flagpole by morning."

Chairs scraped back as the Devil's Hand club filed past the framed pictures of their fallen brothers. Members coordinated their individual plans in low whispers. Larry headed for the door with the others.

Caleb said, "Where're you running off to, Larry? We need to discuss tonight."

Larry spun his six-foot frame around and returned to stand at the end of the table opposite Caleb. Hysko lingered by the exit. When the last member left the room, Hysko closed it, the latch clicking into place.

"Right. When do you want to leave?" Larry asked.

"Sit down. We've got something else we need to discuss," Caleb said.

Larry fell into a chair, nervously scratching the stubble on his chin. "What's that?"

Caleb picked up his gavel and waved it menacingly in the air. "Your future."

"My future?"

Caleb said, "Yes. I'm going to make you an offer that you can't refuse."

Chuckling, Larry said, "Isn't that a quote from *Goodfellas*?"

Caleb and Hysko both groaned, but Hysko had been right. Larry would be the perfect pawn in their game. He was stupid enough to be useful and dumb enough that if Caleb had to sacrifice him, it wouldn't hurt the club.

49

Chapter 12

That same day, Jake sat in the kitchen of Bobby's tiny bungalow. His notes covered the laminated table. The pages were the sum total of Jake's investigation for the last few days. They contained a few clues but no real answers, and nothing new had been added since yesterday. He studied them one more time, hoping to discover a new angle for his inquiry, but he knew it was hopeless. He'd turned the crime scene as well as Tom's life upside down and found nothing.

Surprisingly, Mary had given Jake total access to the couple's phone records and the home computers. Unlike Rick, he hadn't thought that either of them would be involved in an extra-marital affair. Still, he went through their electronic history. Unsurprisingly, there were no jealous lovers for either Tom or Mary.

Furthermore, Tom was also well-liked by his co-workers. Jake had caught a few of them coming out of the office yesterday, and they'd confirmed what Dolan had told Jake— Tom worked strictly on boring corporate accounts. They'd also reiterated that Tom had no personal issues with anyone and had done absolutely nothing to make someone angry enough to kill him. Just the same, Jake would've liked to examine the files on Tom's work computer, but Dolan wouldn't let him anywhere near it during his unannounced visit.

In fact, Dolan had threatened to call the real police on Jake if he didn't leave the building immediately. Jake wished Dolan had; maybe then he could get some facetime with Detective Noles. Because to this point, Noles had ignored Jake's calls, and he certainly wasn't sharing any information with him. And without access to the real evidence, Jake was as useful to the investigation as screen doors on a submarine. Handicapped like he was, Jake had been kidding himself to think he could find Tom's killer.

If there'd been any evidence at the scene, Jake couldn't find it, so the rain, wind, or elements must've destroyed it. Besides, he'd talked to everyone for a mile in either direction, or no one saw a thing. The most helpful person had been Mr. Jones, who thought he saw a biker return to the scene that night. Yet, if it was related, could he have removed a key piece of evidence before Jake's search? Upon further reflection, Jake didn't think so. It was probably a weekend warrior who lost his phone from his pack and came back to look for it.

Jake had one more idea, but it was risky. He wanted to follow Tom's boss to see what he could learn. Something about Dolan bugged Jake even though the background searches revealed the man was as clean as a whistle. Still, it would be worth the inevitable harassment charges if Jake could identify the killer before Noles.

With that thought, Jake placed the call he'd been putting off.

His boss answered, "XP Stampings. Production."

"Hey, Keith. It's Jake."

"Jake, where the hell are you? I was expecting you back today."

"I'm still in Michigan dealing with my friend's affairs."

"Affairs? Are you the executor?" Keith asked.

"No, but his widow needed my help, so I was wondering if I could have a few more days."

"You've got to be shitting me."

Jake grabbed a pen, tapping it on the table. "I wish I was."

"Sorry, I can't do it. I'm up to my asshole in alligators here."

"What if you count days against me for next year?"

"Not a chance. That jackoff running your machine ruined five hundred parts this week. If you're not back here by Monday, I'm going to have to fire you, Jake. Are we clear?"

The phone beeped, alerting Jake to another call. It was Mary's number. "Keith? Can you hang on a second?"

"No. You listen to— "

Jake clicked over. "Hi, Mary."

"Hi, have you left yet?"

"No, but I'll be over in an hour," Jake said, checking the clock on the stove.

"That's why I'm calling. You don't need to come over."

"Why?"

"Because the kids and I took care of the lawn."

He shifted in his chair. "But I said I would help."

"I know, but we have to learn to do this kind of thing on our own."

He shook his head. "Your lawn is so big."

"Tell me about it. I'm sweating like a pig," she said with a laugh.

Jake's phone beeped again.

Mary asked, "Do you have another call?"

"It's fine. It was my boss, but he hung up."

"I'm sorry. Was he checking up on you?"

He picked up his notes and tapped them against the table to straighten them. "No, he told me to be back to work on Monday."

"Monday! That's in two days."

"Yeah. Or I'm fired."

"Fired! Are you serious?"

"It's no big deal. I've wanted to quit that stupid job for a while. Besides, I have a few more things I need to check out with Tom's case."

"Jake, you need to go back to work. You can't lose your job over this. I appreciate all you've done, but— "

"But what?" he asked, louder than he would've liked.

Mary was silent for a moment before asking gently, "Umm . . . aren't the police better equipped to solve Tom's case? I think you should tell your boss you'll be back to work on Monday."

"Fine."

"Jake— "

"Whatever." He ended the call, more upset at his ineptitude than at Mary. Jake redialed Keith's number with a finger that threatened to crack the phone's screen.

"XP Stampings. Production."

"Keith. It's Jake again."

"I'm done talking. I better see you on Monday morning. No excuses."

Jake's shoulders slumped. "I'll be there."

Keith hung up without as much as a goodbye. Resisting the urge to throw his phone at the wall, Jake settled for tossing the pen across the table. It slid on Bobby's ugly linoleum and landed under the fridge. Jake was still staring at the floor when Bobby came home from work twenty minutes later, wearing steel-toed boots and greasy blue overalls. In one hand, he had a large plastic lunchbox, and the other held his mail. Jake didn't look up. Bobby set his stuff down and gave Jake's shoulder a squeeze.

"What's up?"

Jake shook his head. "Absolutely nothing. I've got shit in Tom's case."

Bobby walked to the sink and got a glass of water. "You knew it would be hard, right?"

"Yes, but— "

"Hang in there. I'm sure you'll find something soon. Didn't you find the Silkworm rapist?"

Jake frowned, wishing Bobby would stop bringing up that horrible fact. He said, "It doesn't matter. I'm out of time."

"What do you mean?"

"I will lose my job if I'm not back to work on Monday."

"Shit! That means you have to drive back tomorrow."

Nodding, Jake said, "That's true."

"Well, if you have to go, then you have to go, but we're taking you out tonight to see you off right. What do you think about Mitch's?"

"I'm not sure. I'm kind of tired." Jake stretched his arms above his head.

Digging his phone out of his back pocket, Bobby tapped at the screen with more dexterity than his wide fingers would suggest. "Too late. I texted Rick."

His phone beeped seconds later. Bobby smiled. "Rick's in. Do you want me to text Mary?"

Sighing, Jake shook his head. "No. I'll do it."

"Great. I'll go shower. Tell her to meet us there at eight o'clock," Bobby said as he lumbered out of the room.

"Sure."

Jake didn't want to go back to Chicago and his dead-end job. It should have been him that died, not Tom. People needed him while Jake slid through a worthless existence with an ex-wife that hated him and a daughter he barely got to see. Jake swiped at his notes, and they fluttered to the floor.

Bobby's voice echoed from the back of the small house. "Everything all right?"

"Yeah. Everything's fine." Scooping up his phone, he went to his recent calls and found Mary's number.

A female voice answered, "Hello."

"Mary?"

"No. It's Emma. Mom's in the shower. I answered because I saw that it was you, Uncle Jake."

"Ohh— hi, Emma."

"What's up?" she asked.

"It's kind of silly, but I have to go home tomorrow, and Uncle Bobby insists on taking me out for dinner. You know, to see me off, so I was calling to invite your mom."

"Great. I'll tell her."

"She doesn't have to come if she doesn't want to."

"No. Mom said she needed to run a few errands, but I'll make sure she goes afterward. I can be quite persistent."

He laughed. "I don't doubt that. Tell her we're meeting at Mitch's around eight o'clock."

"I will. Are you going to come here before you go? I'd like to say goodbye too," Emma said.

"I'll see what I can do," he teased. Of all the kids, he felt closest to her.

Emma pleaded, "You have to."

Smiling, Jake rolled his eyes. "Okay. I will."

"Thanks. I'll see you tomorrow. Bye."

Before she could end the call, he yelled, "Wait. Have your mom text me from the parking lot. Mitch's isn't in the greatest neighborhood, especially at night."

"Got it." Emma ended the call.

Chapter 13

The door to Mitch's Bar swung open with a metallic groan, and Mary walked in. Jake stood up and waved to get her attention. She wore a tight pair of jeans, black flats, and a maroon sweater. Makeup covered the dark circles under her eyes, and her hair sported a few curls. Jake, Bobby, and Rick were outclassed in their old t-shirts, making Jake wish he'd put on a button-up long sleeve so that he didn't look like a complete schmuck.

Meeting her in the aisle, Jake gave Mary a hug. "I thought you were going to text me when you got here."

"I forgot. Besides, I found a parking spot right by the door." She gave him a quick peck on the cheek, smelling of lavender and vanilla. "And thanks for turning my kid against me, by the way."

"It was Emma's idea."

"I don't believe you."

Jake shrugged. "Anyway, you look great."

"Shut up. I look like hell."

Rick and Bobby stood, their chairs scraping on the wood floor. Rick said, "I agree. You look like hell, Mary."

Laughing, she hugged him but skipped the kiss. "Thanks, Rick."

"You know me. I'm a lot of things, but I'm not a liar." Rick sat back down.

"But Rick is an asshole." Bobby gave her a big bear hug that squeezed the breath out of her.

Mary pulled out the remaining chair at the table and plopped down with a sigh. Half-full glasses of beer and a soda for Jake rested on the table. Bobby and Rick studied a flat-screen television mounted in the corner with a Detroit Tigers baseball game playing on mute.

Jake fiddled with his straw. "We were worried about you. It was getting kind of late."

She grinned. "I almost called off. After I struggled to decide which bike to buy Hunter for his birthday, I really wanted to go home, put on my pajamas, and eat a bowl of ice cream. But Emma insisted that I come here."

"She said she could be persistent," Jake said.

"Yes, she can," Mary agreed.

Jake grinned. "What do you want to drink?"

"I'll have a rum and diet when the waitress shows up," Mary replied.

Not waiting, Jake waved to their server two tables away, who made her way over. She wore short shorts and an out-of-date hairstyle. Laying her hand on Bobby's shoulder, she gave it a flirty squeeze. Bobby's eyes widened with delight at her t-shirt that was a size too small. Jake snorted and gave her Mary's drink order.

The waitress winked at Rick. "How about you guys? Need another pitcher?"

"You twisted my arm." Bobby jokingly put his hand behind his back before pointing to Jake. "And a Coke Zero for my little friend."

The waitress looked around the table, her big hoop earrings swinging wildly. "Are you ready for food yet?"

"Definitely," Bobby replied. "How about four bacon cheeseburgers and a large basket of fries."

"Sounds good." She grabbed the pitcher and poured the remaining beer into their glasses. "I'll put the food order in and be back with your drinks."

After she left, Rick elbowed Bobby. "How do you know what I wanted to eat?"

Bobby rubbed his belly. "You know they only serve burgers here."

"Yeah, but what if I wanted onion rings?"

"Then order them when she comes back."

Rick shook his head. "No, fries are good."

"Dickhead!" Bobby finished his beer and got up to use the bathroom as Mary and Jake snickered.

Curses erupted at the pool table in the far corner of the bar. Jake turned to find three bikers playing a game of nine-ball, yelling, swearing, and generally being assholes. Not surprisingly, the neighboring tables were empty in the otherwise full bar. The men had long hair and tattoos down to their wrists. On the back of their leather vests was a patch embroidered with a skeletal hand on fire. The outlaws howled with laughter when a pretty waitress dropped off their beer and got goosed as a tip.

"Who are they?" Jake motioned in the direction of the pool table.

"The Devil's Hand. They own all the illegal stuff in this part of town," Rick said, his eyes still on the television.

"The Devil's Hand. I've never heard of them."

"They're local, only the one chapter, so they're not that tough. I'll give you a hundred dollars if you go outside and kick over their motorcycles."

Jake groaned. "I would, but I left my orangutan at home."

The waitress dropped off their drinks. Jake took a sip from his soda. Smacking his lips, he tried to convince himself he didn't miss the taste of alcohol. He wasn't convinced he'd been a certified alcoholic since he hadn't needed a formal program to kick his addiction. But he was wary of his father's example, and it was certainly true that he made enough dumb decisions while sober—he didn't need booze to make things any worse.

Bobby came back from the bathroom and fell heavily into his chair, eyeing the fresh pitcher of beer. "Perfect timing. What were you girls talking about?"

"Jake asked about the motorcycle gang over there," Rick said.

Bobby filled his glass. "I'd stay away from them. They are the real deal, not like those idiots who have a mid-life crisis and buy a Harley to ride on the weekends with their friends."

Jake wasn't surprised by his friends' contrasting opinions, which only highlighted their different personalities.

The baseball game entered a commercial break, and Rick brought his attention back to his friends. "Are you excited to get home, Jake?"

Jake glanced in Mary's direction, but she focused on the red straw jutting from her drink. He said, "I'm excited to get back to Sam, but not my sucky job. I'd like to move home to Michigan one day, maybe when Sam goes away to college."

"That would be sweet," Bobby said. "It's a shame you couldn't get anywhere with Tom's case before you had to go back."

"Me too, but I'm confident the police will get a break soon," Jake lied for Mary's sake.

The waitress arrived with their meals. She brushed her ample bosom against Bobby's arm as she set the food down on the table. The smell of grease and bacon made Jake's mouth water. Everyone grabbed their burgers with two hands and dug in with looks of pure satisfaction. Of course, Bobby finished first, but Jake was a close second. Mary pushed her plate away with half of her burger untouched. Bobby eyed it hungrily but didn't ask to finish it for her. The waitress stopped by again. Mary hesitated but decided against ordering a second drink, while Rick ordered another pitcher for the table.

After she left with their plates, Mary said, "You know I thought I saw him when I was driving here. He was in the car next to me."

"Who?" Jake asked.

"Tom."

Mary's voice cracked as she continued. "I know it wasn't, but for a half a second, I believed it was him. There is still so much I want to tell him."

Bobby placed a hand on her arm. "Mary, I miss him too. I know it doesn't compare to your loss, but I think wherever Tom is, he can hear us."

"I hope so because I talk to him a lot."

With wet eyes, Bobby said, "He definitely can."

Mary smiled at him weakly. The makeup no longer hid the circles under her eyes. She finished her drink and said, "Sorry, but I think it's time for me to go home."

Jake looked down at the floor, wishing Mary would stay a little longer. "It means a lot to me that you came out tonight."

Mary nodded. "Thanks for being there for the kids and me this week. Are you coming by tomorrow before you leave?"

"Emma would never forgive me if I didn't."

Mary laughed. "You got that right."

Wild cheers came from the pool table when the winning ball was put in the corner pocket. Cursing loudly, the losing biker made his way to the bar to buy another round of drinks. Patrons scooted in their chairs to give him a wide berth. Jake understood why; he was menacing, with a large purple scar across his face. Once he'd passed, Mary stood up, followed by Rick, Bobby, and Jake.

"Goodnight." She hugged Rick and Bobby.

Mary went to hug Jake, but he put his hand out. "Let me walk you to your car."

She shook her head. "Fine, but I need to visit the little girl's room first."

"No problem. I need to go too."

Weaving between tables, Jake led the way through the crowded bar and to the restrooms, which were down a wide hallway near the kitchen. After taking care of business, Jake exited the men's room in a rush, buoyed by his empty bladder. He almost ran into the rough-looking biker. They both stopped abruptly, face to face.

More out of habit than anything else, Jake said, "Sorry, my fault."

"Fucking people." The biker side-stepped Jake and entered the bathroom.

"Asshole!" Jake muttered over his shoulder before he turned to find Mary down the hall. Her feet were rooted to the floor. Her face was drained of all the color except bright red dots on her cheeks. Concerned, he rushed to her. "Mary, what's wrong?"

"That guy was wearing Tom's watch!"

Chapter 14

Mary's hands fluttered around like tiny birds as her eyes darted from side to side. "Oh, my God. He's really wearing Tom's watch!"

Jake had been concerned with Mary's earlier admission that she thought she'd seen Tom in traffic. Now she claimed to see someone wearing his watch. This night had been too much for her. He never should've pushed for her to come out so soon after Tom's death.

Jake placed his hands on her shoulders. "Mary, slow down. Who?"

"The biker! I came out of the bathroom and ran straight into him. When he grabbed me to keep me from falling over, I saw Tom's watch on his wrist."

"Was it Tom's watch, or did it just look like Tom's watch?"

"Fuck you, Jake. I'm telling you it was Tom's watch. I'd know it anywhere."

Mary shook in his arms— still, he saw the certainty of what she knew to be true in her eyes. He squeezed her tight to stop the trembling. "All right. I believe you."

"Thank you, but how did the bastard get it?"

"That's a good— "

Suddenly, she stiffened, and her eyes grew as big as dinner plates. Jake glanced over his shoulder to find the biker had exited the bathroom and was coming their way. Jake released Mary, not believing his luck. Tom's killer could be right here in this bar. Whipping around, he blocked the biker's path. The biker stopped and gave Jake a quizzical yet menacing stare.

Without thinking, Jake reached for the man's arm. He had to admit the antique timepiece did look like Tom's watch at a glance. "Excuse me, but I couldn't help but notice your watch. Do you mind if I have a look at it?"

A weird look flashed across the biker's face, but he swiftly regained his composure. He jerked his arm from Jake's grasp. "This old thing. I've had it forever."

From behind him, Mary screamed, "That's my husband's watch! Give it back."

"You're a crazy bitch!" The biker tried to push past them.

There was no way Jake was letting this guy escape until he got some answers. He launched himself at the biker, pushing him into the wall. The biker pulled his arm back to punch Jake and knocked a picture from its nail. It crashed to the floor as Mary screamed. Jake brought his hands up in time to deflect the punch, and then he landed a body shot of his own. The biker grunted in pain and grabbed Jake, trying to pin him against the wall. Jake fought back hard; the muscles in his arm bulged with the strain.

The hallway was wide, but it still offered limited fighting options. Jake needed to end this and fast, given the size disadvantage. He tried to land a hook to his opponent's chin, but it fell short as the biker connected with an elbow to the side of Jake's head, sloshing his brain around. His vision turned gray and narrowed. Jake clutched at the biker's jacket, waiting for the white dots to stop flitting around like fireflies.

Mary's cries grew louder. Jake felt her climbing over his back, clawing at the biker's face with a flash of painted fingernails. Spit, sweat, and curses flew from all three of them. Jake used Mary's distraction to land an uppercut. The biker's jaw clapped shut with a snapping of teeth. Before Jake could finish him, loud shouts ordered him to stop. Had the police arrived that quickly? Turning, he saw two more bikers standing inside the back door; one was the size of a brick shithouse.

Fuck! Jake was in serious trouble.

With the cavalry at his back, Jake's adversary doubled his efforts and pushed him into Mary. She fell on her butt, and Jake tripped over her, cracking his head on the far wall. The biker pounced on Jake, pressing his forearm across Jake's throat. Jake fought for air. Acting out of pure instinct, he thrust his knee up and caught the biker in the family jewels. The biker's face twisted in agony, and his arm fell from Jake's throat so that he could cradle his groin.

Jake grabbed Mary to beat a hasty retreat when he was lifted up by his hair. His feet dangled inches from the sticky floor as he thrashed to get free. The smaller of the new arrivals shouted, "Bring them outside."

It was the larger man who held Jake like a rag doll. However, the smaller man was the one who radiated raw power from his piercing blue eyes. The gang's leader slammed the back door open and exited the building. The giant ushered the scarred biker and Mary ahead of him while dragging Jake behind. Jake wondered where the hell Rick and Bobby were; he could really use their help right now. The Tigers game couldn't be that interesting.

Once outside, the giant threw Jake across the gravel parking lot. Pain erupted across his whole body like a firework's finale. A quick survey told him nothing was broken, but he still struggled to get to his feet. He was promptly knocked back down by the giant's bitch slap.

The gang's leader came to stand over Jake. "You must be pretty fucking stupid."

Jake spit blood on the ground but luckily no teeth. "That's not the first time I've heard that."

"Good, then you won't be surprised when we break both your arms. No one lays a finger on the Devil's Hand and gets away with it."

The other two bikers from the pool table spilled out of the bar to join their friends. It was now five on one. Where the hell were Bobby and Rick?

Mary jumped in front of Jake. "Leave him alone."

"Take care of her," the leader said.

The mountain of a man easily scooped Mary up and held her in a bear hug. The remaining bikers advanced on Jake in the dim light of the parking lot. They formed a circle around him, leaving him backed up against a wire fence with nowhere to run. Mary hissed and fought like a wet cat, but the giant held her tight. The bikers inched forward, casting long wolfish shadows across the parking lot.

Screw it. Jake stood tall and waved them in. The leader laughed.

The back door of the bar slammed open, banging loudly off the brick wall. Bobby ran out with Rick hot on his tail. The men ignored them, their attention on Jake. Bobby skidded to a stop behind the crowd. "Sonny!"

Bobby got no reaction, so he shouted louder, "Sonny! Call it off!"

The gang's leader looked over with mild surprise. "Bobby?"

"Stop. He's with me."

"He is?" Sonny asked. "Because if he's with you, what the hell is he doing picking a fight with Caleb?"

"I don't know, but can we talk about it for a second?" Bobby pleaded.

Sonny gave Bobby a nod and shouted. "Caleb, Hysko, Larry. Hold up."

The three men halted in front of Jake.

With some effort, Jake kept his hands up. The adrenaline was wearing off, and pain set in all over his body. Panting heavily, he looked past his attackers at Bobby and wondered what the hell was going on. Bobby should be busting their heads open, not asking for a conference.

Bobby slipped between the bikers and put a hand on Jake's shoulder. "What the hell is going on?"

Anger bubbled up inside him as Jake pointed at the scarred biker. "He's wearing Tom's watch. I want to know how he got it."

Mary shrieked, fighting to get out of the giant's arms. "Did you kill my husband?"

All eyes turned to the man and the watch. He returned their stares defiantly, exclaiming, "I don't care if they are Bobby's friends. These two are insane. I've had this watch forever. I told them that, and this asshole jumps me anyway— so with your permission, Sonny, I'd like to continue this beat-down."

Sonny bit his lip as he studied all the participants, looking from Jake to Caleb to Mary and stopping at Bobby. Sonny asked, "This Tom, he's a friend of yours?"

"Yes," replied Bobby. "One of my best friends since we were kids. He was murdered last week."

Sonny looked shocked. "Murdered?"

"Yes. Shot in the chest."

Sonny nodded his head slowly.

He turned to the scarred biker. "Caleb, is that your watch?"

"I can't believe you're making me repeat myself." Caleb glared at Sonny. "Yes. It's my God damn watch."

Sonny paused to look in Mary's direction. "Well, there you go. Caleb says it's his watch. Now, I understand how you all must feel, seeing as your friend and husband just died. So I'm going to give you a one-time pass. Leave right now, and I'll overlook your stupidity."

Jake opened his mouth to tell them to go fuck a garbage disposal, but Bobby must have known how Jake would respond. He clamped his hand down tight on Jake's shoulder as Mary writhed in the giant's arms to no avail. For all Rick had done in this encounter, he might as well have been a statue. Jake hated both his friends at this moment, Bobby more so since he appeared to be in bed with these snakes.

Caleb kicked at the gravel. "That's bullshit, Sonny."

"I said it's over."

"It's not over."

"The fuck it is. Now get inside before I decide to kick the shit out of you myself." Sonny pointed to the back door of Mitch's bar before turning his gaze back on Bobby. "And you. Get your friends the hell out of here before I change my mind."

"We need to pay our bill," Bobby said.

Sonny frowned. "I'll take care of it."

"Thank you."

"Go."

The mountain released Mary, who rushed to Jake's side. Hesitantly, Bobby and Rick moved towards their cars. The bikers sauntered back to the bar, led by Sonny, but Caleb didn't follow them. He lingered behind.

Mary whispered in Jake's ear. "We have to go to the police and report this."

Jake's shoulders slumped in despair. He suddenly realized how bad he'd screwed up tonight. Why had he picked a fight with these assholes? That wouldn't get them anywhere. It only showed their hand. Would he ever learn to think before he leaped? He didn't think so. Lost in his thoughts, he never saw or heard the biker rush at him.

The biker landed a haymaker to the side of Jake's jaw. The punch short-circuited his brain. Jake crumpled to the ground, pulling Mary down with him.

Caleb stood over the pair and laughed. "Now it's over."

Chapter 15

Jake's head flopped forward when Mary coasted to a stop in her driveway. A fresh wave of pain erupted in his skull, and he groaned loudly. Mary rushed around the car and opened his door. She tried to take Jake's arm, but he angrily waved her off. Instead, he pulled himself up using the car's frame for support. Once out of the vehicle, he propped himself against the open door while waiting for the earth to stop spinning.

Bobby and Rick hesitantly approached Mary's car, having followed them home. Bobby asked, "Are you all right?"

Jake said, "Yes! But I'd be better if I had that fucker and Tom's watch down at the police station."

"That wasn't going to happen with four of them plus André the Giant," Rick replied.

Jake rubbed his jaw. "No thanks to you guys. Where were you?"

"At first, we thought all the screams were because the Tigers hit a grand slam to win the game. But then someone said there was a fight, and you two were nowhere to be found."

"His name is Aces," Bobby said.

"What are you talking about?" Jake asked, confused. Was his brain more scrambled than he thought? Maybe, he should have let Mary take him to the ER.

"The giant's name is Aces, not André," Bobby said. "And you lost that fight before it started. You fight one of them guys, then you fight all of them. You're lucky that Sonny took pity on us."

"Yeah! What the hell was that about? How do you know them?" Jake asked.

Bobby screwed his mouth to the side. "I guess you could say I'm an associate of theirs. I do some discounted mechanic work for the club, and they look out for me in certain matters."

"So you associate with murderers?" Mary glared at him.

"It's not like that. I thought they only did petty stuff. Some gambling and drugs and loan-sharking."

Jake turned to Rick. "Did you know Bobby had an association with this gang?"

Rick shook his head. "Nope. It's news to me."

Turning back to Bobby, Jake said, "I can't believe you're in bed with them."

"It's not something that I'm proud of, but it's what I had to do to survive."

"Why?" Mary asked.

"When I first took over the garage, I ran into money trouble. The bank wouldn't give me a loan, and the Devil's Hand would. It got me over the hump, but then I missed a few payments, and our relationship got more complicated. Now I fix their cars at cost, amongst other things."

Mary frowned at Bobby. Disappointment oozed from every pore. "That doesn't change the fact that the asshole had Tom's watch. So when it comes down to it, whose side are you on?"

"Tom's side. I swear." Bobby crossed a finger over his heart.

Rick asked, "Are you sure it was Tom's watch?"

Mary's head bobbed up and down. "Positive."

"I saw it too. It was Tom's watch. I bet my life on it, literally," Jake said.

Bobby said, "I believe you, but it doesn't make any sense."

"It does if he killed Tom, and then took his watch," Jake said.

Bobby shook his head from side to side. "But why would he kill Tom?"

"Because he is a rabid monster," Mary spat.

Rick nodded. "True. We all saw how he sucker-punched Jake, but what can we do now?"

Mary said, "I'm going to the police station in the morning to tell them what happened. I'd go tonight, but I want to find a picture of the watch, so they have enough proof to lock that asshole up."

"I just can't believe it," Bobby said.

Jake shouted, "Quit kissing their asses and believe it. Weren't you the one who wanted to get all medieval on Tom's killer?"

Cringing, Bobby said, "You're right. I'll take you to the police station tomorrow, Mary."

"No, I'll take her. I was the one who was assaulted," Jake said.

"Yes, Jake should," Rick agreed. "Plus, if you stay out of it, Mr. Devil's Hand Kisser, maybe you can find out something from the inside."

"Screw you."

"Whatever, fat boy," Rick shot back.

The burger and fries Jake had eaten earlier rose up into his throat. He concentrated on keeping them down, which only made his head hurt more. Afraid he would throw up in front of his friends, he took a step towards the house, but his legs buckled. He leaned back against the car while he took slow deep breaths.

Mary said, "Jake, you aren't looking so good. You should have let us take you to the ER."

"I'm fine." The deep breathing seemed to be helping, but he wasn't sure for how long. "I just need to lay down."

"He can go back to my place. I'll keep a close eye on him," Bobby said.

Mary shook her head. "I'll feel better with him here. I'm pretty sure he's concussed."

"I'm not concussed!" Jake insisted.

Rick laughed. "Dude, you so have a concussion. That guy laid you the fuck out."

"Shut up." Jake pushed off the car and plodded towards the front door. He could feel himself weaving, but he couldn't seem to straighten out his path. Soft footfalls caught up to him, and he felt Mary's hand on his back to steady him.

Bobby called after them, "Do you need a hand?"

"No, we're good," Mary shouted back as she led Jake up the steps and into the house.

Chapter 16

The ground moved under Jake's feet like a Tilt-a-Whirl, so he let Mary guide him up the steps. He looked back at his friends and gave them a reassuring wave. Bobby and Rick were clearly unimpressed as they turned and walked back to their vehicles, casting doubtful glances to one another. Mary opened the front door with a key and led Jake through the kitchen to the family room. They found Emma asleep on the couch in front of a flickering television.

Mary left Jake leaning against a wall while she sat down on the edge of the couch. The nausea had passed, but Jake felt extremely tired. Mary woke Emma up with a gentle nudge. The girl sat up with her eyes still closed, stretched, and yawned, her mouth wide enough to stick a fist inside.

"Sorry we're so late. Where's your brother and sister?" Mary asked.

Emma took in her surroundings and did a double-take when she saw Jake. She said, "Hunter went to bed, and I think Lindsey's in her room watching HBO Max."

Mary stood up and smoothed out her sweater. "We don't have HBO Max."

"Oops."

"How is she watching it?"

"I think she got a password from one of her friends."

"Hmmm. I'll have to talk to her about that. Why don't you go on up to bed? Uncle Jake is going to sleep on the couch tonight. He isn't feeling well. He has . . . food poisoning."

Jake said, "That's if it's all right with you, Emma."

Grabbing her phone from the armrest, Emma said, "Sure, why wouldn't it be?"

"Good, because . . . Yes. I think I ate some bad clams— and I'm not feeling so hot."

Mary gave Jake an icy stare, and he shut his mouth before he said anything else stupid. After Emma left, he stumbled to the couch. With one foot on the floor to steady himself, the room remained motionless, so he didn't think he had a concussion. Back in the day, he'd got a concussion in a game, and it had felt a lot worse than this.

Mary squatted down next to him. "Jake, I want to check on Lindsey and Hunter."

"Go ahead."

"I'll only be a minute."

Jake must have nodded off because when he woke up, Mary stood over him in a pair of sleep pants and a t-shirt. She held a pillow and two blankets. He lifted his head, and she slipped the pillow underneath it. Kicking off his shoes, he placed his feet on the armrest, and she tucked the blanket around him like he was a little child.

"Thank you," he said with a sigh.

"No, I need to thank you." She smiled down at him. "Tonight, you were my hero. You believed me even when I sounded crazy."

Guilt stabbed at Jake's upset stomach. He tried to sit up. "You're wrong. I screwed up. I should have handled things differently with that biker."

She pushed him back down. "It's not your fault. I was the one who freaked out, so stop worrying and go to sleep, Jake."

"Can I sleep with a concussion?"

Smirking, she said, "I didn't think you were concussed."

"I'm serious," he pouted.

"How many fingers do you see?" she asked, raising her hand in front of his face.

"One, and there's no reason to flip me off."

"You're right. You don't deserve that, not after you foolishly took on five men for me." She bent over and gave him a light peck on the cheek.

His whole face grew warm, and the pain temporarily faded. "That's me, your fool."

"Do you need anything?" she asked.

"How about three ibuprofens and a glass of water?"

Smiling, she hopped up and got the pills and water. After he took them and drank half of the water, Mary set the glass on the end table near his head. She asked, "Anything else?"

"I'm good. You should get to bed."

"No, I was serious. I'm going to keep a close eye on you." She sat down in the rocker next to him and wrapped herself in a blanket.

His eyes started to close, but he forced them open. He turned to face her. "I think that asshole murdered Tom."

She nodded her head. "I think you're right, but we're in over our heads. We'll tell Detective Noles to sort it out."

"Yes, this changes everything." He nodded despite the pain. Bobby could provide Jake enough information to close this case.

I don't need to remind you that you still need to get back home to Sam and your job."

"I will, but in a few days after Caleb is arrested and charged."

A creaking sound came from the hallway, followed by light footfalls. They waited to see which kid was coming downstairs. Instead, Socks, the family cat, entered the room and padded towards them. The cat climbed into Mary's lap, purring loudly as she stroked its ears.

She asked, "You won't get fired?"

"No. Keith will be pissed, but I'm the only one that can run that damn machine. He'll have to take me back."

"I hope so."

Maybe it was what happened earlier or the throbbing pain in his jaw. Either way, Jake decided to cross a line that he promised never to cross. But with the sympathy she was feeling for him tonight, perhaps he'd finally get an answer to the question that kept him awake most nights.

With some effort, he sat up. "Do you remember the last time we spent the night together?"

She leaped from her chair; Socks meowed as he hit the carpet. Stomping across the room, she smacked Jake on the arm. Hard. A lot harder than he thought she could hit. "Damn you, Jake. We agreed to never talk about that."

"I know, but it's been eating at me for the last twelve years."

She shook her head. "Stop! It was the biggest mistake of my life."

"Mine too," he agreed, but he was in too deep to stop now. "But I need to know. She's Tom's daughter, right? Not mine?"

"Right."

"Are you sure?"

Her nostrils flared. "A mother knows. She's Tom's."

"I thought so," he lied.

"Good. Not another word, or I swear I'll never talk to you again."

"I'm sorry."

"That's two words." Mary went to the rocker and put her feet up on the ottoman. Socks jumped back into her lap, and Mary rocked them both sullenly. He could sense her eyes on him, angrily boring into his skull.

Despite her bravado, Jake didn't think Mary knew who the rightful father was any more than Jake did, but he'd pushed it as far as he dared tonight. So he closed his eyes, no closer to the truth than yesterday. Frustrated, he didn't want to fall asleep. Besides, he had too much to ponder with the case against the biker, but his body ached, and his head throbbed, making it hard to keep his thoughts straight. Consciousness slowly slipped away from him.

With Jake's snoring, Mary didn't hear Emma creep back up the stairs. She kept her feet to the outer edges of the floorboards to remain silent. The extra pillow she'd brought down for Jake was clutched as tight to her chest as her mother's secret.

Chapter 17

At ten the following day, Jake and Mary arrived at the police station. Forty minutes later, they were still parked in the lobby waiting for Detective Noles. Jake knew the time because he had counted every minute on the large clock on the far wall. His butt ached from the plastic chairs, and his blood was boiling.

A lone clerk sat at the front desk, typing a report into a large desktop computer. Jake exhaled loudly to show his frustration—Mary gave him a dirty look. He ignored her, looking from the clock to the inner door and back again. Jake's obvious irritation had no effect on the clerk, so Jake got up from his uncomfortable seat and paced around the small room to emphasize his point.

Mary said, "Maybe I should've come by myself."

Indignant, he stopped in front of her. "What? We've been sitting out here forever."

"You need to stop. I'm sure Detective Noles will be with us in a minute."

"No, he won't. He's making us wait on purpose. Noles never liked me sticking my nose in his investigation."

"I highly doubt that. He's been nothing but professional. The problem is all in your head."

Jake thought Detective Noles was anything but professional. The man was fat and lazy, and he was screwing up Tom's case. It had taken Jake and Mary's dumb luck to find Tom's watch. Nothing Noles had done would have brought the killer to justice.

Rubbing his jaw, Jake fell back into his chair. "It's not in my head."

Mary frowned. "Did you take more ibuprofen this morning?"

"Yes."

He'd taken four pills, but his whole body ached, both from the beating and the couch that wasn't long enough for him to get comfortable. However, sometime during the night, a thought had occurred to him that he only remembered now. Leaning in, he cupped a hand around his mouth and whispered, "I wouldn't be surprised if Noles was on the take. If this gang— "

Mary slapped his arm. Her aim was impeccable; the blow landed in the same spot as the night before. He watched as her eyes moved in an exaggerated gesture towards the front desk. A large man wearing a short-sleeve shirt and a loosened tie stood at the visitor's gate. He greeted the clerk at the desk and inquired about his family. The clerk returned the greeting, looking relieved that Jake and Mary were now the detective's problem.

Noles opened the half door into the lobby and strode over to them. He extended his hairy hand to Mary and then to Jake. Still shaking hands, he scrutinized Jake's appearance. In a baritone voice, Noles said, "Mr. Bryant, you don't look so good."

"No. Detective Noles, I don't. There was an incident last night."

"That's what I heard. Why don't we go back to my desk to discuss it?" Noles reached back over the wall and opened the door from the inside. He led them into the station, stopping at the entrance to a break room. "Coffee? It's not good, but it's free."

Mary politely shook her head as Jake noticed a coffee stain on Noles's shirt. It went well with the mustard stain on his tie. Jake said, "No, thanks."

"Suit yourselves."

Noles poured himself a cup and steered them to his desk. A wrinkled brown bag sat prominently next to his computer monitor. Noles fervently eyed his lunch as he pulled over a second chair and nodded for the pair to sit down.

The detective's room looked straight out of a television show, with rows of desks, a large whiteboard with assignments scribbled in sloppy handwriting, and a blue water cooler against the wall with a stack of paper cone cups hanging from the side. At the other end of the room, a detective in street clothes answered a ringing phone. Noles centered a yellow notepad on his desk and picked up a ballpoint pen whose cap had several bite marks.

He said, "Mrs. Morgan, you told the clerk that you have information regarding your husband's murder."

In a wavering voice, Mary told the detective the events from the night before. Noles filled three pages of his notebook from top to bottom in large print. He circled some of his text and used arrows to point to others. Noles waited until she was finished before asking a few clarifying questions, which produced more circles and arrows to the pages.

Chewing on his pen top, Noles asked, "How can you be sure it was your husband's missing watch?"

Mary opened her purse and removed the picture she had found this morning. She set it on the edge of the desk. With a shaky hand, she pushed it towards Noles, who picked it up.

Her voice cracked as she choked out the words, "You can't see it very well, but here is a picture of it on Tom's wrist. It is old and has a unique style. There's an engraving on the back. Obviously, I couldn't see that when it was on the man's wrist, but I would know that watch anywhere. It was very special to Tom."

Noles brought the picture to the tip of his nose. "It is unique."

"Yes. It is." Her chin quivered.

Nodding, Noles pulled a file from a desk drawer and flipped through the contents. His eyes traveled up and down the paper several times. A big finger stopped halfway through the file. He looked up shamelessly. "I just wanted to confirm that his watch was missing from the scene."

Mary burst into tears, her face growing red and blotchy. She retrieved a tissue from her purse and used it to dab at her eyes. The makeup she'd spent so much time on this morning was ruined. Jake lost it— he couldn't bear to see her in pain.

"You don't remember?" Jake shouted.

Noles frowned. "It pays to be sure, especially in a murder investigation, but I don't need to tell you that, do I?"

Jake leaned forward in his chair. "You're right. You don't."

Mary laid a hand on Jake's arm. "Sorry, Detective Noles, you'll have to excuse Jake. He's very upset too. Tom was his best friend, and we just want answers."

Noles accepted her apology with two nods of his large head before pulling a magnifying glass from his center desk drawer. He held it close to Mary's picture. The tool looked like a child's toy in his meaty hand. Jake could picture him playing in the dirt after work, lighting ants on fire.

Reading his mind, Mary squeezed Jake's arm harder and said, "Maybe you have some technician or expert or someone who can blow it up, Detective Noles. Then you could see the design, but it shouldn't matter. When you have the watch, the engraving on the back should prove it. The inscription reads, 'To David for all you do, Love Carol' along with the date of their anniversary."

"David?"

"Tom's father. David was killed in a hit-and-run accident when Tom was in high school."

"Oh!" Noles gripped the photograph tighter. "Can I keep this to add to the file?"

"Please."

"Thanks." Noles set down the magnifying glass and rubbed the bridge of his nose with his forefinger and thumb. Looking up, he asked, "Mr. Bryant, did you see the watch as well?"

"Yes, I saw the biker, Caleb, wearing it."

"Can you confirm it was Mr. Morgan's?"

"It was Tom's watch, without a doubt. Like Mary said, Tom loved that watch. The only reason someone would have it is if it was taken off his dead body."

Noles picked up his cup and took a sip. He grimaced. "My coffee is cold. Do you mind if I freshen it up?"

Jake and Mary shrugged, so Noles plodded out of the detective room. Jake considered hiding his lunch on him as a joke, then Noles would jump into action— there would be an APB on the wire within seconds for his missing ham sandwich. But before Jake could find a good hiding spot, Noles returned. Flipping to a fresh sheet in his notebook, Noles wrote three words across the top of the page.

To see them in print made them sound even more ominous. Noles scratched deep lines under each word, then he went back to chewing on the pen cap.

Jake read them out loud. "The Devil's Hand."

Noles whistled in agreement. "The Devil's Hand are as bad as it gets around here. They literally have their hands in everything from drugs to guns to loan-sharking, even the sex trade. I'll contact Detroit's gang department. They should be familiar with most of the members and their whereabouts."

Mary leaned forward. "You will?"

"Yes."

Noles said, "However, a sighting of a supposed watch is not enough evidence to arrest this Caleb person."

Chapter 18

"I know," Jake said with downcast eyes.

"But if you're willing to press assault charges, Mr. Bryant," Noles said. "We should be able to pick him up today."

"I'll do that— definitely. And you should start the questioning before he has time to create an alibi. You'll also need to get a search warrant, so any evidence isn't destroyed."

Noles took a deep breath and sighed. "I know how to do my job, thanks. This is not my first murder investigation."

"It's your second case, right? Congratulations. Look, I was Chicago PD, not some detective from a little town in the middle of nowhere, so I know how to handle a case like this. I'd be working— "

Mary moved her hand down to Jake's knee and squeezed the muscle. He jumped in his seat as he reached for her fingers, but the maneuver effectively cut off his rant. She said, "Detective Noles, you and everyone else here have done a phenomenal job. I know you're working my husband's case as hard as you can, so what Jake is trying to say is— "

"That Noles is a lucky son of a bitch. It took us bumping into the murderer to break the case wide open," Jake said, dumbfounded that Mary would cover for this loser.

Noles dropped the disfigured pen down on his notepad. A vein pulsed in his broad forehead, and his neck grew red. Through gritted teeth, he said, "We would have found him."

White-hot anger overrode Jake's senses. "No, you wouldn't have, but I don't care as long as you get off your fat ass and arrest Caleb today."

"Jake!" Mary hissed. "Apologize to Detective Noles."

"No fucking way. If he can't get it done, I will get justice for Tom."

Noles puffed out his chest. "It will be hard after the mess you made."

"Me?"

Noles said, "Yes. We can only hope the suspect doesn't destroy all the evidence before we can serve the search warrant. He's certainly had enough time."

Shit! Noles had pointed out Jake's worst fears. Of course, destroying evidence wouldn't have been a problem if Noles had done his job properly. If Jake had the detective's resources, then Caleb would already be in jail awaiting trial. Still, Jake had screwed up. He was sick to his stomach all over again. Rising hastily, he kicked Noles's wastebasket over; it clattered to the floor.

Jake muttered, "I'll be outside."

Reaching the lobby, he avoided the clerk's eyes as he rushed outside, but the fresh air didn't calm his insides— they churned like a cement mixer from the guilt. He raced down the sidewalk to Mary's car, the only one in the lot. Leaning against the trunk for support, he sucked in deep breaths like he was practicing Lamaze. He was beside himself. Mary had acted as any grief-stricken widow would have in that situation with Caleb, but Jake was a professional. He knew better.

Jake was still trying to keep his breakfast down when Mary stormed out of the police station, her purse swinging wildly by her side. Without a word, she got in the car and started it up. Jake had to dive into the passenger seat to avoid being left behind.

They picked up lunch for the family after leaving the station. Jake quietly dug in the fast-food bag and pulled out a handful of French fries; otherwise the car was silent. He attempted to settle the guilty void in his stomach with food. Like a mechanical claw from an arcade game, his hand reached in the bag to scoop out more salty fries.

Mary watched him out of the corner of her eye. "Are you going to eat all of those before we get home?"

"You're talking to me now?" He dropped the fries back into the bag.

"I just want some left for the kids— that's all Hunter will eat."

"Sorry," Jake said.

"About the fries?" Mary asked.

"No, about screwing up Tom's case."

She shook her head. "I told you last night that I wasn't upset about that. It was as much my fault as yours. I'm sure it will work itself out. Tom has told me as much in my dreams."

Tom's ghost again? Jake was curious what else his friend had to say, but he'd have to save that for later. Instead, he asked, "Then what are you mad about?"

"I'm mad because you weren't nice to Detective Noles. Your act was extremely embarrassing."

"I understand how you feel, but you need to hear me out."

Jake waited for her to respond, but she didn't. She kept her eyes focused on the road. Her thumbs drummed angrily on the steering wheel. Finally, she said, "I'm listening."

He took a deep breath and did his best to make his case.

"The thing is that some of these small sheriff's departments don't know what they are doing. Their clearance rate on capital crimes can be under ten percent, and the public never hears about it. A lot of them are completely incompetent, so without our lucky encounter, Tom's case may have never been solved."

"I don't believe that. The sheriff wouldn't get reelected if that was the case."

"Believe it because sheriffs are not obligated to release their clearance rates." Jake grabbed another handful of fries. "And I'm pretty sure Noles is on the take."

"Why do you think that?"

"Just a feeling."

Mary gave him a look that would've made Medusa proud, though he'd make a terrible statue with a mouth of half-chewed food. Jabbing a finger at him, she asked, "How can Noles be crooked if he offered to have a police car stationed in front of the house for our protection?"

"He did?"

"Yes."

"Did you take him up on it?" Jake asked.

"Of course. Should I not have?"

"No. You're probably right. It was just weird that Noles knew all about the Devil's Hand."

"It's his job to know about stuff like that, right?"

"Yes, but still . . . "

She slammed her fist on the steering wheel. "Enough. Or I'll send you home tonight."

"My car is at Bobby's house," Jake mumbled.

"No. He and Rick moved it for you. It's at my house now, along with your bag."

"Oh."

That was the last thing that he wanted. Mary still needed him because they were not out of the woods yet. Even if this Caleb character was arrested, there was the rest of the Devil's Hand to worry about. Like Bobby had said, if you fight one of them, you fight all of them, but they should know that Jake wouldn't back down from a fight.

"All right." He smiled. "I'll behave— I promise."

Chapter 19

Later that afternoon, Caleb's cell phone buzzed. Taking a final drag from his cigarette, he unraveled himself from his bedsheets and retrieved the ringing device from the pile of clothes on the floor.

"What?" he yelled into the phone.

"Don't give me that shit!" Sonny said. "Where are you?"

Caleb laughed. "I'm getting myself a grade-A piece of tail."

"Figures," Sonny said with obvious disgust. "Well, they're here. It's a little earlier than we expected— they must have found a judge who wasn't out boating on a Sunday."

"Fuck!" Caleb ran his fingers through his tangled hair.

"Exactly! We didn't need this distraction right now, not with our war with the Outsiders."

"Yeah, I know. So what's the plan?"

Sonny said, "It's simple. You come to the club and turn yourself in. We'll lawyer you up, and you should be out by morning. Have you told me everything— no more secrets like the watch?"

"Yes, but what are you going to do if these charges stick?"

"I'll take care of it."

"Is that a promise?" Caleb asked.

Sonny growled. "Do I look like the promise fairy?"

"Nah, you're too ugly."

"Not half as ugly as you, so get your hairy ass down here. We don't need the cops hanging around any longer than we have to. Who knows what they'll find?"

"Got it, Mr. President. I'm on my way."

Caleb hit the end button and dropped the phone on the bed. The smell of sex and sweat hung in the air of his messy bedroom. He slapped the curvy backside of the body lying next to him. "You awake?"

Jodi rolled over, keeping the sheet wrapped tightly around her. She smiled devilishly. "You're good, but you didn't fuck me into a coma."

"Next time."

"Promises. Promises."

His feet hit the worn hardwood floor with a dull thud. He stretched his arms above his head and let out a loud sigh before picking up his boxer shorts. "I've got to go down to the club."

She stuck out her bottom lip. "Seriously?"

"Yes. The police are there to arrest me."

"You're kidding."

"I wish I was."

"What did you do?"

"It's better if you don't know."

Jodi brought a hand dramatically to her cheek. "Did you kill somebody?"

He dug around in the pile of clothes for his socks. "Murder would be the charge, along with several other felonies."

Jodi sat up in bed, adjusting the pillows behind her, still holding the sheet to her ample chest. She reached for the pack of smokes on the nightstand with her free hand. Using a cheap lighter, she ignited the cigarette and inhaled deeply as a smile crossed her face. "You're a bad man."

"You like that?"

She nodded. "I do."

"Well, I'm bad, but not a murderer. They always try and pin stuff like this on the club. Besides, I was out of the state on the day in question, and I've got witnesses to prove it," Caleb said.

She rolled her eyes. "You sound like Sonny."

"I'm better than Sonny."

She smirked. "Then why are you fucking his old lady? Shouldn't you go find something better?"

"Is that what you want me to do? To go find something younger and prettier?"

"If you do, I'll cut your balls off."

Here we go again, Caleb thought. This girl should've gone into theater, always with the drama. He told himself he would've left a long time ago if she wasn't such a terrific lay, but the truth was that he was madly in love with her.

Caleb groaned for effect. "You heard what I said on the phone. You're the best damn piece of ass I've ever seen, and I've seen a lot of asses. You should be with me, not Sonny."

81

"I should?"

"Definitely," Caleb said.

Jodi's whole face lit up. She took a drag from her cigarette and let the sheet fall to her lap, exposing her chest. They were better than anything found in a museum, erect pink nipples stood out from her round breasts. She reached across the bed to his nightstand, stretching a long arm for the ashtray. The muscles in her legs pulled taut, presenting her ass perfectly.

Exhaling thin white trails of smoke from her nostrils, she asked, "So this ass is grade-A?"

He slowly sucked in a breath. "You know it is. In fact, I think I may have to break off a piece to take with me."

Caleb lunged for her, catching a cheek in each hand. He squeezed her butt hard while making animal noises. Jodi squealed, trying to fight him off, but it quickly developed into heavy petting. She seemed excited at first, but then her arousal faded. The kisses grew cold, and she rolled out of bed.

"What's wrong?" Caleb asked.

"Didn't you tell Sonny you were on your way?"

"Screw Sonny!"

Pawing through the clothes on the floor, she found her tank top and pulled it over her head.

She walked around the bed towards him. "I think Sonny is getting suspicious."

"You worry too much."

Her bare ass didn't allow him to think about anything else, his mouth hanging open. She waved a manicured nail at him like he was a little child. She found her pants amongst the dirty clothes on the floor. Turning away, she slipped into them without any underwear. He enjoyed her jiggly dance as she struggled to get her butt into her pants.

Jodi turned around and planted a kiss on Caleb's lips. "You're probably right, but I think maybe we should lay low for a while. Sonny has been acting weird lately."

"He's got a lot on his plate right now."

She shook her head. "He's always thinking about the club. I'm sick of it."

"That's what happens in our business. Get used to it. If you don't, you wind up dead."

She said, "I know. I worry myself sick over both of you."

"Both of us?" He frowned. "What would you do if Sonny died?"

"What are you saying?" She tried to back away, but his fingers were locked in her belt loops, holding her in place.

"I'm saying any one of us could die. I could get shanked in jail by a rival gang, and here you are not letting me have any."

"Fine." She pulled his fingers from her pants and commanded playfully, "Sit on your hands!"

He complied.

She turned around seductively and shimmied against him, gyrating and rubbing down one of his thighs and up the other, dancing to music only she could hear. Her experience as a retired stripper was on full display. She straddled him and flipped her hair, hitting him in the face as she pulled down the front of her tank top. He flicked his tongue out, catching the nub of flesh. She moaned in delight. Scooting forward, she let him suckle on it. However, when she got too excited, Jodi jumped off his lap. He tried to grab her, but she was too quick.

Laughing, she said, "You need to go."

He reluctantly nodded. "Lock the door behind you."

"Sure."

Looking around the room, he added, "You could do a little cleaning before you go too."

She rolled her eyes. "I don't clean my own house."

"Spoiled."

She nodded. "I could give you the number of my housekeeper."

"Maybe when I get out."

From the dresser by the door, Caleb grabbed a watch— one that looked similar but was not the watch he'd worn the night before. The back of this watch was plain, without an engraving.

Chapter 20

The rocking chair was empty. Jake had insisted Mary sleep in her own bed tonight. At least one of them should get some rest. It would be impossible for Jake— the couch was too soft, the pillow was too hard, and the house made a lot of weird noises he wasn't used to hearing. Besides, guilt still racked his burger-filled belly.

Detective Noles had called earlier to inform them that Caleb was in custody, but it had done little to ease Jake's mind. Tom's watch would not be enough evidence to hold Caleb. They'd need more physical evidence, either blood, hair, fibers, or the murder weapon. Otherwise, a decent lawyer would get Caleb released, and once that maniac was out, who knows what he'd do. That was if the Devil's Hand didn't silence Jake and Mary first— a dead witness can't give testimony.

Jake tried to change positions on the couch, but the blanket caught underneath him. He jerked it free, almost tearing the material in half. He growled in frustration. Light footsteps pattered down the stairs and went into the kitchen. Cupboards were opened and closed, so it was not Socks the cat.

Light from the refrigerator hit his half-opened eyes, and Jake saw Emma adding milk to a bowl of cereal. It was the first time he'd seen her since yesterday. She'd been locked in her room all day. Mary had explained it away as a bad day for Emma emotionally, so Jake hadn't inquired any further. They were all having bad days.

Jake stole a long look at her. Emma smiled when Jake caught him studying her. He thought he saw something familiar in her features, but he smartly drove those thoughts to the dark corners of his mind.

"Uncle Jake?"

"Hi, Emma," he said, sitting up.

"Did I wake you?"

"No, I was just lying here. I've got a lot on my mind."

"Me too. Do you want some cereal?"

He kicked off the itchy blanket. "No, but I'll sit with you."

"Cool." She went back to eating.

He asked, "Are you feeling better?"

"I just wanted to be alone."

"I understand."

"And I miss my dad," she whispered.

"I miss him too."

"I bet," Emma said. "You two were like brothers."

"We were." The words caught in his throat.

"He talked about you a lot."

Jake blinked away his tears. When he could, he said, "Your dad talked about you a lot too. He was very proud of you."

"Do you think?" She set down her spoon.

"One hundred percent."

A tear slipped out the corner of her eye. She brushed it away with the back of her hand. "I hope so."

"I'm proud of you too. You're a smart beautiful young woman. I bet there's nothing you can't do if you set your mind to it."

"Thanks." Blushing, she changed the subject. "How much longer are you staying in Michigan?"

He frowned. "Probably another day or two, then I'll have to go back to work."

Looking at him sideways, she asked, "Are you feeling better after your food poisoning?"

"Yes, all better now. Since it was going to go to waste, I ate your lunch along with my own." He patted his belly, hoping she ignored his bruised jaw.

"That's good." She smiled. "But then how come you aren't sleeping at Uncle Bobby's house tonight?"

Jake lied, "Bobby snores really loud. He sounds like a grizzly bear who swallowed a bees' nest and is trying to kill them with a chain saw."

Emma giggled, and the crisis was averted.

Bobby did snore like a freight train, but Mary had chosen not to tell the children about the events at the bar or Caleb's arrest. There had been too much turmoil in their lives. Besides, why upset them until there was something concrete to report. However, Jake wouldn't have been surprised if Emma had guessed something was wrong. She was an intuitive girl, and she had to have noticed the police car parked in front of the house.

Suddenly, a loud motor revved down the street. It sounded like a motorcycle. Jake jumped to his feet and raced to the front of the house with Emma trailing behind him. Creeping to the large front window, he pulled the drape open an inch and peeked outside. The street was empty, no cars or trucks, and no Harley in the driveway.

But more importantly— no police car.

Where was the black and white cruiser? It had been parked there less than an hour ago; Jake had checked.

Did the Devil's Hand have their protection removed? Were Jake, Mary, and the kids about to be eliminated? Jake should have trusted his instincts; Noles was crooked. It was up to him to protect Mary and the kids.

Out of sight, the motor revved again. Jake left the window and went to the front door. Turning to Emma, he said, "Lock this behind me. If I'm not back in five minutes, dial 911."

She looked at him quizzically. "911?"

"Yes. Can you do that?"

"I guess."

"Good girl."

Jake opened the door and cautiously stepped outside. The crescent moon lit up the night in muted colors. Emma followed his orders, and the deadbolt clicked into place behind him. Hugging the side of the porch, he stealthily moved into the yard, where the grass was cool on his bare feet.

Crickets chirped melodically in the yard, but the insect noise was drowned out by Jake's thumping heart. As usual, he'd ran off half-cocked with the element of surprise his only weapon. He wished he had his pistol, but it was back in Chicago. Hunter probably had a baseball bat in the garage though he didn't want to turn back now and scare Emma.

Surveying the neighborhood, nothing looked out of the ordinary to Jake. The street was now eerily silent. He didn't like that— not one bit. Something bad was about to go down. Jake could feel it in his bones. But he wasn't about to sit back and wait, he'd meet it head-on.

Crouching down, he ran to the side of the house. He stuck his head around the corner and pulled it back quickly. Nobody was there, so he ran to the rear of the house. Getting low to the ground, he studied the yard carefully. There were a lot more places to hide back there amongst the landscaping, but the shadows remained shadows. So he stood up and ran around the deck with his legs tingling.

The far side of the house contained the attached garage. Its side door would be the perfect place to enter the house undetected. The lock wouldn't be as secure, and the noise might not travel to the living spaces. Jake listened intently. No sounds came from within the garage, so he jogged over to the door. The knob held firm, and the lock appeared secure.

Maybe this whole thing had been in Jake's head, a figment of his over-active imagination and a desire to be the hero. However, as he trudged back to the porch, Jake heard loud voices followed by a burst of shrill laughter. The blood turned to ice in his veins. Quickly, he took in his surroundings, but the street was still empty.

Or was it?

Chapter 21

Jake thought he saw a man pressed against a tree a few yards down. He studied the figure carefully, but it didn't move— not one inch. Damn, his mind must be playing tricks on him, which wasn't a surprise with all the stress he was under. Even more worrisome was how much time had he'd spent chasing shadows. Had he been gone five minutes? It felt more like ten. Jake rushed to the front door, hoping to catch Emma before she dialed 911.

When he was five feet from the porch, the mysterious motor roared to life. Jake spun around. Every hair on his body stood on end as he looked for the source of the noise. He quickly spotted a pair of headlights three doors away. The car's white bulbs glued Jake's feet to the ground. They'd been watching Jake the whole time as he'd made of fool of himself running around the house.

Before he could decide if he should dive for cover or go on the offensive, a teenage girl climbed out of the car. She yelled something incoherent, laughed, and slammed the car door closed. The driver revved the engine loudly in response. Running up to her house, she never gave Jake a second look. Nor did the muscle car with the bad muffler as it sped down the street, leaving a wide patch of rubber.

Jake let out the breath he'd been holding and walked up the porch steps. He felt a little silly at his overreaction but not too badly. A gang, like the Devil's Hand, would do anything to protect one of their members. With his hand on the knob, Jake knocked lightly on the door, trying not to alert anyone but Emma. However, before she could answer, a black and white police car screeched to a stop in front of Mary's house. The searchlight landed on Jake's back, pinning him in place.

An officer hopped out of the vehicle with his gun drawn. He shouted, "On the ground. Now!"

Jake stepped off the porch and got down on one knee, his hands in the air.

The second officer joined the first. His elbow rested on an open car door, steadying the pistol aimed at Jake. "Do it!"

The pair were looking for any reason to shoot him, so Jake hastily dropped to the grass and laced his fingers behind his head. He calmly said, "My name is Jakob Bryant. We met at the beginning of your shift. My identification is in my back pocket."

The first officer extracted his wallet while the second kept his weapon trained on Jake. Using his flashlight, the officer read his driver's license then apologized while he helped Jake to his feet. "Sorry! Someone called 911."

"Yes. I heard a loud engine, so I had one of the kids call it in while I went out to investigate. But it turned out to be a neighbor's hot rod instead of a motorcycle."

The second officer holstered his gun. "No problem, but you should have waited on us to respond."

"I know, but I was concerned when I didn't see you out front," Jake said, his voice tinged with accusation.

The officers looked at one another before the first officer said, "We got called out to assist in a high-speed chase. Luckily, it went in a different direction. We were on our way back here when we got your call."

"All right—" Jake brushed off his pants, not entirely convinced.

"We shouldn't have to leave again, Mr. Bryant. You can reenter the residence and lock up. We'll do a walk around to make sure everything is secure," the second officer said with a nod of his head.

With no other choice, Jake thanked them and climbed the porch steps. Emma stood behind the screen door in her pink pajama pants and a white t-shirt, her phone in hand. She opened the door. "I called just like you said. Is that all right?"

"Yes. You did great."

"But why did you rush outside? What's wrong?"

He shut the door and engaged the deadbolt. "Nothing is wrong. I thought I heard Rick's truck, so I went out to meet him. I didn't want him to knock on the door and wake everyone up," Jake said. He knew it sounded lame, but he couldn't come up with anything else quickly.

"And you wanted me to dial 911 on Uncle Rick?"

Jake didn't want to dig himself any deeper, so he went with a half-truth but tried to keep it vague. "It might not have been Rick. It could've been someone else, someone . . . not nice."

Emma's mouth twisted into a half grimace, but she didn't ask any follow-up questions. Jake was glad. They returned to the table, and Emma fixed herself another bowl of cereal. She mixed up the contents of her bowl with her spoon. "Are you really going home tomorrow?"

"Probably tomorrow or the next day— unfortunately."

"Yeah, I bet Sam misses you. You've been gone a long time."

"She does, but she understands." Jake had been too busy lately to check in with her, but he thought she would.

"I haven't seen Sam in a long time."

"I know. It's been years since she's been to Michigan. Maybe she'll come next time I visit. Would you like that?"

"Yes," Emma said. "I follow Sam on Instagram. She is super pretty."

"She looks more and more like her mother— every day, which is good. It would be bad if she looked like me," he said with a laugh. But more importantly, Jake was glad that Sam treated people like he did and not like her mother, who could be a world-class bitch.

"People say that Lindsey and I look a lot like Mom. What do you think?"

"I think you do. You're lucky— your mother is a smart beautiful woman."

Blushing, Emma looked down at the table. Her index finger traced invisible lines on its surface. "You know, I was looking at old pictures this morning."

"I like doing that too, but it can make you sad," Jake warned.

"The thing I noticed in the pictures is that even though Lindsey and I look like Mom, and Hunter looks like Dad— we all have Mom's eyes, and Hunter and Lindsey have Dad's nose, but I don't have a nose like either of them."

"Genetics are a funny thing. I don't understand any of it." He shrugged.

"In fact, I think my nose looks exactly like Sam's nose."

Not sure where she was going with this, he said, "Really?"

"Yes. Did you ever notice that?" she prodded, leaning forward in her chair and watching his reaction.

Why was she asking these questions? Why now? Emma couldn't have overheard his conversation with Mary the other night, could she? No. There was no way, she'd been upstairs asleep. Even though Jake thought Emma might be his, it was better not to think about it. Not if he wanted to remain friends with Mary. Not if he wanted to stay in the periphery of Emma's life.

Jake met her stare with his best poker face. "No. I never noticed that. Besides, everyone says that Sam has Kate's nose. I'm pretty sure that you didn't get your nose from my ex-wife. Did you?"

"No." Emma forced a laugh, but her face dropped in disappointment. The hallway clock chimed once. They both jumped in their seats. Jake sighed, "It's late."

She nodded slowly. "I guess I should go to bed."

"Yeah. Me too."

She collected her bowl and set it in the sink. The ceramic flatware made a metallic thud against the stainless-steel surface. Jake helped by putting the milk back in the refrigerator and the cereal box in the pantry. He turned to find Emma standing in front of him. She hugged him, her arms landing just above his waist. She squeezed him hard as he patted her gently on the back. She released him and padded down the hallway. He wished he could have told her the truth, whatever that was, but the words died on his lips.

The clock ticked in the hallway. Floorboards creaked upstairs and a bedroom door shut. His mind raced, and he took several short quick breaths to try and calm the crazy thoughts. Did Emma really think Jake was her father? He considered telling Mary about Emma's questions, but she'd been crystal clear that Jake was never to bring up that subject again. So instead, he walked from window to window around the house.

Under the pale light of the moon, he saw nothing unusual in the backyard. The night appeared quiet. At the front window, the police car idled quietly. Two dim shapes moved inside. His head still hurt, so he found some ibuprofen in the bathroom cabinet and swallowed three pills with a handful of water, before returning to the couch to stare at the ceiling. He still wasn't sure he trusted the police, not completely. Had they acted suspiciously, or was Jake's imagination in overdrive? There was a strong case for either possibility, so he lay awake, fighting off sleep and listening for the tiniest sound in the house.

At dawn, sleep snuck up on him like a thief.

Chapter 22

The next day, an unwatched television played for Jake and Mary. They sat on opposite ends of the couch, waiting anxiously for an update from Detective Noles. If the police couldn't find more evidence on Caleb, Jake knew Tom's case would go unsolved because Caleb was undoubtedly the killer. Jake was sure of it— he could feel it in his bones. And the more he thought about it, the more Jake was sure Tom's death had been because of a stupid traffic altercation, which made Jake mad enough to kill that psychopath, Caleb.

Just when they had given up on hearing anything, the doorbell rang. Jake and Mary raced past Emma, who'd been reading a book in the living room. Looking out the side window, Jake saw Noles staring down at his shoes with the afternoon sun at his back. Jake prayed he was here to deliver good news. Mary swatted at Jake until he stepped aside.

Taking a breath, she forced a smile and opened the door. "Detective Noles."

"Ms. Morgan." He paused before adding, "Mr. Bryant."

"Please, it's Mary. Would you like to come in?"

"Are your kids home?"

Mary looked over at Emma, who stared back at her, the book now closed on her lap. "Yes."

"Maybe it's better if we talk out here."

"That's probably a good idea." Mary turned to Emma. "We're going to need some privacy for a few minutes."

Raising one eyebrow, Emma said, "All right?"

Following her outside, Jake shut the door behind him. The covered porch spanned the length of the house and was the perfect place to spend an evening watching fireflies. So it would suffice for their impromptu meeting to discuss Tom's murder investigation.

Mary took a seat on the porch swing. Noles angled a wicker chair towards Mary. It groaned under his weight as he fell into it. Jake leaned against the porch railing, completing their triangle.

Noles pulled a notebook from his pocket. Dark circles colored his face under both eyes. He said, "Unfortunately, I have bad news."

Mary's shoulders slumped. "How bad is it?"

Frowning, Noles opened the small pad. "Caleb Clarke was arrested yesterday and questioned. We were able to obtain a search warrant for his home and vehicles. The watch found on his person was similar but didn't match your description or the picture you provided. Also, there was no engraving on the back face."

Mary gasped as Jake muttered a string of obscenities.

Noles continued, "The preliminary results from his vehicles show no evidence linking him to your husband's murder. In addition, Mr. Clarke had several guns registered to his person, and all of them were recovered. However, none matched the caliber that we believe killed your husband— "

"Shit!" Jake growled.

Noles took a deep breath and continued. "Furthermore, Mr. Clarke was out of the state at the time of your husband's murder, which was confirmed by multiple witnesses."

With her voice barely above a whisper, Mary said, "I see."

"Fucking God damn it! He manufactured an alibi too!" Jake slammed his hand down on the railing. He'd screwed up everything by attacking Caleb. How stupid!

Ignoring Jake's outburst, Noles said, "We will still consider Caleb Clarke a person of interest. However, he was released pending the discovery of new evidence relating to the murder. And it is the department's belief that he poses no future threat to you or your family, but we can post a car on the street again tonight if you want?"

She stood up. "Thank you, Detective Noles, but I think we'll be fine."

"Again, I'm truly sorry, Ms. Morgan, and I want you to know that your husband's case remains my top priority."

"I appreciate you coming out to tell me in person. Now if you excuse me, I think I'm going to go inside and . . ." Mary trailed off before walking robotically into the house.

The front door slowly closed behind her. Noles struggled from his seat and returned the chair to its original position on the porch. With a nod to Jake, he made to leave.

Jake called after him. "Detective Noles, can I have a minute?"

The big man sighed, "Yes."

Jake swallowed his pride and said what needed to be said. "I'd like to apologize for yesterday. I know it was cheap theatrics, but I was frustrated and mad. Mad at myself more than anyone, but I lashed out at you. I'm sorry."

"I accept your apology," Noles said, looking very tired.

"Thank you."

Noles leaned against the spindled railing next to Jake. "I have to admit that when you first came around asking if you could assist in Mr. Morgan's case, I looked into your history."

Jake nodded glumly. "I'd be surprised if you didn't."

"Truthfully, it wasn't that hard to find with the publicity around the Silkworm rapist case. It was national news, after all. I recalled the headlines, but I wasn't familiar with some of the details."

"And?"

"I think there's a lot more to the story than what was published. I'm betting you took the fall, so the politicians could get re-elected, and the higher-ups could save their own butts. So I'd love to hear your side of the story— if you want to share it."

Jake had never really shared his tale outside the official questioning, but maybe it would help him get some answers out of Noles that he wouldn't get otherwise.

"Why the hell not?"

"Great. I'm all ears." Noles walked back to the swing and eased himself down onto it.

Shoving his hands in his pant pockets, Jake dragged those terrible memories from the dark recesses of his mind. "I'd been a violent crimes detective for a short time. I'd solved some cases. My career was on the rise, so it was an honor when they asked me to assist the senior detective on the Silkworm Rapist case.

"The whole city was scared. There was a big push from city hall to close the case fast. The perp had already beaten and raped five women. He attacked them as they entered their vehicles and slipped a silk bag over their heads, so they couldn't identify him."

Noles asked, "Did you have DNA to work with?"

"No. He always wore a condom."

"Damn."

"I know." Jake nodded. "So anyway, one afternoon, a credible tip came in on a suspect, so we went out for the initial questioning. The man had been on a list of perpetrators with a violent sexual past, but we hadn't gotten to him yet. The suspect worked as a transporter in the same hospital that two of the other victims were employed. The senior detective, Detective Hill, figured we could get him to consent to a DNA swab if he wasn't our guy. If he was, well . . . you never know."

"I'm always surprised when they willingly consent to the swab when they're the perp."

"Yeah. So we knocked on the door and waited. Leroy Jones, the suspect, lived in a low-income townhouse with his mother, girlfriend, son, and baby. He saw right away that we were cops and slammed the door in our face. From within the apartment, my partner and I could hear yelling and screaming and what sounded like a scuffle."

Noles leaned forward in his chair, his elbows resting on his knees.

"Detective Hill called for backup, and then he went around back to cover the rear exit while I stayed at the front door. One of the voices was a female's, and she was begging him not to do something. 'No', 'Please God', and 'Don't do it' and stuff like that."

"Wow! What did you do?" Noles asked.

"I kicked the door down." Jake's heart raced as he recalled the scene. "Inside, I found Leroy wrestling with an adult female over an object. Leroy was an African American, six foot three, two hundred fifty pounds, who was a former college basketball star with a bum knee that kept him from going pro. The woman was also African American and half his size.

Noles interrupted Jake's monologue. "His girlfriend?"

Jake shrugged his shoulders guiltily. "I should have suspected it, but I didn't because it all happened too fast. I was full of adrenalin, and I needed to be prepared for the worst-case scenario. In retrospect, I don't think it would've made a difference who I thought she was because Leroy threw the woman to the floor. I screamed at him to freeze, but he didn't. The object was a gun. He turned and aimed it at me. You could see the fear and hate in his eyes."

"Shit! It was you or him," Noles said.

Jake sighed, "You're telling me."

"So what did you do?"

Chapter 23

Jake sat down heavily in a wicker chair. "I saw the muscles in Leroy's hand tense. I knew he was going to shoot me. No amount of de-escalation would change that— so I pulled the trigger."

Anxiously, Noles kicked the porch swing into motion. The chains whined under the effort. He didn't say a word as he waited for Jake to continue.

"My aim was off. Instead of a chest shot, the bullet hit Leroy in the stomach. He dropped his pistol and fell to one knee. I moved in to secure him, but before I could, he ran. I don't know how, but he ran."

A low whistle escaped Noles's lips.

Jake said, "I chased after him. In the back of the townhouse was a small boy holding a baby. I couldn't risk another shot with innocent bystanders in the way, besides that, Leroy was unarmed, and Hill was at the rear exit."

"But Hill didn't get him?"

"No. Leroy ran straight through the sliding screen door, knocking Hill over, breaking his leg. The whole scene was chaotic. The girlfriend was yelling at me for shooting her baby-daddy, the boy was crying, and the baby was screaming its little head off. I don't know where Leroy's mother was, maybe at work, and now Leroy had disappeared into the park behind the townhouse."

Noles ran a hand over his head, leaving the hair standing up wildly. Jake felt himself warming up to the big detective.

Jake said, "Hill verified that backup was minutes away and sent me after Leroy. The park had children playing in it, and I could only guess what he'd do to avoid arrest. If he was hopped up on drugs or something, even with the gutshot, he could easily snatch up a kid and use him for leverage.

"The park was a big place, but he was easy to find with the blood trail. He'd collapsed near a pick-up baseball game. An elderly man out for a walk helped me clear away the ten-year old boys, and I moved in to find Leroy leaning against the trunk of a giant oak tree. He was dying— his shirt was drenched in blood, his breathing was short and raspy, and he was looking off into nowhere. There was nothing I could have done that would have saved him. I knew that. And at the time, I didn't feel bad because he'd put himself there. It was by my hands, but what choice did I have?"

"Right. You had no choice," Hill agreed.

"Before Leroy died, I attempted to question him. I knew it was the only chance we'd have, but he swore that he wasn't the Silkworm Rapist with his dying breath."

Noles shifted in his seat. "Shit! Sounds like every cop's worst nightmare."

Jake nodded. "And that's the whole truth— or my version of the truth."

With some trepidation, Noles said, "But the newspaper story said Jones didn't have a weapon."

"Yes, the official reports say it was a TV remote, and he and his girlfriend were fighting over what show to watch." Jake snorted. "Which anyone with half a brain will know is bullshit."

Noles leaned forward in his seat, resting his elbows on his knees. "So what happened to the gun?"

"I have my suspicions."

"Like what?"

Jake ran his fingers through his hair. "It doesn't matter. It wouldn't change anything."

"But you were cleared of any wrongdoing?"

"Yes and no. After a long Internal Affairs investigation, the shooting was deemed justifiable. However, I was still put on administrative duties, given the publicity of the case and the racial tensions in the city. Riding a desk wasn't what I signed up for. Within a year, I was no longer with Chicago PD, divorced, and had a drinking problem."

"Damn! That sucks," Noles said.

"Shit happens. What are you going to do?"

"Still."

Jake bobbed his head. "Yep."

"Do you think Jones was the Silkworm Rapist? The story was a little vague on that point."

Rubbing his chin, Jake said, "No evidence was found to link Leroy to the crimes. However, the rapes stopped after his death."

"Then he was the rapist?"

"Maybe. I don't know."

"Well. Either way, it's quite a story."

"I guess." Jake turned to face Noles. "So now that I've shared my sordid past with you, I was hoping you'd share something with me."

"Like what?"

"Like details about Tom's case."

Noles bit his lip.

Jake continued, "Do you think that Caleb switched the watches?"

The detective didn't deny it, which was all the answer Jake needed.

"Do you believe his alibi?"

Noles got up from the swing. "It doesn't matter what I believe. It only matters what I can prove, and right now, I have nothing I can charge him with outside of your assault, which wouldn't stick since you admitted to striking him first. You'll be glad to know that he chose not to press charges."

"No jury would convict me of that crime," Jake laughed.

Noles tucked his notebook back in his pocket. "Probably not."

Jake turned away from Noles and stared out at the yard. He asked, "Off the record, do you think Caleb murdered Tom?"

Noles shuffled from foot to foot without looking Jake directly in the eyes. "You and I both know there is no such thing as off the record, but I do know the world would be a better place without men like Clarke in it."

Shaking his head, Jake asked, "Are Mary and the kids safe?"

"Clarke is a free man. We have no case against him, so I highly doubt the Devil's Hand would draw more attention to themselves by attempting something stupid here."

"I sure hope so." Jake released the railing and looked down the street. Normal life continued for the rest of the world. Kids rode their bikes down the street, and a neighbor washed his car as a woman walked her dog.

Noles put a hand on Jake's shoulder. "I know we got off on the wrong foot, but given different circumstances, I think we could have been friends, so I want you to know this— I'm not giving up on this case. Maybe the murder weapon will turn up, or I'll punch holes in his alibi. We have a subpoena for the phone records, and there are still more pawnshops to check. But . . . "

Jake could guess the rest, but he wanted to hear Noles say it. "But?"

"I can't make any promises."

"I wouldn't ask you to."

Noles nodded. "Are you going to be all right?"

"Sure."

"Please don't do anything stupid."

Jake smirked. "I can't make any promises."

Chapter 24

Across town, Dolan rapped his knuckles on the door to Sonny's office. He didn't get a response, so he knocked louder.

"Come in," Sonny shouted.

Dolan strode inside. "I hope you don't mind that I didn't call ahead."

Sonny sat up straight and cleared his throat. "No. You can stop by anytime."

A large oak desk occupied most of the room. A pair of filing cabinets stood in the corner. On the wall behind the desk hung a framed reproduction of *A Friend in Need*. Dolan hated that stupid picture of the dogs playing poker— the bulldog wouldn't slip his friend a card to win the hand. Everyone knew it was every dog for himself.

Sonny opened a desk drawer and placed a tattered red book inside.

Dolan said, "I find that book helpful as well."

Nodding, Sonny said, "I find a new nugget of wisdom every time I pick it up."

"How many times have you read it?"

"At least fifty," Sonny answered.

"I'm not surprised," Dolan said. "You know you are way too philosophical for this business."

Sonny shrugged. "I have to be to deal with a lot of assholes. It's the only way I stay sane."

"Speaking of assholes, I hear your brother was arrested." Dolan took the chair opposite Sonny without asking for permission.

"Yeah, for a simple assault— our lawyer already has him out. They wanted to tie him to Tom Morgan's death, but they have nothing on him."

"Great. I don't have to tell you how bad it would be if Caleb was charged with murder."

"Don't worry. If that happened, the club could squelch it."

Dolan raised an eyebrow. "Could you?"

"Yes."

"Good, because if I had to handle it, I'd just wipe out your whole club."

Sonny pursed his lips. "You could try.

Pointing a finger at Sonny, Dolan said, "Count on it unless you get me that thumb drive."

He was bluffing, of course. Dolan didn't have the resources, not since he left the agency. However, if they forced his hand, he'd kill this thug and his dumb brother and skip town before anyone was the wiser. He should do it anyway; they'd only done half of the job.

Dolan knew the file was on a thumb drive from their internal CCTV footage, the same system that put him in this mess. Stupid! Why had he ever installed it? Luckily, just a single copy should exist. Files could only be extracted if they were write-protected and encrypted. He'd at least been that smart with the system settings. However, if Tom had become a computer whiz in his spare time and made a duplicate file, these thugs were useless. But Tom hadn't— Dolan was sure of it. If Tom had more than one copy, he would have turned it over to the police, and Dolan would also be looking at the wrong side of the grass.

Sonny stuck his chin out. "We'll find it."

"Your brother should have beaten the hiding spot out of Tom before he killed him. Why didn't he?"

"Things got out of control. He wasn't expecting your boy to put up such a fight."

"Christ, I thought you were professionals."

"Caleb handled it, but a heads-up would have been nice. If I'd known, I would have sent Aces instead."

"You should have— your brother is a fuck-up. Wasn't it supposed to look like a robbery?"

Sonny gritted his teeth. "There was a change of plans. Morgan stopped to save a turtle."

"A turtle?"

"Yes, so Caleb thought it should look like a random fight between two motorists. It was pretty smart if you ask me."

Growing frustrated at his excuses, Dolan ran his fingers through his thinning hair. "Then why did he take the watch?"

"The watch was a mistake— but Caleb took care of it."

"How?"

"It's at the bottom of a landfill," Sonny said.

"It better not turn up."

"It won't."

Dolan asked. "So how are you going to find the thumb drive?"

The answer to that question was why he'd personally come to this shithole of a club— that and to see if he could still trust Sonny. His source had already told him about the details of Caleb's arrest. Thankfully, Sonny hadn't tried to deceive him. Sonny was a lowlife, but he was honorable.

Sonny said, "We tailed Morgan for days. He only went to the office and home, so that drive is in his house somewhere. We'll break in and toss the place."

"When?"

"First chance we get. They've been at home mourning, but they have to go back to work and school eventually. Unless you want us to murder his family too?"

Dolan shook his head. "No, let's give it a few more days. Who are you going to send?"

"Aces."

"Good."

"What do you want us to do if we can't find the file? He could have a good hiding spot inside the house."

Dolan smiled. "Burn it to the ground."

Chapter 25

When Jake reentered the house after his conversation with Noles, he found Emma's nose was back in her book, but Mary was nowhere in sight. Emma set down her John Green novel and studied him with pinched eyes. "Looking for Mom?"

"Yeah. Do you know where she went?"

"She went upstairs, probably to her room."

He gave her an awkward smile. "Thanks."

"Is everything all right? She looked pretty upset."

"I'm not sure." Jake exited the room before Emma could ask any more questions.

Upstairs, he timidly searched the bedrooms, but the only open door was to Mary's room. She was perched on the edge of her bed, staring at the floor. Jake knocked on the door frame. "Can I come in?"

Mary looked up slowly, her face etched in pain, but she gave her consent. He entered the room and closed the door behind him. The latch snapped into place. He sat down next to her and glanced around. A lot of Tom's stuff remained in the room. Jake didn't blame Mary; he wouldn't want to part with it so soon either.

On the nightstand, covered in a thin layer of dust, was Tom's favorite book, *A Wrinkle in Time*. He must have read it a hundred times when they were kids. Jake never understood how; he could barely read a book once. In the open closet hung Tom's shirt and pants. A white sock peeked out of a closed dresser drawer. In the master bathroom, his shaving cream, mouthwash, and deodorant were on the counter.

He stopped his survey to find Mary watching him. She blinked away her watery eyes, which tore Jake's heart in two. He could deal with his own pain, but hers was too much. His chin quivered as he said, "I'm so sorry."

The tears spilled down her cheeks. "I was so sure that it was Tom's watch— I needed that closure. I'm fighting to keep it together here, but I fear I'm going crazy."

He laid a hand on her shoulder. "You aren't crazy."

A manic giggle escaped her lips. "How do you know? You thought it was his watch too. Maybe we are both crazy."

Jake shook his head. "Mary, it was his watch."

"No, it wasn't. Detective Noles said it was similar, but that it wasn't Tom's watch."

Reaching for her hand, he said, "I screwed up. I shouldn't have confronted Caleb that night. It gave him time to destroy Tom's watch and get a new one to make us look stupid. He did it— he killed Tom."

"No, he couldn't. Caleb had an alibi." She pulled her hand away. "He couldn't be the killer."

"Caleb's friends lied for him," Jake sighed. "After you went inside, Noles confided in me that Caleb Clarke is most likely Tom's murderer, not that he can prove it."

"Most likely?"

"Yes."

"I can't believe the police would let a murderer go."

"They had to."

"How can you be so sure?"

"It's just a feeling. I'd bet my life on it, but I can't prove it either."

She wiped away her tears. "Then, for my own sanity, I have to move on and put the pieces of my life back together for the kids."

Scooting away from her, he knew he had one more thing to tell her, and he knew it wouldn't go over well. "About the kids . . . "

A hand shot to her chest. "What about the kids? Are they in danger?"

Grimacing, he knew he had to cross that line again. "Nothing like that, but I think Emma heard us talking the other night."

Her hand clenched into a fist. "You promised."

"I know. This is the absolute last thing I want to do right now, but Emma brought it up. Not me."

"When?"

"Last night."

Fresh tears streamed down Mary's face making Jake feel worse than before. He took a couple of deep breaths as he wiped his sweaty hands on his pants. "It was stupid, but pretending that it didn't happen is not going to make it go away. We had a one-night stand, and Emma thinks I might be her dad."

"She said that?"

"Not in so many words."

Mary wiped a hand across her face. "Tell me what words she used."

"She was comparing my facial features to hers."

"Ok? What else?"

"She said that her and Sam have the same shape of nose."

Mary threw her hands up in the air. "That's all?"

"She acted weird too," he added, realizing how stupid he sounded.

"Oh, I see. Detective Bryant thinks that Emma is his daughter because they have the same nose, and she was acting weird."

He cringed. "That's a low blow. And I don't think that— Emma does."

"But she's not."

"How can you be so sure?"

"I just am. I wish I could take it back. It was the worst mistake of my life."

Standing up, he paced back and forth in the confined space. "Mine too."

The two of them had said little after their tryst except to swear an oath of secrecy. The revelation would have destroyed their lives and Tom's as well. Jake couldn't do that to his best friend— better to carry the guilt on his back like a two-ton weight.

On some level, Jake knew why he'd done it. He'd always had a crush on Mary, even freshman year when she'd been skinny with braces. She had a special aura about her, but then Tom and Mary started dating, and Jake was relegated to the friend zone, at least until that night.

With Jake visiting Michigan and Tom traveling for business yet again, he had asked Jake to get Mary out of the house since Lindsey was so colicky. Tom's mother had kept the baby for the night, so at dinner, they both had a few drinks, and later while watching a DVD, they'd had a few more. This was before Jake's drinking had become a problem, or maybe it was the start of it, he wasn't sure— Jake had plenty of troubles of his own.

Katey, his ex-wife, was sassy and driven, a real spitfire in and out of the bedroom. Great qualities in a girlfriend, but not so much when you were trying to build a family. Nothing Jake did was ever good enough, so it was no wonder in a moment of weakness, he'd sought comfort in another woman's arms. However, the reason for Mary's bad decision had always eluded him.

Knowing he might never get this chance again, Jake asked, "Why did you sleep with me?"

Mary picked a piece of lint from the comforter and dropped it to the floor. "I was feeling fat and lonely, and you were so sweet to me that night."

"That's all?"

She hesitated. "No, it was also revenge. I thought Tom was cheating on me."

Chapter 26

Dropping back on to the bed, Jake said, "You can't be serious. Tom cheated on you?"

"He didn't, thank God. But I was sure of it at the time."

If what Mary said had been true, it would have turned Jake's world upside down. He was a screw-up, and Mary had a moment of weakness, but Tom was practically a saint in Jake's eyes. "He'd never do something like that— not to you!"

Mary's mouth twisted up like a pretzel. "Tom's not as perfect as you think."

"True. Nobody's perfect, but . . . "

"You don't know him as well as you think you did. Tom had his secrets."

"Like what?" Jake's phone buzzed in his pocket, but he ignored the call.

"I don't want to get into it, but he hid more than his relationship with Kelly from us."

"Who's Kelly?"

"An attractive single woman on Tom's consulting team. He traveled with her all the time, and they would spend whole weeks together in fancy hotels."

"That doesn't mean anything. It was his job."

"It was more than that. I found out they talked and texted, even when they didn't have to and not about work stuff. They were close, a lot closer than I would've liked. Maybe Tom wasn't physically cheating, but he was emotionally cheating, and I hate the little homewrecker. To this day, I fucking hate her."

Jake knew Mary had a temper, but he'd never seen this jealous side of her before. He guessed there was a lot he didn't know about either of his friends or their marriage, but he still felt the need to defend Tom. Jake said, "I'm sure you had nothing to worry about."

She said, "No, I did. I saw Kelly at the company Christmas party. She was gorgeous with long dark hair, a perfect body, and perky tits that never nursed a baby."

"See, I was right. You had nothing to worry about— Tom was an ass man."

"Kelly had a great ass too, better than mine."

Jake shook his head. "You are selling yourself short. You have a great ass."

"Shut up." Her brow pinched tight.

Shrugging, he said, "It was just a friendly observation."

"Stop looking at my ass." Mary frowned. "Anyway, I know that I can get jealous, and that I probably had nothing to worry about, but Tom spent a lot of time with her. A lot of time! And Tom was a good-looking man— women wanted him."

"But he'd never cheat on you," Jake insisted.

"You're right— he didn't. At least, I think he didn't because when I confronted him, Tom swore up and down that he'd been faithful. And I believed him, but . . . "

"But what?"

"It was a feeling deep down in my gut. He was different. He started working out, and he bought new clothes and an expensive bottle of cologne. After he returned from trips, sometimes he'd attack me, and other times he couldn't be bothered."

"Interesting," Jake said, trying not to sound patronizing. To him, it sounded like Tom was an average guy who wanted to stay attractive for his wife.

"It was interesting, but if Tom was cheating, I should've divorced him, not been fighting fire with fire. I would've liked to blame our affair on postpartum depression, but in reality, I was a stupid bitch. I should've had been tarred and feathered or at least been beaten with a belt. I never told him the truth, so I guess living with my guilt will have to be punishment enough."

Mary had a strict Catholic upbringing, so he wasn't surprised by her statement— Catholic girls were fueled by their guilt. They wore it like armor.

Jake sighed, "I'm sorry. I should've never let it happen either, but I was going through some stuff of my own. Kate and I were separating. There was the whole Leroy Jones thing. I was a little messed up in the head."

Ignoring his admission, she asked, "Did Tom ever say anything to you about Kelly?"

"No. This is the first time that I've heard of her."

"And you never told him about us?"

"No way."

"Good."

"So, what do we do now?"

"I guess we move on with our lives. Like you said, we focus on the family that is still here." Jake paused before cautiously adding, "And you really need to say something to Emma, so that this whole thing doesn't mess her up too. Lie if you have to."

"I know. I will. Tomorrow," Mary said.

"Promise?"

"I promise. When are you leaving?"

Jake said, "In the morning. I should get back home, see if I still have a job, and return to my normal life."

"Good. You need to."

Jake had lied too— he'd be back every weekend. He couldn't let Caleb get away with it. Maybe Noles wasn't a bad guy, but Jake couldn't rely on him to solve Tom's case. He'd still do his own investigation, even if it was a waste of time. He had to do it for Tom. And for Mary.

Maybe he could find a witness to refute Caleb's alibi or a pawn shop that had bought Tom's watch from Caleb or sold the new watch to him before his arrest. Jake would find a way to get him convicted, but there was no reason to get Mary's hopes up yet.

"Can I do anything for you or the kids before I go back to Chicago?" Jake asked.

"No, we're fine."

"I could stay here tonight?"

"I think it would be better if you went back to Bobby's. Sorry."

"I understand." He'd pushed too hard with Emma. With regret, he opened the bedroom door. "Bye, Mary."

"Bye, Jake. Drive safe." A deep sorrow etched her features, but behind Mary's eyes, a fierce resolve still burned. She was one tough woman— Tom had been a lucky man.

"I always do."

Chapter 27

As the setting sun turned the horizon purple, Jake found the perfectly round rock exactly ten paces from the rear corner of Bobby's service station. He dug it from the ground with his fingers. A key rattled inside the fake stone. After he'd checked the shadows for witnesses, Jake retrieved the key from behind the plastic flap and returned the rock to its hiding place.

The phone call Jake had ignored earlier while talking to Mary had been from Bobby. His voicemail had given detailed instructions on finding the key. Jake rang Bobby to report his success. "Okay, I found it, but I still don't understand why this couldn't wait until morning."

"Jesus!" Bobby shouted. "Because I need to call that guy about those parts tonight, or I won't get them in time. Can't you do me this one favor? The papers are right on my desk."

Rolling his eyes, Jake said, "Don't get your panties in a bunch. You want me to put the key back in the rock when I'm done?"

"No, I want you to leave it in the door, so I can get robbed blind!"

"All right, smartass. See you in twenty minutes."

Jake walked around to the front of the garage. Cars and trucks waited on the cracked asphalt for their turn to be repaired. Cautiously, he glanced over his shoulder but didn't see anyone or anything suspicious, so he used the key. A brass bell hung above the door. It tinkled hauntingly in the station's lobby, causing a chill to run up Jake's spine.

The shiver made him feel silly. There was nothing to fear in the empty garage, but he still prioritized finding the light switches. The fluorescent bulbs flickered to life with a dull hum. To get his bearings, Jake approached the front counter and drummed his fingers on the laminated surface. It had been years since he'd been in here, but not much had changed.

The smell of oil and rusted metal brought back memories from his youth when they waited for Bobby's shift to end. Vic's Garage had been in business for nearly fifty years. For its first forty years, Uncle Vic owned and ran it before he succumbed to cancer. Like his uncle, Bobby did honest work at a reasonable price. He had a loyal customer base who used him religiously. Bobby would never be rich. Yet he could afford a two-week vacation in Florida every year to watch the Tigers spring training.

The outdated customer area appeared to have a thin layer of dirt, but Jake knew it was clean. It was the kind of grunge that collected over time and couldn't be scrubbed away. Old *Sports Illustrated* and *Good Housekeeping* magazines littered a chipped coffee table. Along the opposite wall, a door led to the garage, and behind the counter was an office with a one-way glass window. The office door was closed.

Before he got the papers, Jake decided to have a look around the garage for old times' sake. It was well-kept and organized, but the layer of dirt looked thicker out here. He walked around the hoists and racks filled with parts, tires, and fluids. His footfalls thudded dully in the normally loud garage. The eerie feeling returned, but he pushed it down to the pit of his stomach. His bladder fought back, making him cut his trip down memory lane short.

Inside the employee bathroom in the rear of the garage was a sink with a cracked mirror, a toilet, and a plunger that probably saw a lot of use. On the back of the door hung a girly calendar. Miss April was buxom and blonde with long legs and a groomed patch of pubic hair. After he finished ogling her, he took care of business, flushed the toilet, and turned on the water to wash his hands when the bell tinkled above the front door again.

Jake froze— the soap lathered thick on his hands. Was that really the bell, or was his mind playing tricks on him? He thought he'd locked the door, but now he couldn't remember. He muttered a curse for his poor memory. Finishing up quickly, he turned off the water and dried his hands with brown paper towels while straining his ears for another sound. He heard nothing.

Pushing open the bathroom door, he shouted, "Bobby, is that you?"

His voice echoed through the empty garage. He waited and then yelled again. No one answered, so he hesitantly made his way across the garage. Two steps away from the lobby, he paused to listen, but all remained quiet. However, his intuition told him the space was occupied by someone or something, so he called out again.

Still no response. Could somebody be robbing the place? The neighborhood had gone down in recent years, so it wouldn't be a big surprise. Bobby should really think about installing an alarm system with all the expensive tools scattered around.

Jake tentatively poked his head into the office area for a quick look. The door to Bobby's office was open an inch, and light poured from the crack.

"Bobby?"

"In here," a muffled voice responded.

Ignoring the alarm bells clanging in his head, Jake rushed into the office. "What? You don't trust me?"

Jake stopped dead in his tracks. It was not Bobby sitting behind the desk.

The leader of the motorcycle gang laughed. "I don't know. Can I?"

Jake mumbled, "What are you doing here— ?"

Shit! Jake couldn't remember his name. It was something stupid like Junior or Rocky— no, it was Sonny. The man was too pretty to be a gangster. He looked like he would be more at home on the movie screen with his long blonde hair falling across his brow.

Sonny raised a flat black gun and pointed it at Jake's head. "We need to reach an understanding."

Jake tried to back up, but a second gun was jammed into the back of his skull. The cold metal prickled his scalp. Sonny had backup, which meant Jake was totally screwed. He had nowhere to run. The blood in his veins turned to ice as Sonny's grin grew wider.

Chapter 28

"Don't do anything stupid," said a gravelly voice.

The owner sounded like he voluntarily gargled with razor blades. Jake didn't need to turn around to know the voice belonged to the giant biker. Jake let loose a string of profanities but didn't make any sudden movements, not with the gun at his head. Damn! How could he allow himself to be cornered like this?

"Sit down in the chair, nice and slow," Aces ordered.

Jake weighed his options. He could either avoid multiple bullets like he was Neo, or he could do what they said. Sonny couldn't take a shot without putting Aces at risk. However, the giant had Jake dead to rights. A shot aimed low to high would take the top of Jake's head off and leave a hell of a mess all over Bobby's office. Jake decided to play along— at least until he got an opening because he was sure they intended to kill him. With Jake eliminated, the investigation would go cold, and Caleb and his gang would have nothing more to worry about.

"What are you waiting for?" Aces pushed Jake with his free hand. He stumbled towards the cracked leather chair facing the desk. Sonny kept his gun trained on him the whole time while Jake pulled it out and sat down.

Frustrated, Jake said, "If you're going to shoot me, do it and get it over with."

"Why would we shoot you? I only want to talk."

"Fuck off! I've got nothing to say to you."

Aces delivered a backhand to Jake's ear that bounced his head off his shoulders like a pinball. Stars danced in front of his eyes. When his head cleared, he turned to face the big man, his anger getting the best of him. "Touch me again, and I'll rip your dick off."

Shifting his gun to his left hand, Aces pulled his right hand back to punch. Jake prepared for a strike of his own. Any chance for a surprise groin shot was lost with his threat, so he'd have to settle for ramming his head into Aces's chin. If Jake didn't land it, he knew he'd be torn apart.

Sonny calmly said, "Aces, enough."

The giant frowned but lowered his hand. He moved to Jake's side, so he'd no longer be in Sonny's shooting lane. Jake slumped back in the chair— it was checkmate. He only hoped that they'd be satisfied with killing him as a warning for Mary to be quiet.

As if reading his mind, Sonny shook his head. "We're not going to kill you! I only want to talk. Aces, why don't you leave us alone for a minute?"

Aces looked as shocked by the request as Jake, but he lowered his gun. "I don't think that is a good idea."

"You're not going to try anything during our little discussion, are you, Jake?

Jake shook his head. "Nope."

"See." Sonny smiled. "Besides, Jake isn't half as quick as me, and I have the gun."

Aces glared at Jake. The meaning was clear— if something should happen to his boss, what remained of Jake's life would be very painful. "Fine. I'll be right outside this door."

"No. Have a cigarette and check the street for Outsiders. We wouldn't want them sneaking up on us," Sonny said, still grinning.

Aces stuck his Glock in a holster at his ribs. "Ok."

Sonny and Jake watched as he stomped out of the room, leaving the door open behind him. The bell rang over the front door. Jake shifted his gaze back to Sonny. He judged the distance to the gun pointed at his head; it was way too far away to try anything, especially with the desk between them. Sonny looked down at the gun and scowled like he had forgotten that it was in his hand.

Removing his feet from the desk, Sonny set the weapon down in the vacated space. "That better?"

"Yes."

Jake had his opening. He managed to keep his eyes on Sonny to not give away his true intentions as he nodded his aching head. If he could get his hand on the pistol before Sonny, then he stood a good chance of shooting his way out of here.

Sonny pulled out an eight-inch long knife from a sheath at his belt. The mirror-like finish cast Jake's image back at him. Sonny used the point of the blade to dig in his palm. "Good. Because I want you to be able to focus on our conversation."

Jake shifted uneasily in his chair. Now the thug was just fucking with him. "You can cut the bullshit intimidation tactics. It's not going to work."

Sonny continued to dig at his hand with the knife. "Sorry. I've got a splinter, and it hurts like a son of a bitch."

"Whatever. Get on with it. Talk."

"So, you and Tom Morgan were best friends?"

Jake nodded his head. "Yes, but you already knew that."

Pulling the knife away, Sonny brought his hand to his mouth and extracted a sliver of wood with his teeth. He spat it on the floor. "I've got a few old friends. I'd do anything for them, and I know they would do anything for me. I'd lie, cheat, or steal for them."

Jake's stomach clenched. "Good for you."

"I'd even kill for them."

Jake glanced down at the pistol. "I bet."

"Would you kill for Tom?" Sonny asked.

"Yes," Jake said without hesitation. He'd kill every last gang member for what they did to Tom and his family.

"Interesting." Sonny sucked at the wound on his hand.

Jake dove for the pistol. With blinding speed, Sonny brought the knife down. The tip buried itself a quarter inch into the desktop. Jake jerked his hand back quickly, but the blade still nicked the webbing between his thumb and forefinger. Blood seeped from the cut. Shit! He'd been so close to getting Sonny's weapon.

Sonny grinned. "I was hoping you'd try that."

Jake exhaled slowly to keep his cool. "Why?"

"Because. I saw it in your eyes at Mitch's bar— you don't back down from anything. You would've torn Caleb apart with your bare hands if you weren't outnumbered."

Jake wiped the blood on his pants. "I'm glad you feel that way because I would've killed you too if I'd gotten my hands on that gun."

Snorting, Sonny tossed Jake the weapon. "It's not loaded."

The gun felt light, but Jake checked to be sure. The clip and the barrel were empty. He shook his head at Sonny. "You're insane."

"I must be," Sonny said. "Because I'm here to make you the offer of a lifetime."

Chapter 29

Jake grunted in disbelief. "You're crazy if you think I want anything to do with you. You killed Tom."

Sonny nodded. "I might be crazy, but I didn't kill Tom. Caleb did."

"Same difference. He's in your club."

"Normally, I'd agree with you, but things were different with your friend. Will you at least hear me out?"

"Why should I?" Jake asked.

"Because if you do, you'll walk out of here without a scratch— no matter what you decide."

"I don't believe you, but what choice do I have?"

Sonny set the large knife on the desk next to the gun. "I'll take that as a yes."

Jake ignored both weapons, choosing to watch Sonny for signs of deception. "Whatever, let's get this over with so that I can go home."

Sonny stroked his goatee. "Fine. I'll get right to the point— I want you to kill Caleb."

"Excuse me?" Jake's chin hit his chest.

"You heard me right. I want you to kill Caleb."

"Why me?"

"Great question, Jake. I'll get to that in a minute, but first, you need to understand that Caleb and I have a complicated relationship because he is my brother."

"Yes, I know. He's in your club."

"No— Caleb's my brother. He is my baby brother."

Disappointed in himself, Jake slumped back in his seat. They had enough of the same features. Jake should have seen the resemblance in the two men.

When Jake didn't respond, Sonny said, "Caleb has to die, but I can't do it."

"Why not?"

"It's a long story— I could kill anyone else, even my old lady, but not Caleb."

"I have the time. Your goon outside will make sure of that."

Nodding, Sonny let the silence fill the room before he said, "Caleb and I grew up in a broken home. Different fathers and a drug-addicted mom who had a new boyfriend every month. Some were bad, but more were really bad. Me, being the big brother, I tried to protect Caleb. I can't tell you how many beatings I took for him."

"That sucks," Jake found himself saying as he thought of the beatings he received from his drunken father.

"Yeah, one of those fuckers kicked my ass so bad, I thought he'd killed me. I had to spend a week in the hospital."

Sonny clasped his hands in front of his face and exhaled slowly. He stared at the ceiling. Jake looked up but didn't see the Sword of Damocles hanging about his head. Instead, Sonny must be reliving his past up there; Jake waited somewhat patiently while he finished.

Sonny continued, "However, there was a time when I was twelve, and Caleb was ten. He said something that he shouldn't have, and I got mad and hurt him. Hurt him bad, and all he ever did was look up to me. I felt terrible. I wanted to die— so I promised myself I'd never hurt him again, and I'm a man who keeps his promises. In my world, you're nothing if you can't do that."

"Ok?" Jake said, unsure what else to say to his monologue.

"Anyway, we survived, and with a childhood like that, we couldn't lead a normal life. Luckily, my mother's brother founded this club and eventually sponsored Caleb and me.

"We loved everything about the outlaw life and became full members. Time passed. Guys fell to jail, age, and death, so I ended up the president, and I made Caleb my vice-president. He was happy with that at first, but a year ago, things changed."

"How?"

"Nothing specific, just a feeling."

Jake understood intuition; sometimes it was a detective's best tool. "And?"

"And I believe Caleb is plotting to kill me and take over the club."

Jake leaned forward in his seat. "And you want me to kill him before he kills you?"

Rubbing his temples, Sonny said, "I do. And I know you want him dead as well, so I thought we could reach an agreement."

Sonny's offer was too good to be true. Yes, Jake would love to kill Caleb and skip all the red tape, but that was not how things worked. Vigilante justice was a pipe dream. In the real world, the guilty were arrested, tried, and sentenced for their crimes. Sonny was playing Jake somehow, and if he didn't watch it, Jake would be the one locked up in prison for murder.

Stalling, Jake asked, "Why me? Why don't you get somebody else in the club to kill him?"

"I can't. I believe Caleb's got other members involved, but I don't know who. The only one I know I can trust is Aces, but Caleb would expect that, so I need someone from outside the club to do it."

Jake had heard enough; he wanted no part of this scheme. His chair scraped loudly on the floor as he stood up. Jake turned to leave, hoping Sonny would hold up his end of the deal.

"I'm out of here. I don't need to kill Caleb. Eventually, Noles will get the evidence against him, and he'll go to prison for his crime."

Sonny leaned back in his chair and laughed. The man was obviously crazy, so Jake chuckled along with him. However, the laughter was cut short, and Sonny looked at Jake with dead eyes. "That won't happen."

"Why? Is Noles crooked?"

"Who?"

"Noles, the lead detective on Tom's case. Is he in your pocket?"

Sonny shook his head. "Sit down, detective. I don't have anyone on the inside. Caleb won't go to prison because he'll kill everyone involved, so it won't matter what you find."

Alarm bells went off in Jake's head, but it wasn't Aces returning to the garage. Jake was in deeper than he thought. He sat back down. "How did you know I was a detective?"

"I've done my homework. I know your high school GPA and the name of the girl you banged at prom. I know how many tackles you had over your high school football career, and I know about your dad, your divorce, and your kid. I know about the rapist too."

"Who did I bang at prom?"

"Julie Gray."

Jake's skin crawled. This was bad. How did he find out about that, and what did Sonny know about Sam? He leaned back in his chair and tried to play it cool. "Shit! I guess you have done your homework."

"I have, and what I learned is that you're one tough son of a bitch. You can definitely handle the hit on Caleb, and maybe one day, I can talk you into joining my club."

Jake was in trouble. This madman wanted to add Jake and his police knowledge to his collection of misfits. Jake's best play was to let Sonny think he was still interested, or he'd kill Jake where he stood. He said, "If this scheme with Caleb is real, then I might do it, but I don't want your life."

"I think you're lying."

"I'm serious. I have no interest in being an outlaw."

Sonny smiled. "No. You're lying about Caleb. You should know that if Caleb kills me and takes control of the club, he'll go after you and Tom's family next."

"He will?" Jake almost fell out of his chair. He thought back to the other night with Emma. It could have just as easily been an assassin out there in the dark instead of horny teenagers.

"Yes, to cover his tracks. Plus, you did lay hands on him. He's old-school like that. You know, fire and brimstone, scorch the earth, kill seven generations, and all that biblical stuff."

"Now I think you're lying," Jake said.

"I wish I was," Sonny replied. His face could have given lessons to a stone. "You should really listen to my plan— it's a good one."

Jake tried to swallow, but his throat was too dry. He now believed Sonny. Caleb would kill them all. Not that Jake had agreed to murder yet, but the least he could do was hear Sonny out. "Fine. I'll listen, but I want some time to think it over."

Sonny put his feet back up on the desk. "I can give you twenty-four hours, no more. We can meet back here for your answer."

Chapter 30

An hour later, on the Southside of Detroit, Caleb sped down a dark suburban street. The Harley Davidson's chrome sparkled in the moonlight. He slowed in front of a house in the middle of the street and turned down its narrow driveway, following it to a small garage in the back. The garage door closed as Caleb shut off the rumbling engine.

A tall man with a bushy beard and long black hair stepped into view, a hand behind his back. Caleb put a hand inside his jacket. The man took another step closer, and Caleb put a finger on the trigger of his pistol. The man stepped past him and peeked out a window set in the garage door.

"You weren't followed?" Alex asked with the garage remote clutched in his hand.

"I'm not stupid." Caleb removed his hand from his jacket and eased the bike down on its kickstand.

"We can't be too careful. If we're seen together, we're both dead men," Alex said.

"No shit!"

It was the reason they'd met at Alex's mother's house. They couldn't chance a meeting on the street nor at their own residences— not with both clubs on high alert. The wrong person might see them. Caleb reached into his pants pocket and pulled out a thick wad of cash bound in banker's paper. He tossed it across the garage to Alex, who snatched it from the air like a flyball.

Alex inspected the amount and then pocketed it quickly, nodding a thank you. He pulled a cigarette from his pocket. The leather jacket bore a president patch on the chest and the Outsider colors on the back. He offered a cigarette to Caleb, who shook his head and pulled out his own pack. The pair lit up.

Alex held the butt away from his mouth and frowned. "The Devil's Hand tried to burn my clubhouse down."

Caleb shrugged his shoulders. "It couldn't be helped. I had to respond, or somebody might put two and two together about our relationship."

"If it happens again, we won't have a relationship."

Alex walked past Caleb and leaned against a dirty tool bench in the back of the garage to tap his ashes in a glass ashtray. Tools lay scattered on the bench's surface, rather than being hung on the pegboard above the bench. A lamp waiting for repair sat off to one side. They both smoked their cigarettes, waiting for the other to speak. Caleb knew Alex wanted an apology. He wasn't going to get one. Caleb never lost a pissing contest.

Puffing on his cigarette like it was a lifeline, Alex's eyes darted around the cramped garage. Finally, he said, "You're fucking lucky no one got hurt."

"We're all lucky." Caleb snorted. "How many guys in your club know what's really going on?"

"Two," Alex said.

Caleb believed him. Any more than that, and it would be hard to keep the secret. Emotions would be high, particularly if men died in this manufactured war to benefit Alex and Caleb's personal interests. Their respective clubs would crucify them if they found out.

"I've got about the same number myself," Caleb said.

The cigarette fell from Alex's hand, and he ground it into the concrete with a heavy boot. "The Devil's Hand will back your presidency after all this shit is over?"

Caleb nodded. "They're sick of Sonny and all of his philosophical bullshit. They're ready for an ass-kicker like me."

"Good, because I'm really sticking my neck out here!"

"What the fuck do you think I'm doing?"

Alex held up his hands. "All right, but I'll need to be compensated more than what you just gave me for the damage to my club."

Scratching his chin, Caleb asked, "How much we are talking about?"

"I was thinking about something different than money."

"Oh, yeah?"

Alex grinned. "I was thinking about ten more blocks of territory."

Caleb's lips tightened to a fine line as he shook his head from side to side. "No way is that going to happen. You got all the territory I'm going to give you."

"Fine. What else can you offer me?"

"How about a kilo of smack on the big night?"

"Make it two kilos," Alex said, shifting nervously from foot to foot.

Caleb made him wait before saying, "I can do two kilos."

"Deal."

Alex pushed off the tool bench and peeked out the window again. "My guys are itching to settle the score for the firebombing, so I need this to happen soon."

"Give me a couple more days to set things up with Sonny."

"No more than that."

Caleb bit his tongue. Alex would get his soon enough too. "I'll call you with the time and place. We can't risk another meeting."

Alex paced back to the tool bench. "Yeah, good idea. Call me."

With a push of a button, the engine to Caleb's bike rumbled to life with a throaty growl. Alex opened the garage door with the remote. Caleb rocked the bike off its stand and used both feet to push the heavy motorcycle back into the driveway before dropping it into gear. He dumped the clutch and roared off into the night, feeling good about himself. The meeting had played out just like he'd hoped. How someone as dumb as Alex had risen to be president of the second-best club in Detroit was hard to believe. This would be like taking candy from a baby.

Chapter 31

Jake found the side door unlocked, but out of respect, he knocked before entering his childhood home. Good thing his mother had nothing worth stealing because her idea of security was leaving the light on above the stove. Surprisingly, she'd only suffered one break-in. They'd tossed the place but only took some costume jewelry and her tip money from the dresser. Jake called out, but luckily no one was home. He didn't feel like talking, not even to his mom who must be working the late shift at the diner.

Pangs of guilt stabbed at his heart as he kicked off his shoes on a green rug older than him. Jake could have stayed at his mom's house this visit— except Nancy drove him nuts with her constant questions. He loved her for all that she'd sacrificed for him, but the admiration wasn't enough for a week-long stay.

However, since he was too angry to go back to Bobby's house tonight, Jake had decided to spend the night here. If he saw Bobby right now, Jake would punch him in his fat nose. He was such an asshole. Was Bobby so far up the club's ass he'd do whatever Sonny asked, including setting up a deadly ambush on a friend?

Jake's boyhood home, like most houses in Westland, had a well-worn but homey kitchen. He took in all the familiar sights and smells. The aroma of beef, potatoes, and coffee permeated every corner of the room, complemented by the comforting hum of the outdated refrigerator. A tattered window shade bulged around the potted plants eternally stationed on the windowsill. Dishes, silverware, and a pot dried in a rack by the sink on an otherwise spotless counter.

Inside the fridge, he found the basic staples of milk, eggs, and condiments. The bottom drawers held apples, oranges, and cheeses. The freezer was better stocked with frozen low-calorie dinners and sugar-free ice cream. Jake wasn't really hungry, so he let the doors slide shut and moved into the living room.

A couch and an easy chair faced an old-style tube television in the corner of the room. He'd considered buying his mom a flat screen, so she could enjoy technology from this millennium but had decided against it. Nancy wouldn't want to learn to operate a fancy remote control. The couch was new, but the recliner was the same one from his childhood, the material shiny from wear. A cable box sat on top of the console, which was pointless since Nancy only watched network television when she wasn't wearing the treads off another pair of shoes at the diner.

Plodding down the threadbare carpet to the back of the house, he stopped at the door to his mother's bedroom. A queen-sized bed with a depression on the left side of the mattress filled the tiny room. Besides a polished dresser, the only other piece of furniture was a nightstand holding a large digital clock, a romance novel, and a pair of reading glasses.

Across the hall was Jake's old bedroom. The room gave him an odd sense of comfort that no other bedroom had since. He supposed that was true for everyone. The furniture was the same, but the walls were now bare, the posters of rock bands, supermodels, and athletes long gone. Nancy had ripped them down when he'd moved out. All his trophies, baseball cards, yearbooks, and forgotten toys had been boxed up and sent to Chicago. She'd been angry and hurt when he left to work a high-paying job for his father after graduation. She'd gotten over it eventually, but she'd been right— Chicago had been a mistake. Adding insult to injury, after his divorce, a fire broke out in his storage locker, and he'd lost those keepsakes along with everything else.

Jake's phone buzzed in his back pocket. He pulled it out and looked at the screen— another text from his treacherous friend. Bobby had tried calling him three times and had sent a dozen texts since Jake's meeting with Sonny. Annoyed, he shut off his phone and set it on the nightstand before dropping onto his old bed. His butt touched the box-springs through the aged mattress as he looked around the room. The bare walls and empty shelves glared back at him. Losing all that old stuff bothered him more than he'd like to admit, especially after he lost a marriage and a job. It made him feel like a child's lost balloon, untethered to the world.

Kicking up his feet, Jake laid down. The bed protested loudly. He closed his eyes but didn't think he could sleep with so much on his mind. Sonny's plan gave him a lot to consider, so he laced his fingers behind his head and let his mind wander. Old memories came flooding back with Jake and Tom playing in this very room, pushing Matchbox cars across the carpet, building Lego structures on the bed, memorizing baseball and football stats for all their favorite players, and later talking about girls— of which they knew next to nothing about but pretended otherwise.

Laughing, he recalled the time they'd snuck some whiskey from the kitchen cupboard. Tom ended up puking in the bathtub. Almost throwing up himself, Jake had a hell of a time cleaning the tub to its usual pristine condition before his mother's shift ended. Good ol' Tom. A tear slid down Jake's cheek. He brushed it away while he pondered his options.

Could Jake really find enough evidence to have Caleb arrested? Probably not, especially if Caleb intimidated or killed witnesses that could refute his alibi. Could Jake trust Sonny? Doubtful. So, should he walk away and let karma run its course? Not if what Sonny said was true— Jake, Mary, and their families could wind up dead by Caleb's hands. Damn. He didn't know what to do. Yes, Jake had killed before, but it hadn't been premeditated, no matter what the media and the public believed. Did he have the guts to pull off a calculated assassination?

Jake was screwed either way. Maybe meditation would help him find the answer— not that he'd had any luck with it before, even with the app on his phone. He steadied his breathing and forced himself to relax. Concentrating on a void, he tried to think of nothing as he waited for the solution to bubble up, but his thoughts wandered, and he remembered all the times he masturbated in this room.

At fifteen, he'd set a personal record of six times in a twenty-four-hour period. Six! Jake dared anyone to top that. He considered rubbing one out for old time's sake but dismissed the idea given his injured hand. Furthermore, he was no longer a teenage boy who got excited by a stiff breeze; he wouldn't be able to conjure up the right imagery without an internet connection. Yet this exercise proved Jake was no yogi. Meditation wouldn't provide the answers that he sought, so his thoughts returned to Tom.

His best friend was gone. God, did Jake miss him. Tom had always been there for Jake. No matter how bad Jake had screwed up, Tom stuck with him, never judging, always helping him get back on his feet. Didn't Tom deserve retribution? Jake wished that if he were murdered, someone would seek revenge for him. Jake wanted to be loved that much. He loved Tom that much. Didn't Jake owe him that for betraying their friendship and sleeping with his wife? He hoped Tom could forgive him in death.

Overwrought with emotion, Jake pushed himself to a sitting position. He knew in his heart what he should do. Still he wanted a nudge in that direction from his best friend, though Jake wasn't sure what kind of answer that he'd get.

"Tom? Are you out there?"

No response. No audible noise. No creak. No knock on the wall, but Jake waited intently.

"Tom! I could really use your help."

He listened carefully, trying to pick up even the slightest sound, but he heard nothing. Yet the temperature in the room grew colder, and he felt different in some indescribable way. Better. Happier. Like a weight was being removed from his chest.

"Tom, is that you?"

Nothing.

"Tom?"

Nothing.

"Tom, I'm stuck. I need your help just one more time. Should I kill Caleb? If I don't, he might kill your wife and kids. Please tell me what to do. Give me a sign or something."

Something.

It was a noise. It sounded like a throat being cleared, but Jake couldn't be sure. It could've been his imagination, so he sat there, dead still for two whole minutes, but he didn't hear it again. It wasn't the house, so it must have been Tom's spirit.

"Thanks, buddy."

Jake laid down and fell fast asleep— his decision made— the path set— Caleb would die by Jake's hands.

Nancy found him after her shift, snoring loudly. She laid a blanket over her baby boy, turned off the light, and crept to her own bedroom with a smile on her face.

Chapter 32

The next morning, Jake parked down the street from the industrial park where Rick's crew was working. With a groan, he pulled himself from the driver's seat with a full belly. In addition to a full breakfast of eggs, bacon, sausage, toast, and piping hot coffee, his mother had also cleaned and bound his hand so it would heal properly after Sonny's knife attack. Luckily, she was used to his half-baked lies and hadn't probed when he told her that he'd cut it helping Bobby at the garage. It had been a nice visit, but by the end of the meal, Nancy was already driving him crazy, so he made an excuse to leave with the promise of returning before he left town.

However, going back to Chicago right now was out of the question— not with Jake's decision on Caleb. So he'd left a voice mail with his boss, Keith, informing him of Jake's decision to quit. He was nearly broke. Thankfully, Kate didn't need his child support with as much money as she made, but he'd catch up on his payments with his next crappy job. There was a slim chance Keith would hire him back since Jake had rigged his machine so that only he could run it properly.

Jake made his way to where Rick operated a large blower to clean the sidewalks of stray grass clippings. Approaching cautiously, he tapped him on the shoulder, but Rick still jumped. He turned off the machine and removed his ear protection.

"S'up?"

Jake held up his bandaged hand. "We need to talk."

"Don't blame me for your friction burns. I told you to use lube."

"Ha-ha." Jake slapped his knee with his good hand. "That would've been funny back in middle school."

Rick grinned. "Gotta love the classics."

"This is serious."

"All right."

"Dead serious," Jake said, emphasizing the first word.

"Ok, I hear you. Hold on a minute."

Sticking two fingers between his lips, he whistled loudly, getting the attention of a twenty-something kid with long hair. The man-child finished loading a mower onto an open trailer and jogged over. Rick handed him the blower and led Jake to a back corner of the lot away from his nosy crew. Jake told him the story of his encounter with Sonny. Rick interrupted him with countless questions.

After Jake finally finished, Rick punctuated the tale in a fashion that would've made Samuel L. Jackson proud. "Fucking motherfucker!"

"Got that right," Jake agreed.

"We should kill that big asshole too."

"Aces?"

"No, Bobby."

Jake shook his head. "Shut up, he's our friend— though we're going to have a long talk about whose side he's on. But there's only one man I'm killing, and that's Caleb."

"So you're going to do it?"

Looking from side to side to ensure none of Rick's crew had snuck up on them, Jake said, "Yes."

"You don't really have a choice." Rick spit on the ground. "Like Sonny said, if Caleb takes over the club, he'll kill you for sure. Mary too. Jesus Christ, maybe he'll come after me too."

"You? What threat do you pose?" Jake asked.

Looking a little insulted, Rick said, "Either way. I want to help."

"That's kind of why I'm here. Does any of your crew deal in black-market guns or know someone who does?"

"Why? Won't Sonny give you one and then take care of it afterward?"

"That's just it. I don't trust Sonny, so I want to stay one step ahead of him. I'd rather have a gun that I know is clean, and I dump myself."

"That's smart." Rick's head bobbed up and down. "But none of my guys are into big stuff like that. They could sell you pot if you wanted."

"I'll pass." Jake snorted.

"Then you're out of luck here."

"Shit!"

"If I were you, I'd go to the Gibraltar Trade Center."

"On a Tuesday? The gun and knife shows are on the weekend."

"They still have permanent dealers there all week. With the right amount of money, I'd bet one of them would sell you what you're looking for."

Jake scratched his chin. "I bet you're right. Thanks."

"No problem." Rick placed a hand on Jake's shoulder. "You're going to let me help you, right? Tom was my friend too."

"Sonny's plan is risky."

"I understand. I wouldn't expect Caleb to go down without a fight."

"Good, because I could use you. And Bobby too."

Rick's hand dropped. "Bobby? You're going to trust that fat bastard after he set you up? You could've been killed if things went sideways."

Jake had given that a lot of thought this morning, and he'd come to a conclusion that he believed was true. He explained, "Bobby's a simple man. He didn't think that I was in any real danger. I'm sure he thought he was brokering a deal between two people with the common goal of killing Caleb."

"You give him too much credit."

"Why? What do you think it was?"

"I think Sonny has Bobby under his thumb. Bobby was just doing what he was told without thinking of the consequences." Rick spit on the ground again. "If I were you, I'd at least punch him in his nose."

"Don't get me wrong. I'm mad as hell at him, and I may punch him, but he's still our friend. He'd never intentionally betray me. I bet he'd take a bullet for me if it came down to it."

"I hope you're right." Rick looked up. The sky had grown darker and more menacing since Jake had first arrived, with a thunderstorm rolling in from the east.

"Me too. I'm betting my life on it," Jake said. Yet there could be a lot of truth to what Rick said. He had a knack for seeing through all the bullshit. All the bullshit except his own, or else he wouldn't be stuck cutting lawns at almost forty years old.

The wind ruffled Rick's hair. "I should get back. My guys are probably screwing around, and we really need to finish before the rain."

Jake took in all the grass and landscaping at the industrial park. It would require weekly maintenance to keep things looking professional. "You must make a lot of money on a place like this."

"Not as much as you might think. Landscaping is a cutthroat business— I need to find an easier way to make a buck. Maybe when you move back to Michigan, we could open a PI business together."

The suggestion caught him off guard. Jake hadn't thought of what he'd do for employment once he moved back here— probably just take a crappy factory job. There was an abundance of those in Michigan.

"Maybe." Jake nodded. "If we don't wind up in jail. Or dead."

Chapter 33

Heavy rain pelted his windshield as Jake entered the Gibraltar Trade Center. The parking lot of metro Detroit's largest flea market stretched for a mile. The cracked asphalt was uneven, and weeds grew a foot tall in the less-traveled paths. The marketplace attracted sellers of knock-off watches, hand-made crafts, exotic pets, and firearms. Jake dodged potholes that were large enough to double as swimming pools on his long drive to the front doors.

A reputable gun store would require all the proper permits and background checks as well as submit a public record of the purchase— one that would look suspicious when Caleb ended up dead. This was the exact opposite of what Jake wanted. Bad enough, if Noles discovered Jake was still in town, he didn't need to put a bell around his neck too.

If their website was up to date, the flea market had three permanent gun dealers. Jake hoped at least one was unscrupulous; otherwise, his next choice would be to pull some Jack Reacher stuff and steal a gun from a drug dealer in Detroit. However he didn't think he could pull it off, that was for damn sure. Maybe, they'd sell him one if they didn't carjack him first.

On this Tuesday afternoon, less than twenty cars were parked outside the center. Perfect. This type of transaction would only work if Jake could have a private conversation with the weapons dealer without other people nosing around. He parked the Focus two spots away from a rusted-out pickup truck with a car seat in the middle of the bench and sprinted to the building to avoid getting soaked. The entrance opened to a dim hallway. A skinny security guard with bad acne sat on a padded stool by the door. He looked up from his phone and nodded, and Jake nodded back.

Jake's shoes squeaked on the floor as he walked past the booths of baby clothes and crafts. He kept his head down to avoid making eye contact with the lonely sellers, not wanting to give them false hope. A man with a graying beard dressed as a pirate stood in front of an exotic pet booth. Wire cages with rabbits and tanks of fish and lizards haphazardly lined the exhibit. The scrawny pirate wore a three-pointed hat, red bandana, and eye shadow. Beads dangled from his long hair, and a blue parrot sat perched on his shoulder.

The bird called out to Jake, "Heello."

Jake gave them a quick wave and tried to walk by.

The pirate held out his hand. "Stop and look, my matey. Not all treasure is silver and gold— sometimes it has fur or scales."

Not stopping, Jake said, "No, thanks. I'm not looking for a pet."

"Arrrgh, you sure?"

"Yes." Jake laughed.

The pirate winked at him. "I have a feeling you'll be back."

"I don't think so."

From a booth away, the bird squawked, "Issehole."

Jake turned around. The pirate tried to look indignant but failed miserably. "Polly! Don't talk like that to the nice man."

"Shittforbraiins."

The want-to-be Captain Jack shrugged, his shoulders nearly touching his cap. "Sorry. I can't do a thing with her."

Smiling, Jake left. It was a good gimmick. On weekends, it probably brought the kids to his booth in droves, much to their parent's dismay. He could still hear the parrot insulting him as he came to the first of the gun dealers' booths. Long glass display cases formed a rectangle. In the center, racks held shotguns, long guns, and assault rifles. Oriental rugs lined the space, giving it a classy look. As he perused the cases filled with rows and rows of neatly organized weaponry, Jake's brow furrowed. Someone who put this much care into his space probably didn't perform under-the-table transactions.

A heavy-set man wearing a faux bowling shirt got off a stool and ambled over to Jake. "Can I help you?"

"I hope so. I was looking for a Glock 19."

"A Glock 19 is a solid choice. I'd be glad to show you my inventory, but first, do you have your purchase permit and the PSR?"

"PSR?" Jake asked.

Chins wobbled as the man shook his head. "A pistol sales record. You'll need it in triplicate to purchase from a dealer."

Jake's assumption was confirmed. So, the dealer wouldn't report him to security, Jake bluffed, "Sorry. I have a FOID."

"A what?"

"A firearms owner identification card. It's required in Illinois."

The man shook his head as he made his way back to his stool. "We're not in Illinois, are we? No reputable dealer will sell you a pistol without the permit and the PSR."

"I understand."

Jake moved on to the next dealer. This one was ex-military with a buzzcut, cargo pants, and a jaw that could double as an anvil. A tight black t-shirt stretched over a muscular frame. Jake didn't even slow down. He could tell this guy would not budge from his high horse draped in the American flag. Which left him one more option before he had to take his chances on the streets of Detroit.

The last dealer was tucked in a dark corner of the building. Three unadorned glass cases faced the aisle, with racks of long guns behind them. The glass was smudged, and the floor was bare concrete— no fancy rugs in this booth. A skinny man leaned against the counter and stroked a graying goatee, pulling at the wiry follicles. He wore a fraying t-shirt advertising his Second Amendment rights and a pair of stone-washed jeans. His beady eyes glanced from his gun catalog to Jake and back again.

Jake couldn't have imagined a better dealer to negotiate with. He entered the booth and studied the contents of the glass cases. He bent over for a closer look. Several Glock 19s sat on an inner shelf lined with faded orange material. The man closed his catalog with a snap and tucked it behind the counter.

Looking up, Jake said, "You have some nice merchandise."

"Affirmative. What are you looking for?"

"A Glock 19. How much for that one there?" He pointed to the compact black gun near the top of the case.

The dealer rubbed his goatee. "Hmmm. That one goes for $549, but I could cut you a deal. $500 out the door."

Jake stood up, resting his hands on the edge of the case. "Wow. That's a good price."

"You bet your ass it is. I have the best prices in town. Do we have a deal?"

Pulling out his wallet, he laid six crisp one hundred-dollar bills on the polished glass. "I'd love to make a deal, but I don't have one of those pesky permits. Can we work something else out?"

"I think you have the wrong guy."

Jake pulled out another bill and set it on top of the stack.

The dealer's eyes darted from side to side. "Are you a cop?"

Shaking his head slowly, Jake said, "No. I'm just a guy who doesn't like all of big brother's rules. Do we have a deal?"

The man performed some mental calculations that Jake hoped would unethically fall in his favor.

"We have a deal, but I can't sell you that one. I have another 19 for this type of transaction."

"It's not some piece of junk. It shoots straight?"

Indignation fell across the man's face. "All my merchandise is in tip-top operating condition."

"It better be." Jake's fingers tapped the glass.

The man nodded. "For another hundred, I have a Glock 18 that might better suit your needs."

"No. I don't need the full auto. The 19 is good enough."

"All right, put your money away."

"Wait," Jake pleaded. Beads of sweat popped out on his forehead. "We still have a deal, right?"

"Sure." The man waved Jake's concern away with the brush of his bony hand. "But I can't do this type of transaction out in the open. I'll lose my license. Did you see the pirate on your way over here?"

Jake nodded. "The one with the swearing parrot?"

"Yes, that's the one."

"Then I saw him."

"Good. He's my brother. Go back to his booth and tell him you want the 'special' jet pump for your fish tank. Pay him, and he'll give you a brown paper bag with a box in it. Take that to the food court and wait for me."

"A 'special' jet pump," he repeated, gathering up his money and putting it back in his wallet.

"Yes."

"Do we really need all this cloak and dagger stuff?"

"Do you want the gun?"

"Fine." Jake left the booth.

Looking back over his shoulder, he saw the skinny man typing on his phone, so Jake wandered towards the exotic pet booth. His path avoided the previous two dealers and their moral principles. At the opposite end of the flea market, the pirate stood in the aisle-way, smiling widely. Several teeth were missing from his grin. An old woman at a craft booth across the way frowned at them as she knitted a scarf.

"I knew you'd be back, matey."

"SonnofaWhorre," the parrot squawked.

Feeling a little bit ridiculous, Jake said, "I hear you have a 'special' jet pump that will fit my nineteen-inch tank."

"I do. Follow me." The pirate led Jake past the tanks of lizards and fish. He walked behind the counter and leaned towards a large bird stand. The parrot hopped off his shoulder onto a horizontal wood post. It stretched its wings wide and cocked its head at an impossible angle.

"Polly wants a cracker."

The pirate dug behind a counter. Over the fishy smell of the exhibit, Jake caught the faint smell of marijuana and the stronger scent of body odor. The man's costume was due for a good wash. He came back up with a plain white box.

"Here we go. One 'special' jet pump."

Jake laid seven crisp one hundred-dollar bills on the counter.

The pirate counted the cash and frowned. "This is a little light."

"That's the price your brother agreed to," Jake growled.

Captain Jack laughed. "You heard my feathered friend. She needs a cracker— an extra fifty dollars should cover it."

The pirate removed the box from the counter and scratched the bird's head. The parrot lifted its foot in pleasure. Jake wanted to reach over the counter and choke the bastard, but the old woman still watched them from across the aisle. Instead, Jake opened his wallet and laid his last bill, a twenty, on the counter. The pirate eyed the amount carefully.

Jake said, "That's all I have— looks like Polly is getting off-brand crackers."

The man tilted his head back and laughed heartily. "Arrgh, you drive a hard bargain. Twenty it is."

"Frooocker," the parrot cawed.

His owner scooped the cash off the counter, put the box in a brown paper bag, and handed it to Jake, who snatched it up quickly and left the booth without another word to the crooked pirate. In what must have been a practiced speech, the man called after him, "This is the day you'll remember as the day you got swindled by Captain Jack."

"Sooloing Succcker," the parrot yelled.

Still steaming, Jake waited in the food court. The paper bag sat on top of the table in front of him. His stomach growled from the smell of deep-fried corndogs, elephant ears, and French fries. After ten long minutes, the skinny gun dealer took the seat opposite him. He set an identical bag on the table next to Jake's.

"Not eating?" the man asked.

"Your brother stole my lunch money."

Tipping his head back, the gun dealer laughed— a laugh that matched his brother's. He stood up and took Jake's bag, leaving his behind. "Too bad. The pizza here is excellent."

Jake waited a minute before picking up his bag off the table. It was heavy. He sighed with relief as he exited the flea market to deal with his next problem— Bobby.

Chapter 34

Caleb stepped out of the shower to find an empty towel rack. Water dripped into his eyes, and he swiped it away with his hand. Scanning the floor, he found his dirty jeans, t-shirt, balled-up pair of socks, and a stiff towel. Caleb brought the towel to his nose and inhaled. It didn't smell like ass, so he used it to dry off and tossed it back on the floor.

Going into the bedroom, he rummaged in his closet until he found his favorite pair of jeans and returned to the bathroom to examine himself in the mirror. He poked and prodded at the spots that showed his age. But after flexing his pecs and biceps, Caleb decided that he still had it— if only he didn't have the purple scar that ran from his left eyebrow to his jaw. It was a wonder he hadn't lost an eye.

With all the blood, he'd thought the wound was fatal, but he'd been a stupid ten-year-old kid at the time. Yet again, Caleb's mom had dropped him and Sonny off at her brother's farm, so she could run off with her latest loser. She was a mother of very questionable morals but smart enough to know they'd be arrested for stealing if she left them alone for three days. What choice would they have with no food in their rundown apartment?

Uncle Jim was the only decent role model the boys had, which meant he put them to work when they visited the farm. Everyone had to earn their keep. On this particular rainy autumn day, he had the brothers mucking out horse stalls. Sonny moved around stiffly from the beating that he'd received from their mother's boyfriend, who got too handsy with Caleb. Apparently, this one was into little boys and used their mothers for access.

The night before, Caleb had woken up with his shorts pulled down and a hand over his mouth to muffle his screams. However,

Sonny still heard and attacked the creep. He got the worst of it, but all the noise woke up their mother, who should have questioned why he was in Caleb's room in the first place. She should've kicked him out on the spot, but she didn't. In fact, she had yelled at her sons for starting the fight. That was why she had gone away for the weekend, so she could make it up to him. The joke was on her— he wouldn't be that into her, she had a mature woman's genitalia. He was gone by the next week, and a new jerk took his place.

Caleb hated her. She was a whore, and they deserved better than that bitch. There in the barn, he said as much— and that was why Sonny hit him. He had felt the need to defend their mother's worthless honor.

The shovel caught him in the side of the head. Caleb saw it coming but was too shocked to move. He fell to his knees as white stars filled his vision. Sonny swung a second time; the edge of the shovel dug into his face. He fell backward, cracking his head on the wood floor. The ringing in his head didn't stop for a week.

As Caleb lay there on the barn floor, crying, bleeding, and with horseshit on his face, Sonny had made him swear he'd never bad-mouth their mother again. And it was that day that his hatred for Sonny took seed. Their mother had always put herself first, but Sonny had been the one person Caleb could count on. Then he'd scrambled his brain and given him a permeant reminder that he was all alone in this cruel world. Caleb was a quick learner; he never needed a second lesson.

Caleb gave the scar one more caress before he shook his head to bring himself back to the present. On his nightstand in his bedroom was a framed picture of a man with his face scratched out, courtesy of his mother. It was the only photograph he had of his father, who'd run off before Caleb was born. The man wore a flannel shirt, and on his wrist was a watch eerily similar to Tom Morgan's, which was probably why he'd stupidly taken it from the dying man.

An acoustic guitar stood in the corner. It was a Gibson Les Paul with a wood grain front and a marbled brown pickguard. He sat down on the corner of the bed and picked at the strings. It was horribly out of tune. After adjusting the tuning pegs, he played through a few of his favorite Led Zeppelin songs, but he grew bored quickly and laid down on the bed to stare at the ceiling and reanalyze his plot to murder Sonny. He didn't feel the least bit guilty for wanting to kill his brother. If he was any kind of leader, he should have seen this coming. It was classic fratricide, but Sonny was too dumb and vain to notice.

Truthfully, Caleb wanted Jodi more than he wanted control of the club— not that he didn't want that too. She deserved to be with him. Sure, their affair made Sonny look like a pathetic cuckolded stooge, but for their relationship to be out in the open and not a badly kept secret, Sonny had to die. There was no other way, just like there was no other way to deal with Alex and his gang.

Alex was too hungry for more territory to suspect a double-cross from Caleb. With Sonny and the Outsiders gone, Caleb would own Detroit with Jodi at his side. He laughed manically. The sound echoed through the empty house. Books and quotes were not Caleb's thing, not like his brother, but there was something their Uncle Jim used to say that Caleb never forgot— *Tough times don't last, but tough men do.*

Caleb knew he was tough, and he'd burn the whole city down to get what he wanted. Sighing, he stood up and brushed his long hair from his face. He wished Jodi was here because this whole thing was stressing him out. She'd make him forget about everything with those lips that could remove the chrome from a trailer hitch. But she wasn't, so he finished getting dressed.

Checking his new watch, Caleb saw he was late for his meeting at Sonny's house. Screw him. Sonny could wait. Maybe Caleb could sneak in a quickie with Jodi while Sonny's back was turned. Jodi would really be turned on by that, and his useless brother wouldn't even notice. Not until it was too late.

Damn. It couldn't get here fast enough. Just two more days, and the club and Jodi would be his.

Chapter 35

Jake sat at Bobby's kitchen table, waiting on his supposed friend. He tapped his fingers on the chipped oak surface, counting the minutes until Bobby would get home from work. The loaded pistol lay hidden in the trunk of Jake's car underneath the spare tire. After leaving the flea market, Jake had purchased several boxes of bullets and tested the weapon in a field out in the country. As promised, the gun shot straight and true.

Twenty minutes after five o'clock, the back door creaked open. Jake's fists clenched tight. The big man walked into the room, setting his lunchbox on the counter next to the fridge. Wearing greasy overalls and a guilty look, he tried to win Jake over with a goofy smile. The anger simmering in Jake's gut threatened to boil over— no way he was getting off that easy.

Bobby said, "I know what you're going to say."

"Screw you. How do you know what I'm going to say?" Jake leaned forward in his seat.

Putting up both hands, Bobby said, "I know you're pissed, and you've got a right to be, but I've known these guys for a long time, and I trust them. Sonny guaranteed your safety."

"Safety!" Spit flew from Jake's mouth. "Sonny guaranteed my safety!"

"He did, I swear."

Jake launched himself across the room and pinned Bobby up against the fridge. The contents rattled inside. Jake's forearm dug into Bobby's windpipe. "Sonny's gorilla pressed a gun to my head and then slapped the shit out of me. I'd hate to see what would happen if I was in danger. Would I have died like Tom?"

"That's a low blow," Bobby managed to choke out.

"I'll show you a low blow." Jake punched Bobby in the stomach. Hard.

The blow caught him off guard. Bobby doubled over in pain and fell to his knees. Begrudgingly, Jake took his seat at the table as Bobby coughed and wheezed, sounding like a donkey with asthma. When he could talk, Bobby said, "I suppose I had that coming."

"You did," Jake agreed.

Using the kitchen counter, Bobby pulled himself up. "But I had to do it."

"Why?"

Bobby wiped his sweaty palms on his overalls and looked out the kitchen window. After some hesitation, he answered, "Because Sonny asked me nicely."

Rick was right. Bobby was under Sonny's thumb, and he wanted Jake there with him. Jake could punch him again.

Bobby massaged his stomach. "What did Sonny want?"

"You don't know?"

"No."

"I'm not sure I want to tell you," Jake said.

"Why?"

"Because I don't think I can trust you."

"What's that supposed to mean? Of course, you can trust me."

Jake shook his head. "I'm not so sure."

"You should know I didn't sleep a wink last night. I was worried half to death when you wouldn't return any of my calls or texts."

Jake noticed the dark circles under his eyes and took some pleasure in that. "Good because those assholes could've killed me."

"I don't believe that."

"Did you not hear me say that they put a gun to my head?"

"Ok. I'm sorry about that, but I did what you guys asked— I worked it from the inside. And when Sonny asked for a surprise meeting, I panicked."

Jake had forgotten Bobby's assignment, but that was still no excuse for hanging Jake out to dry. "You should've warned me."

"You're right." Bobby nodded. "Do you want to hit me again?"

"Maybe." Jake stood up and walked across the kitchen.

Bobby closed his eyes and put his hands behind his back, leaving himself defenseless. "Go ahead. Do your worst."

Jake pulled his fist back and lined up a punch to Bobby's chin. The blow would knock him out cold. The seconds ticked by. Bobby never cracked an eyelid or tried to avoid the hit. Jake relaxed his arm. Bobby had passed the test. It wasn't so much that he was open to the beating. It was what Jake saw in Bobby's eyes right before he shut them, the disappointment in himself. He never thought Jake would get hurt at the meeting. Jake was sure of it.

Jake returned to his seat. "Fine. I forgive you, but do something like that again, and we're done."

"I won't. I swear." Bobby nodded nervously.

"Good," Jake said.

Bobby opened the fridge, pushing aside jars of pickles and mustard until he found a cold drink in the back. He popped open the can and took a long drink before saying. "Please tell me what happened with Sonny."

Since Bobby asked nicely, Jake told him everything that happened the night before from the moment he entered the garage until Sonny and Aces drove off. Bobby sat down at the table, halfway through the story. Mesmerized, he took in every detail and didn't interrupt Jake like Rick had. And although Bobby would probably believe him, Jake didn't tell him about his conversation with Tom's spirit. That was Jake's secret, one he'd never share with anyone, except maybe Mary.

"Well, what do you think of Sonny's plan?"

"I like it," Bobby said, rubbing his hands together.

"We are talking about murder."

Bobby sniffed. "Oh, because I thought we were talking about the weather."

"Shut up. So you want to be a part of it?"

"Hell, yes."

"I was hoping you'd say that because I need three people to pull this off."

"You ask Rick?"

"Yes. He's in too."

"Good. Then it's settled." Bobby smiled and stood up. "I'm starving. Do you want something to eat?"

"Really, you can think about food right now?"

"I skipped lunch. I couldn't eat since I was so worried about you."

"What are you making?"

Rubbing his sore belly, Bobby said, "My favorite. Breakfast for dinner."

"I guess."

Kneeling, Bobby dug in his cupboards and found two large pans. With some effort, he worked himself back to standing and arranged the items on the stove. The gas burners clicked and flickered to life. Blue flames licked the bottom of the pans. Bobby went to the fridge and pulled out a one-pound package of bacon and a dozen eggs. He lined up several pieces of bacon in the larger pan. The meat sizzled as its delicious aroma filled the room.

While he waited, Jake's thoughts turned back to Sonny's plan. It was risky. Any one of them could catch a stray bullet, and Jake couldn't afford to lose any more friends. Besides, if Jake died, who would protect Mary and the kids? What Jake needed was his own plan, but he needed to know how Sonny would react if Jake went off script but still got the result he wanted— Caleb eliminated.

Jake said, "Tell me more about Sonny."

"Like what?"

"First, is Sonny his real name?"

"No. I think his real name is Brian Donovan. I'm not sure where Sonny came from, but all those guys have nicknames."

"Maybe it's because of his sunny personality." Jake chuckled.

"I somehow doubt that."

"How long have you known him and the club?"

"Five years, and they've never tried to cheat or steal from me in all that time. In fact, they've given me a ton of work. I probably would've gone out of business during the recession if not for them."

"So, they're great guys?"

"Kind of," Bobby said as he added more bacon to the pan.

"But they killed our best friend."

"Caleb did that, not the Devil's Hand."

Jake tended to agree with Bobby. Caleb was a psychopath, the exact type of guy who would get involved in a road rage incident. But that didn't mean Sonny wasn't capable of murder himself or ordering the club to execute them.

Cracking his knuckles, Jake said, "True, but I'm worried about what happens to us after we kill Caleb. If I was Sonny, I'd want to tie up the loose ends."

Bobby studied the ceiling, nodding when he came to his answer. Jake swore he saw a light bulb appear above his head. Bobby said, "No. He wouldn't do that. It would be against his code."

"Code?" Jake asked. "The same code that won't let him personally handle Caleb?"

"Exactly," Bobby said.

"I'm not buying it."

"Sonny likes you for some reason, Jake. I don't think he'll kill you or us."

"What about the rest of his club? They are outlaws who would kill you as soon as look at you."

"Not if Sonny forbids it."

"And the club does whatever he says— outside of Caleb?"

Bobby turned around to face Jake, ignoring his cooking duties for the moment. "Without a doubt. He's the president. That's the way it works. Everyone follows his orders."

"Everyone?"

"Everyone, and he can be so damn persuasive. Sonny always gets what he wants."

Jake had heard enough. If Sonny and his silver tongue always got their way, he'd never expect Jake to act on his own. Jake could kill Caleb ahead of time and be back in Chicago before Sonny knew what happened. And Jake could tease Sonny by telling him that he'd consider joining the club when his daughter went away to college. However, if Jake's plan didn't work . . . well, worst case, he could follow Sonny's plan. With Rick and Bobby's help, Jake should be able to kill Caleb.

Jake said stupidly, "I wish I could tell Mary."

"You can't. She wouldn't approve."

Sighing, Jake agreed. "You're right."

"Of course, I'm right."

Smoke curled up from a pan. Jake asked, "Are you burning that bacon?"

Bobby spun around quickly and flipped over the bacon as it popped and crackled. Grease jumped out of the pan and landed on the stove's surface. Bobby danced around the fatty explosions like a ballerina. A paper plate wrapped in a paper towel waited on the counter for the finished product. Bobby removed several pieces and gave them a minute to cool. While he waited, he added more bacon to the pan.

"Do you need any help?" Jake asked.

"I'm good," Bobby replied, shoving a piece of bacon in his mouth. "Maybe I should've been a short-order cook instead of a mechanic."

"You are a good cook."

"How do you want the eggs? Over easy or scrambled?"

Jake shrugged. "I guess scrambled."

"Good choice."

"I'm glad you think so," Jake said, realizing their meal reflected his brains after all the scheming— deep-fried and scrambled.

Chapter 36

"Knock. Knock," Caleb called out as he entered Sonny's house.

Remy and Romy ran to meet Caleb in the foyer. Circling him, they nipped at his heels. His boot connected with Romy's butt, pushing him several feet across the marble floor. The dog howled in pain but quickly resumed barking at him as he made his way through the small mansion.

Sonny sat at the kitchen table with a phone to his ear. A cigarette smoldered in an ashtray near the edge of the table along with a black handgun. Sonny held up a finger indicating Caleb would have to wait— and that pissed him off. The dogs continued to yip at his ankles, so Caleb pulled his foot back for another kick.

Jodi bustled into the kitchen. "Don't you dare hurt them."

Caleb growled but lowered his boot to the floor. Jodi smiled and bent at the hips to retrieve a pan of bubbling lasagna from the oven. Her thin sweater rode up her back, exposing an inch of milky skin. Caleb stole a sideways glance and licked his lips. She turned and caught him studying her ass, and her eyes widened with fear and excitement. As she set the pan on top of the stove, she looked guiltily at Sonny, who was still absorbed in his phone call.

Removing her red oven mitts, she shook her head at Caleb.

"Remy! Romy! Stop it. Be good boys." She pulled out a box of dog treats and shook it.

Both pugs skidded to a halt, let out a final obligatory bark, and ran to her. She held two biscuits high in the air. They jumped up and down with no hope of reaching them, their curled tails bouncing like springs. She let one drop. Remy swallowed the treat whole. Jodi threw the second treat to Romy, but Remy pounced on his back and stole it. Romy barked wildly at his brother as Remy ran away with his prize.

Laughing, Caleb pulled out a chair and sat down at the table. Sonny ended his call and set the phone down next to his gun. He glared at Caleb and said, "Jealous fucker, always wants what his brother has."

Shit! Did Sonny know? And why was his gun on the table? Caleb's heart pounded in his chest, and his left eye twitched. He tried to remain calm since there was no way Sonny could know unless Hysko or Larry had ratted him out. Fuck! Who had been on the phone?

Jodi scooped up the remaining pug. With her free hand, she pulled down her sweater that had crept up two more inches. "I'll leave you boys alone. The lasagna needs some time to cool, and I have some laundry to fold upstairs."

Sonny winked at her. "Thanks, baby."

She swayed out of the room with the squirming pug in her arms. Caleb didn't try to sneak another peek as she left; all his attention was on Sonny. Did his comment about the dog mean something? Probably not— Caleb was just being paranoid.

Sonny drummed his fingers on the table. The gun rattled on the hard surface. "You're late."

"I got hung up. It was unavoidable."

Sonny frowned but remained silent.

Screw that. Caleb was not going to apologize. "Who was on the phone?"

"Hysko."

"Hysko?" Caleb reached inside of his jacket, pretending to reach for his cigarettes.

"And he had something very interesting to tell me."

"What was that?" Caleb asked, with his hand resting on the butt of his own pistol.

"Hysko told me the street value of heroin is going through the roof. The mafioso are having a supply line issue out of Chicago. We have eight bricks down at the club that we can sell them. The new price should offset the costs of this little war we are in with the Outsiders."

Sonny's hand moved away from his weapon, and Caleb relaxed. Since it was integral to their plan, Hysko was supposed to have told Sonny that lie earlier at the club. But the old guy must have a good reason for changing things up. Caleb pulled the cigarettes from his inside pocket and slapped the pack against his thigh until a filtered end poked out of the opening. He brought the pack to his mouth and removed the cigarette with practiced ease.

Through clenched lips, he said, "That's good news."

"It is."

Caleb lit the cigarette and inhaled deeply. "Speaking of the Outsiders, do you trust me?"

Sonny nodded his head.

"Good." Caleb returned his lighter to his pocket. "I got a call from Alex, their president today— that's why I'm late."

Sonny moved his hand back to the table. "Why did he call you and not me?"

"He didn't have your number."

"But he had yours?"

"Dale gave it to him."

"Who?"

"The fat guy who owns that crappy bar downtown. Anyways, I knew you have plenty of other things to worry about, so I decided to see what he had to say."

Sonny crossed his hands in front of him. "And?"

"Alex wants a truce, but I told him if that's what he wanted, then it would cost him all of their territory south of Eight Mile. Otherwise, we would wipe his whole crew off the map."

"What did he say?"

"He agreed, but only if you agree to the deal in person."

Sonny closed his eyes and pinched the bridge of his nose.

Caleb shifted in his chair. "I hope I didn't overstep my bounds."

Shaking his head, Sonny said, "You did, but I'll forgive you because that's one hell of a deal."

Keeping up his act, Caleb let his shoulders slump with relief. "Funny that Hysko brought up the issue with the smack. Alex asked me if he could buy two kilos from the club. He's willing to pay a premium. They can't meet their demand either."

Sonny reached for his cigarette in the ashtray, which had burned down to the filter. He ground it out and lit a new one. "When is the meeting?"

"Tomorrow night."

"Use the warehouse out in Brownstown. It's in the middle of nowhere, so we can control who comes in."

"Great minds think alike," Caleb said with a smile.

Sonny asked. "Who do you want to run security?"

Hesitantly, Caleb said, "It's my meeting, so I'll do it."

"I'm good with that."

"Why don't you show up late?" Caleb suggested. "Then I can make sure everything is safe. And keep Aces with you, so he can watch your back— that's what he does best."

"Anything else?"

Caleb shook his head. "Nope. I'll get word to Alex that you agreed to the meeting."

"Sounds like a plan. Do you want to stay for dinner?"

"No, I already ate. Give my regrets to Jodi." Caleb pushed back his chair and stood up.

"Suit yourself."

Caleb exited the kitchen and entered the foyer. At the top of the staircase, Jodi leaned against the railing and waved to get his attention. He gave her a quick wink. She mouthed something to him, but Caleb didn't understand it. He raised his hands to his side and shrugged, so she repeated it, exaggerating the words with her lips.

He thought she said, *"Your nose."*

He gave it a quick rub, but she was wrong. No boogers were hiding in his nostrils.

Jodi shook her head and tried again, emphasizing each syllable. *"He knows."*

Caleb laughed. No way. Sonny didn't know, or he would've shot Caleb in the kitchen. Sure, Sonny had promised to never hurt Caleb after nearly bashing his head in with a shovel, but he'd broken that promise a hundred times over. It was just more theatrics from Jodi. Sonny didn't know shit. When would she stop it with all the drama?

Rolling his eyes, Caleb left. The large oak door thudded shut behind him.

Chapter 37

Jake leaned back in Bobby's desk chair. It creaked loudly from supporting his weight over the years. Afraid that it would break, Jake brought it to rest on all four legs. Bobby stood in the corner of the room with his butt pressed against the wall. He glared at Jake.

"I should get the chair," Bobby said.

Jake shook his head. "Sonny enlisted me to kill Caleb, so I get the chair."

Bobby rested a meaty arm on the top of a metal filing cabinet. "It's just because you used to be a detective, and you'll know how to commit the perfect crime."

"There is no such thing as the perfect crime."

Before Bobby could offer a rebuttal, motorcycles roared from the parking lot. Their engines revved loudly and then shut down. Bobby shifted anxiously from foot to foot. He removed his elbow from the cabinet only to place it back again. The bell on the front door rang, followed by heavy footsteps. A large fist pounded on the outer wall before Aces's hulking frame filled the office doorway.

"Is your jackass friend going to behave himself tonight, Bobby?"

Jake waved at the giant. "I can speak for myself."

Ignoring him, Aces asked Bobby, "Does he have a weapon?"

Bobby hesitated. "No."

"Are you sure?"

"Positive," Bobby said, sticking his chin out.

"Good. I believe you— I know you would never lie to us."

Bobby looked down at the floor. "Got that right."

Aces grinned and then shouted over his shoulder, "All clear."

Sonny stalked into the office and took the seat in front of the desk. Aces moved to a spot against the wall behind Sonny.

Jake folded his hands in front of him. "Sonny."

"Hi, Jake. I knew you'd be back."

"I had nothing else to do tonight." Jake shrugged. "I washed my hair yesterday."

Sonny said, "Funny. Have you reached a decision?"

"Yes."

"And?" Sonny's eyes bored into Jake's. "What's your answer?"

Taking his time, Jake stretched his arms above his head then crossed one leg over the other. Sonny leaned forward, and the muscles in Aces's neck visibly tensed. Jake relished making them wait.

When he couldn't drag it out any longer, he said, "Yes. We'll kill Caleb."

"We?"

"Me, Bobby, and Rick. I need someone to watch my back."

"I'm fine with Bobby, but who's Rick?"

"Another friend. He was there that night at the bar."

Sonny said, "All right, but I don't know him, so he's your responsibility."

"I'm good with that— I trust Rick completely."

Bobby nodded his head. "He's good people."

"For your sake, I hope so." Smiling like the Cheshire Cat, Sonny pulled out a Glock 19 from inside his leather jacket. "I have a present for you."

It was the exact same model of pistol tucked in Jake's waistband. Sonny examined it for a moment and then slid it across the desk. Jake picked it up. The weapon felt light and therefore unloaded. "It's just my size. Thank you."

"It's a clean gun. Never been used before. No serial numbers, either. I assume you're familiar with it from your police days?"

Jake nodded. He doubted how clean it was, but he verified the chamber was empty as well as the clip. He dry-fired it towards the opposite wall. The weapon appeared to be in perfect working condition. From his other pocket, Sonny pulled a burner phone and a folded piece of paper.

"Leave your own phones at home."

Jake picked up the paper and the phone. "Of course. I have no intention of leaving an electronic trail."

"That's why I picked you, Jake. You're smart. If something changes, then I'll call you on the burner. My number for the night will be the first one on the speed dial but don't use it."

Unfolding the paper, Jake read the text. "I assume this is the address for the hit."

"Yes. It's the old farm we talked about."

Aces shook his head, and Sonny said, "Shut up. He'll be there."

"It'll be both our asses if you're wrong," Aces said.

"Trust me, Caleb thinks he can outsmart me, but I know my brother. He'll want to exact his revenge in that barn."

"What are you talking about?" Jake asked.

"Nothing you need to worry yourself with, except that our plan changed a little."

Jake frowned. "How?"

"Caleb invited a rival gang to the party, so I assume he intends to double-cross them before I arrive. He'll tell me the Outsiders had planned on killing all of us to take over the whole city, and while I'm thanking him for saving my life, he'll put a bullet in the back of my head, and Hysko or Larry will put one in Aces's skull too."

Jake said, "Another gang? No way!"

"You can handle it," Sonny replied.

"It was only supposed to be Caleb at the location."

"It's fine," Bobby said. "We can handle it."

Jake rolled his eyes. "Really? How?"

Sonny said, "I'd suggest you get there early and hide in the loft of the barn. If they find you, you best start shooting, but I don't think it will come to that. Just wait until after Caleb and his fellow traitors take care of the other club, then he's all yours."

"What about Caleb's friends?"

"You'll have to kill them too."

The blood boiled in Jake's veins. He knew he should've never gotten in bed with these devils. "I'm not killing anyone besides Caleb."

"Let Rick or Bobby take them out. That's why you wanted back-up, right? Believe me, they all deserve it," Sonny said.

Moving to stand next to Jake, Bobby asked, "What do we do when we're done?"

"Use the second number in the speed dial. It's for a cleanup crew. When they get there, they'll take care of the gun, the phone, and the heroin."

Jake threw his hands in the air. "Heroin? This keeps on getting better and better."

"Yes, it's part of Caleb's game to double-cross them," Sonny said.

"This thing is turning into a complete cluster fuck."

Sonny nodded. "I agree."

"What if I want out?"

"Go ahead, and when Caleb takes over the club, he'll kill you and the widow. Or did you forget?"

Jake said, "And what about you? You'll let Caleb kill you over a promise."

Smiling, Sonny said, "I don't have to worry about that because you won't let that happen."

Jake's secret plot better work because Sonny's new plan sucked. It should; Jake's was simple. He'd wait for Caleb outside his house and put a bullet in his head as soon as he took off his helmet, quick and easy. Caleb wouldn't suffer like he deserved, but it would have to do.

Still playing his part for Sonny, Jake said, "Fine. I'll do it, but nothing else better change."

Sonny stood up and smoothed out his jacket. "I can't make any promises."

Jake snorted, and Aces glared at him. Sonny turned to leave as well, but Jake said, "Wait."

Sonny stopped, looking over his shoulder. "Yes."

"I have one more question."

"What?"

Jake asked, "Why do they call you Sonny if your real name is Brian?"

Sonny smiled grimly, the sort of smile that concealed a set of well-used fangs. "When you join the club, I'll tell you my secret. Good night, gentlemen."

Sonny left the office, followed by Aces, his shoulders brushing each side of the doorframe. The giant's absence made the room seem a whole lot larger but no less disheartening.

Chapter 38

An overgrown bush stood at Caleb's backdoor. Jake hid between it and the brick wall of the home. Caleb would most likely park in the detached garage behind the house since there was a motorcycle-sized hole amongst the garbage inside. His large black truck sat in the driveway, the hood cold to the touch. Jake assumed he only used it when the bike wouldn't suffice.

The house's exterior light was off, and the moonlight that broke through the clouds offered Jake limited visibility. That was fine. It was perfect for concealment, and Jake wouldn't need much to put three bullets in Caleb's head at this range.

A branch jabbed Jake in his stomach, so he broke the offending stick and returned to his vigil. Jake had been in position for hours, unsure when Caleb would return home. The address had been easy enough to find on the internet. Caleb lived in a rundown part of town where the lots were close together, so Jake parked his car two streets behind Caleb's house and snuck in at sundown. After he completed the deed, Jake should have no problem sneaking away undetected with the bulb removed on his license plate lamp.

A cramp formed in his leg, and he quietly rubbed it out. The time must be well after midnight. It didn't matter; he was prepared to stand here all night if necessary. He could recuperate in Chicago, his mind at peace knowing Caleb was dead. That was if Caleb came home. Jake's plan didn't account for him sleeping somewhere else.

Before Jake's fears got the better of him, he heard the low rumble of a carbureted engine from a block away. He'd been fooled earlier by a car without a muffler, but as the sound grew closer, it was undeniably a Harley Davidson, so Jake removed the pistol from his pocket. Every muscle in his body tensed with anticipation.

A lone headlight flashed across the neighbor's house and proceeded down the narrow driveway. It avoided the parked truck and entered the garage. The loud growl echoed off the junk-lined walls. Peeking through the branches and leaves, Jake made out a figure with Caleb's size and shape. He rested the bike on the thick metal kickstand. With a turn of the key, the motor sputtered to a stop, and the light was extinguished. The yard plunged back into darkness.

Silently, Jake raised his weapon and waited for Caleb to reach the back door. His heart pounded in his chest as the anger welled up inside him like a bubbling volcano. His revenge was seconds away. Jake knew Caleb was the right guy; he had no doubt. Noles had said as much, and Sonny had confirmed it.

The gun remained steady in Jake's hand, but Caleb didn't come. It shouldn't take this long to walk from the garage to the back door. Caleb couldn't have seen Jake in the dark; he'd been as quiet as a clam, so where was the son of a bitch? Shifting to find an opening in the shrub, Jake peered out into the dark, but he couldn't see a thing until metal scraped on flint. A tiny flame erupted in the dark, just two paces from the garage. Caleb puffed until the cigarette glowed orange.

Really? Well, Jake guessed even Caleb deserved a last cigarette.

Jake could only assume the man was enjoying the beautiful night. The temperature was perfect, and a mild breeze had kept the mosquitos away from Jake. Yet the rage didn't dissipate while Jake waited. Time wouldn't change his mind— Caleb deserved to die. However, Jake lowered his arm quietly to give the muscles a rest as he watched Caleb intently.

The smoldering butt paced back and forth in front of the open garage. Jake grew impatient, but he couldn't risk a shot at this distance. He might miss and allow Caleb to escape into the night. Nor could he sneak up on him; the rattling of the shrub's branches would give him away. It couldn't be that much longer unless Caleb decided to chain-smoke his whole pack while he star-gazed.

Luckily, Caleb tossed the butt down, and a boot ground it into the pavement. Hard rubber soles made their way towards Jake, so he silently raised the pistol and readied himself again. At this distance, there'd be just enough moonlight for Jake to make a positive identification before he fired.

Caleb drew closer.

Jake's finger tickled the trigger.

Any second now.

Suddenly, the sound of Caleb's boots was joined by a pair of high heels clicking up the driveway. Jake's sphincter tightened, and he hoped that his mind was playing tricks on him, but it wasn't.

A woman whispered loudly, "Caleb, baby, where are you?"

"Over here."

"Where?"

Jake saw the outline of a woman come into view. Caleb stepped out from behind the truck and grabbed her by the waist. "Boo!"

Surprised, the woman screamed and dropped her bag.

A window screeched open at the house next door. A gruff voice shouted, "Is everything all right out there?"

Caleb yelled back, "Mind your own fucking business, or I'll break my foot off in your ass."

The window slammed shut.

The woman smacked Caleb's arm. "You don't have to be so mean."

"Then don't scream and wake up half the neighborhood."

"But you scared me."

"That's because there is only a quarter moon out, but I can fix that." He pulled her in close and tugged at her skirt.

Jake stifled a groan. If he had to stand here and listen to them do it in the yard, he might turn the gun on himself. However, if they went into the house, then Jake would miss his chance. Either way, he was screwed. He couldn't eliminate Caleb with the woman here. What were the chances that he'd be satisfied with a kiss and then send her home? Jake was no statistician, but he'd probably have better odds jumping over the moon. The real moon, not the one Caleb was trying to get his hands on.

"Not out here," the woman said. "Someone might see us."

"You just got done saying how dark it was. Besides I thought you liked danger."

"No. I don't. Let's go inside."

"Fine." Caleb released her, and she bent over to retrieve her bag. The contents clunked inside. He asked, "What's in there? Got some new toys?"

"Yes. Also, my toothbrush and jammies."

"You're spending the night? You've never done that before."

Jake clenched his jaw. That was it. If this woman was staying the night, Jake couldn't wait until she left. He'd counted on using the cover of darkness for Caleb's murder. By morning, there would be too many potential witnesses. He'd be easily identified during his escape. Jake would have to slink off with his tail between his legs as soon as they went inside.

"I know, but I want to wake up next to you." She walked towards the back door. "I don't think we have much time left together."

"What are you talking about? Are you breaking up with me?"

"God, no. I love you to death, but that's what I'm afraid of. I think Sonny knows, and something is going to happen to one of us."

Caleb groaned. "Is that what you were trying to tell me yesterday?"

"Yes."

"Why do you think that? Did he say something?"

"No. It's just a feeling."

Caleb put a hand on her arm, stopping her from reaching the door handle. "You always have a feeling."

"But he was acting strange."

"When are you going to learn that Sonny can be a moody fuck?"

"I guess. Because if Sonny knew I was screwing his brother, he wouldn't wait to kill me. He'd stick a knife right through my cheating heart."

"Jodi, will you stop with the damn theatrics?" Caleb hissed.

The final piece of the puzzle fell into place.

Jake silently drew in a breath. This woman was Sonny's girlfriend. If Caleb was banging his old lady, Sonny couldn't have someone from the club kill him. Caleb would sing like a canary, then everyone would know, and Sonny would lose face. That's why he needed an outsider for the job. That's why he recruited Jake.

Jodi stamped her foot. "He would."

"Stop. I'm tired. I have a big day tomorrow."

"What's tomorrow?"

"I have to go by the club to pick up something, and then Sonny and I have a business transaction."

"You'll have to tell me if he acts funny towards you too."

"Jesus Christ." Caleb pulled open the screen door and ushered Jodi into the house. They passed within feet of Jake, but neither one saw him. The door slammed shut behind them.

Jake waited two minutes before creeping off into the night. In his head, the seeds of a new plan to kill Caleb took root, and it had to work because it would be Jake's final chance.

Chapter 39

The next day, Caleb sat alone at the bar in the Devil's Hand clubhouse. He checked his phone for the hundredth time, but there was still no return text from Jodi. Since she left his house this morning, he hadn't heard a word. Knowing her, Jodi had probably forgotten to charge the damn thing, and it died. Caleb finished his beer, slamming the glass mug down on the bar.

Across the room, a cue ball cracked into a newly racked set of billiard balls. The shooter, Wild Bill, howled as a ball fell into a corner pocket off the break. Three Hand-Maidens clapped and squealed at his skill. Jimmy, his opponent, grumbled about it being a lucky shot, which made Wild Bill howl even louder.

With downcast eyes, Phil brought Caleb a fresh beer. He twitched nervously as he backed away, holding the empty mug with his good hand. Caleb smirked and nodded a thank you at the pathetic man. He savored the cool amber liquid as it slid down his throat; his lips left an imprint on the cold rim.

Caleb resisted the urge to check his phone again. Instead, he half-followed the game of eight ball while ogling the young girls. They cheered on the handsome Wild Bill, who didn't disappoint as he sank the eight ball off of a bank shot to win the game. He took the wad of bills from the side of the table and tucked it into the brim of his black cowboy hat.

Before the next game could start, Caleb heard the floorboards creak, announcing Aces's arrival. His hulking frame slid on to the stool next to Caleb. Looking at the clock on the wall, Caleb said, "You're late. I thought you'd stood me up."

From inside his jacket, Aces extracted an envelope, smoothed it out, and set it on the bar in front of him. "You know how it is— no rest for the wicked. Sonny sent me on a job that took longer than planned."

"What job was that?"

"The one you screwed up with the accountant. Good thing I found what Dolan wanted; otherwise, the orders were to burn the place to the ground."

Sneering, Caleb pointed to the letter. "I thought Dolan wanted a thumb drive?"

"He'll get the drive, but not this letter. So forget you saw it, or I'll bust your head open like an egg."

"Fuck you."

Aces smiled. "Fuck you too."

"Whatever. Where's Sonny? Why did he pawn me off on you?"

"Sonny had an issue he had to deal with personally."

"What kind of issue?"

"Don't know. He didn't want my help, so it can't be that big a deal."

Aces turned to Phil and gave him a wave for a beer. The hanger-on rushed to the freezer to get a fresh mug. Aces redirected his attention back to Caleb. "Sonny told me you need two kilos of smack for the meeting tonight."

"I do."

"That's a lot of H."

"It is a lot of H, but the Outsiders agreed to pay top dollar for it. They must be having the same supply trouble the mob is dealing with."

"I'm not sure we should give them our supply," Aces said as Phil dropped off his beer before leaving quickly.

Caleb's pulse quickened. He needed the smack. The plan was to hit the Outsiders while they were distracted with checking the product. "Jesus Christ, I gave my word."

Aces sat forward. He rested his hulking arms, as big around as most people's legs, on the bar. A vein pulsed in his thick neck. "Your word means shit."

Caleb pushed himself up; his chair slammed to the ground. All heads in the bar turned to the sound. With fists clenched, they stared each other down. Now was not the time to pick a fight with Aces, but he couldn't help himself.

Caleb said, "Why don't we take this discussion outside?"

"I was hoping you'd say that."

Aces interlaced his fingers and cracked his knuckles. He twisted his neck from side to side, and more joints snapped and popped. Standing up, he gestured to the back door. "Let's do this."

Wild Bill ambled over like a gunslinger from an old Western and got between them, the cue stick at his side. "Fellas, no need for that. We're all on the same team. Aren't we?"

They studied each other, neither man was willing to back down. The tension in the room could be cut with a knife.

"Aren't we?" Wild Bill repeated.

Caleb gave in first, knowing Aces' would get his later. "Yes."

"That's what I am talking about. Now, I'm over there with three lovely ladies, and there's only one of me. So, what do you say, Aces?"

Aces grinned. "They are pretty."

"Good because that little brunette has been eyeing you up for a while. She was wondering if you're big everywhere, if you know what I mean?"

Wild Bill raised a hand and motioned the Hand-Maiden over. The girl was a stunner with long silky hair, perky breasts, and curvy hips. His devious thoughts were obvious in Aces's smile, but he held a hand up to the girl. She stopped in her tracks, a look of disappointment on her lovely face. He said, "I need a minute to finish up here."

"All right," she replied meekly.

"You two play nice, or I'll have to smack both of you around," Wild Bill said, pointing a finger at both of them.

Caleb and Aces both laughed at the smaller man, and the tension dissipated. Caleb righted his chair and sat down. Wild Bill sauntered away, and the girl followed him back to the pool table as Aces stared at her round butt out of the corner of his eye. Thinking about great asses, Caleb checked his phone — still no text from Jodi. Damn it! He took a drink from his beer and set it down on the damp napkin.

Aces finished off his beer in one gulp and signaled for another round.

He turned his attention to Caleb. "Can you play nice?"

"No."

"Me either, but we can save this for another time."

They both chuckled. The pair made empty small talk about other club business, their bikes, and the state of the Tigers while the people in the room watched them, waiting for the next dust-up. It didn't happen. They finished their beers politely like old English gentlemen sharing tea. The whole time Caleb was thinking about how much fun it would be to put a bullet in Aces's skull.

Finishing the second beer, Caleb stood up. "I really need the smack now, so I can get out to the warehouse to run security."

Aces pulled a key from his pocket and slid it across to Caleb, glancing in the brunette's direction. "Here's the key."

"You were fucking with me this whole time, weren't you?"

"Yep."

"Asshole!"

"I never claimed to be anything different." Aces crammed the envelope into his jacket pocket and headed towards the pool table and the pretty girl.

Caleb picked up his phone and the carrier bag he brought for the drugs and went up the back stairs. The door thudded shut behind him. After two flights, he reached the top floor, only slightly out of breath due to his smoking. He paused to look at his phone but still nothing. Scowling, he slid the phone into his pocket and proceeded down the hallway to Sonny's office. He slipped the key into the slot and unlocked the door. Closing it behind him, he walked over to the framed reproduction of *A Friend in Need* that hung behind Sonny's desk. He rotated it on its hinges to expose the safe recessed into the wall. He'd never opened the safe without his brother present. Sonny had trusted him with the combination long ago but not the key to the office. Maybe, Sonny was smart, after all. Caleb spun the knob right and left, entering the number sequence, Sonny's birthdate in reverse order, and turned the handle.

Inside the safe was easily two million dollars, along with a gun, property deeds, some stocks, and eight kilos of muddy brown heroin wrapped in plastic bricks. He took two kilos out and placed them on the desk. Before he closed the safe, he grabbed a bundle of bills and shoved it inside his pants pocket— it would be his money soon anyway.

A door closed in the hall. A bead of sweat grew on his temple and trickled down his cheek to his neck. Caleb quickly sat down in Sonny's chair and dropped the bag to the floor. A hand knocked, and the handle turned slowly, opening the door partially.

Jimmy stuck his head inside the room. His mouth turned into a small circle. "Caleb?"

"Yes."

"Is Sonny here?"

"Nope."

Looking at the open safe, Jimmy asked, "He knows you're in here?"

"Yes. I'm taking care of something for him."

"Ok?"

"Check for yourself. Aces gave me the key."

"I don't need to do that. What kind of club are we if we can't trust one another, right?"

Standing up, Caleb closed the safe and spun the combination knob. "Exactly. Did you need something?"

"No, I didn't think Sonny was here, but I saw his door open. Anyway, I will leave you to your business." Jimmy gave him a short wave and left.

Footsteps retreated down the hallway. The stairwell door creaked open and closed with a bang. Exhaling, Caleb sat back down at Sonny's desk and put his feet up. He would keep the desk, but the stupid dogs playing poker picture would have to go. Caleb decided to go through the drawers to see what else he could take. The bottom one on the left held file folders, lots of them. He tried to flip through them out of amusement but got bored quickly and closed the drawer. In the middle drawer sat the red book on military strategy that Sonny was always reading. Caleb looked forward to throwing it away too. If Sonny had learned anything from it, he would have seen his empire crumbling beneath his feet. The other drawers held boring office supplies, so he carefully set the drugs inside the bag and left the office, closing the door behind him.

The bag heavy on his shoulder, he raced down the steps. He found Aces at the bar with a grin on his ugly face, a fat cigar between his lips, and the cute brunette perched on his knee. A cloud of white smoke hung above the pair.

"Took you long enough," Aces said.

"Sorry, I'm not a minute man like you."

The girl giggled at Caleb's joke. Aces growled, removed her from his lap, and sent her on her way with a smack on the rear. When she was out of earshot, Aces said, "You only take the two kilos?"

"Of course." Caleb set the key on the bar, the money burning hot inside his pocket. It had been dumb to take it, but he couldn't help himself. He said, "Remember to wait until you get the call to enter the warehouse."

Aces released a fresh plume of smoke. "I remember. You sure Sonny will be safe?"

"I guarantee it. I want my brother to get everything he deserves."

"I wish I had a brother like you."

"Aren't we all brothers, Aces?"

"Yes, we fucking are." Aces nodded. "I'll follow you out. Got to make sure you're safe too."

The pair left the bar and stepped onto the asphalt parking lot as Caleb wondered why Aces wanted to follow him out. Had Jodi been right? Had Sonny killed her while Aces was sent to dispose of Caleb? Too many questions were bouncing around Caleb's head, and they were giving him the creeps. No, Aces couldn't possibly plan to kill him out here. The club was downtown, and people crowded the street. There'd be civilian witnesses.

Who would be stupid enough to do that?

If Aces was going to do it, he should have done it inside. Still, Caleb couldn't shake the eerie feeling growing like a weed between his shoulder blades. It felt like he was being watched.

Caleb found his bike amongst the other chrome-laden motorcycles. The messenger bag barely fit inside the hard side case. He closed the lid and sat down on his bike; the suspension settled under his weight. Aces watched his every movement. Nervously, Caleb pulled his phone from his pocket and unlocked it with a finger swipe. He had one message.

With a sigh of relief, he read the message from Jodi. **Sorry, I forgot to charge my phone. Can't wait to see you between my legs. TTYL.**

Thank God! And it was short and to the point. It didn't have any of the stupid emojis that Jodi usually added. Caleb hated those damn emojis.

Chapter 40

Jake watched Caleb store a carrier bag onto his motorcycle while Aces looked on. Jake couldn't hear their conversation from the opposite side of the street, but it didn't matter. He didn't need to listen to put a knife through Caleb's heart. No— Jake would stab Caleb in his liver, stomach, small and large intestine, and finally, his heart. Jake wanted him good and dead.

A knife would be silent, better than a gun in the middle of the afternoon on a crowded street, but Jake needed to get close enough to use it. In the ensuing chaos, he should be able to discard his costume and disappear. His Focus was parked three blocks away in a commercial alley with the Glock in the trunk for insurance. He prayed it wouldn't be towed, yet if he'd parked it on the street, the tires and rims would have been gone in five minutes. And, in a parking structure, he might be picked up on video surveillance, so he chose the option with the least risk.

To get close enough to attack, Jake had dressed up as a homeless man. He'd bought clothes from a thrift store and then rolled around the filthy alley. He smelled like a sewer, and his fake beard itched like crazy. The only part of his outfit in pristine condition was the large hunting knife on his belt that he'd purchased at a hardware store with cash. If he succeeded, it would all be worth it, though he'd have a rash on his face tomorrow. An unexpected bonus with the costume was that he'd already collected enough spare change to buy a cheap bottle of wine to celebrate afterward.

However, Jake would need Caleb to pause long enough for him to strike. For that, Jake had a shopping cart full of junk, including a board laden with sharp nails that he'd assembled with supplies from the same store as the knife. As Caleb exited the club on his motorcycle, Jake would toss the board in front of him. Caleb would get a flat, causing him to dump the bike. With him on the ground, Jake could get stabby. The only issue was if Jake misjudged his board toss, then his next stop would be the barn and a gang shootout.

Across the street, the motorcycle's starter whined, and the engine roared to life. Caleb rocked his bike off the kickstand and dropped it into gear. Jake edged his cart closer to the curb as Caleb nodded at Aces and released the clutch. Jake narrowed his gaze and slowed his breathing, forcing himself to calm down. He'd missed his chance last night. He wouldn't let it happen again.

Doing his best to look inconspicuous, he grabbed the board from the cart and lined it up with Caleb's expected path. The big toss was only seconds away.

"Hey, buddy!" said a voice over his shoulder.

Jake ignored it, studying Caleb intently.

"Buddy, you're not supposed to be here," the voice called out again.

Caleb goosed the throttle, and the bike shot forward.

A hand tugged on the sleeve of Jake's tattered coat. "What're you, deaf?"

Caleb slowed at the sidewalk, looking both ways for traffic. They were only twenty feet apart. Jake was invisible to him across the street, just part of the scenery. He pulled the board back, preparing for his throw. Every muscle in his body tensed in anticipation.

It was now or never.

A hand grabbed Jake's shoulder. He tried to shrug out of its grasp, but it held tight.

Caleb punched the gas.

"Don't do it!" the voice yelled.

Ignoring his guardian angel, Jake heaved the board into the street.

"Fucking bum!" Caleb shouted as he swerved to avoid Jake's makeshift spike strip.

The board came within inches of piercing Caleb's front tire, but it came up short. Stupidly, Jake yanked the knife free from his belt and leaped after Caleb while he was still somewhat close in a desperate attempt to slice him open.

A bum snagged Jake by the collar, nearly yanking him off his feet. "Are you trying to get yourself killed?"

"Let go of me!" Jake shouted.

The motorcycle roared down the street with Caleb alive and not full of holes. Jake had missed his second chance, a whole day waiting in smelly clothes for nothing. Intent on saving Jake from God knows what, the bum never saw the knife as Jake dropped it into his oversized pocket.

The mocha-colored hand kept its grip on Jake's collar as the man tried to steer him away from the club. "I don't know what he did to you, but you gonna die if you mess with them. I've seen it happen."

"Seen what happen?"

"I've seen it all, and God will bring into judgment both the righteous and the wicked, for there will be a time— "

Jake jerked himself free. "Enough with the sermon!"

"Don't be stupid." The bum shook his head, his white frizzy-haired waving wildly. "I'm trying to help you."

With his anger spilling over at his missed opportunity, Jake pushed him. The bum stumbled backward but stayed upright.

"Motherfucker!"

"Not so godly now, are you?" Jake said.

"Well, screw you then. Try and help somebody out, and this is how I get paid. Vengeance will be mine."

Behind the wide eyes of the crazed man, Jake saw movement. A large shape stomped towards them. The reptilian part of his brain told Jake to flee, but it was too late. Aces stopped in front of them, blocking out half the street.

"I thought I told you people never to hang around here."

The bum puffed out his chest. "That's what I was trying to tell him, but he wouldn't listen. He must be stupid because anyone with any smarts knows to stay off your street."

Aces glared down at Jake. "You stupid?"

"No."

Jake looked down to avoid Aces's eyes. Cursing under his breath, he realized that his shoes were his own. They were too good to be from the streets. Would Aces see through his lame costume? He prayed not. At least he'd missed his board toss, or this dialog wouldn't have been with words.

"Then give me one good reason I shouldn't give you a beat-down."

Jake turned to leave. "Sorry. I'll never beg here again."

Yanking him back, Aces placed a finger the size of a cigar on Jake's forehead. He tilted Jake's head back and studied him intently. "You look familiar."

Every pore in Jake's body oozed sweat, and the glue loosened on the beard. It slid a fraction of an inch. He stuttered over his words. "I . . . I shouldn't. I just got to town."

"Are you sure I haven't smacked you around before?" Aces asked, removing his finger.

Jake dropped his head again. "No. I would've learned my lesson and never came back."

"Got that right. It only takes one time."

The bum stood nearby, watching the show. "I'se tried to tell him."

Aces shifted his gaze to the old man. "Shut up. I've heard enough out of both of you. Get out of here and don't come back."

Jake spun on his heels and left. Unfortunately, the bum followed. Jake sped up, but the man matched his pace, weaving as he walked. Jake scratched at the fake beard and tried to slide it back into place.

"You forgot your cart. Don't you want your stuff?" the man asked.

"I'll get it later."

Too loud for Jake's taste, the man said, "Is that a fake beard?"

Jake shushed him, knowing it would do no good. This plan was stupid and desperate. His impulsiveness would get him killed. When would he learn?

"Don't hush me." The bum stopped. "I bet that big man would like to know you're not really from the streets."

Checking over his shoulder, Jake saw Aces still standing there watching their progress with a questioning look on his face. Jake yanked the bum forward. They were nearly out of earshot. "Stop it, and I'll give you twenty dollars."

The bum pulled free and took a swig from a bottle tucked away in his jacket. "Make it fifty."

"I only have forty," Jake pleaded.

The man looked from him to Aces and back. Jake prepared to run. Finally, the man said, "Forty dollars and your jacket."

"Deal, but let's go around the corner."

The bum frowned. "I ain't down for no funny business."

"Don't worry, I'm not either."

As they turned down the next street, Jake stole a glance back. Aces stomped back to the clubhouse, not looking in their direction. Jake heaved a sigh of relief, removed his jacket, and handed the bum the contents of his wallet. Without so much as a thank you, the bum bee-lined for the closest liquor store. Scowling, Jake high-tailed it to his car but not before the phone buzzed in the pocket of his stained pants. He looked at the number and answered it.

"Hello."

Mary was panting heavily on the other end of the line. "Jake, we've been robbed."

"What?"

"Someone broke into the house while we were gone."

"What did they take?"

"I don't know. I can't tell. The whole place is trashed."

He broke into a cold sweat. At least everyone was fine. "You should call Detective Noles, so that he can file a report, and I'll stop by tomorrow to check things out. I'm kind of in the middle of something right now."

"You don't have to drive in from Chicago to help."

Without thinking, he almost admitted he was still in Michigan. Instead, he said, "It's only a five-hour car trip."

"No. We'll be fine."

Jake wiped at his brow with a dirty hand. "Are you sure? I don't mind."

"I'm sure," she said hesitantly. "I better go call Detective Noles."

Mary hung up. Jake wished he could go to her, but there was no time. He was already late for his rendezvous with Rick and Bobby.

Chapter 41

After Caleb left the clubhouse, he met up with Hysko and Larry at their warehouse outside of town. If he hadn't been running late, he would've handled the bum himself, but he trusted Aces to smack him into next week. His co-conspirators each sat astride their motorcycles in the gravel lot behind the cement block structure, killing time until the meeting with the Outsiders. Caleb tossed aside a half-smoked cigarette; its glowing red tip smoldered in the dirt. Hysko looked longingly at the cigarette while Larry got off his bike and twisted his spine, producing several loud cracks. Following suit, Caleb and Hysko also dismounted and stretched.

A breeze rattled the branches of a nearby stand of trees. Caleb studied the dense foliage and scowled as the hairs stood up on the back of his neck. Since he'd arrived, he couldn't shake the feeling of being watched.

Larry noticed Caleb staring into the woods. "You feel it too?"

"Feel what?" Caleb snapped.

Larry paced around his bike. "The feeling of eyes on you."

Hysko reached for his pistol. "Do you think someone is out there?"

Caleb kicked at the gravel under his boot. "Hell no. It's just nerves. We've got a lot of killing ahead of us tonight."

Larry took a couple steps back. "I think I saw a Samsquatch."

"What?"

"You know, a Bigfoot."

Caleb howled with laughter. "You believe in that shit?"

"You don't?" Larry asked.

Caleb said, "Of course not. I'm not ten years old."

"Whatever," Larry said.

Hysko coughed. "It's almost seven. Isn't it time to make the call?"

Caleb lit up another cigarette, still laughing. "Not yet, I don't wanna give Alex time to think about it, or that asshole might chicken out."

"What I don't get is why are we waiting at the warehouse instead of at your uncle's barn?" Larry asked.

"Because this is where Sonny thinks we're meeting. If he comes early, we'll ambush him here, but I'd prefer the farm— it's more secluded."

Larry scratched his head. "I'm confused. Why didn't we just set up the meeting at the farm then?"

"Because it would look like an obvious setup— this way, Sonny doesn't have time to think about it either. Do you think he's as stupid as you?"

"No." Larry returned to his bike and leaned against it, sparking up his own cigarette.

Caleb could almost hear the hamster wheel that Larry called a brain, spinning noisily inside his head, thinking of the next question to ask. He hadn't shut up since they got here. Caleb silently cursed Hysko for suggesting that Larry join their coup.

As expected, Larry asked, "Do you think the club will believe it?"

Caleb sighed. "Believe what?"

"You know— the story you're going to tell them about what happened tonight."

Pulling a pack of gum from his pocket, Hysko shook his head. "What's not to believe, greenie?"

Larry looked at them but didn't answer. He was probably too afraid after being called stupid. Hysko snorted as he shoved the gum into his mouth. Crumpling up the wrapper, he tossed it over his shoulder.

Caleb took a deep breath and answered. "They'll believe it because this shit happens all the time in our business. A deal goes south, and weapons get pulled. People die, and new people take over."

"I guess," Larry said.

The three men laughed, but then an awkward silence fell over them. Caleb stared into the woods again. He thought he saw movement, but he couldn't be sure it wasn't a bird or the wind in the trees. Damn Larry had him chasing shadows, so he turned away in disgust and stared at the back wall of the warehouse instead.

Looking at his feet, Hysko asked, "You don't feel the least bit guilty for what we're about to do, Caleb?"

Caleb squinted at Hysko and kicked at the loose gravel with his boot, exposing fresh dirt underneath. "No, I don't. We agreed that Sonny would've run this club into the ground, and Aces couldn't be reasoned with when it comes to Sonny, so we'd all end up dead, and our old ladies would have to sell their asses to buy groceries."

"Really?" Larry asked.

Caleb nodded. "Hell, yes."

Hysko muttered, "Sonny and Aces. They're good men, and we shouldn't take killing them lightly."

"I'm not." Caleb rested his hand on the grip of his handgun. Damn. He'd really thought the threat of exposing Hysko's homosexual tendencies would keep him in line. "But are you having second thoughts?"

Hysko stood very still, hands down by his sides. "No. Not at all, Caleb. I'm one hundred percent behind you."

"Good." Caleb relaxed but didn't move his hand. "I agree— they're our brothers, and they deserve respect for all they've sacrificed for the club. But they forced us into this. You know that."

Hysko said, "I know. I was just saying . . ."

"Well, stop saying it. I need you to focus on what we need to do tonight. Got it?"

"Got it."

Clueless to the seriousness of the conversation, Larry looked down at his wrist. "Probably time to make that call, huh?"

"Is that the watch I gave you?" Caleb asked.

Larry hid his hand behind his back. "What watch?"

"THE watch!"

"Maybe."

Caleb's trigger finger itched. "Dumbass! I told you to get rid of it."

"Sorry, I keep on forgetting."

Damn it. Why had Caleb trusted this dumb ass with something so important? Why? Because he couldn't do it himself. The police had been watching Caleb like a hawk, even picking through his garbage at the curb. Caleb should have had Hysko take care of it. What had he been thinking?

Grinding his teeth, Caleb said, "If I see it on your wrist tomorrow, I'm shoving it down your God damn throat."

"I'll take care of it. I promise." Larry crossed a finger over his heart.

"You better."

Caleb pulled a pre-paid phone from his pocket along with a piece of paper with Alex's information. He punched in the number and brought the phone to his ear. Pacing, he waited for Alex to answer his call. The gravel crunched under his boots. At the edge of the parking lot, he stopped and stared off into the woods but saw nothing unusual. In fact, the scene was picturesque; the sky was a vibrant shade of pink and purple, and the sun was a big orange ball crashing towards the horizon.

After the fifth ring, he heard a click. "Hello."

"Alex. It's Caleb."

"Is there a problem?" Alex asked.

"A small one, but it's nothing to worry about."

"What is it?"

"People are working in the warehouse next door. They're usually gone by now, but there's no sign they'll be stopping soon, so I'm moving our meeting. We don't want any witnesses."

"That wasn't part of the deal," Alex growled.

"I understand, but the new place is better, and it's only twenty minutes from the warehouse. It was my uncle's farm. It is abandoned, so it'll be perfect. It's miles from the closest neighbor, and all the rednecks out there are always shooting off their guns so no one will think twice."

"Caleb, I don't fucking like this."

"You worry too much, Alex— you're going to give yourself ulcers."

"Screw you."

"Do you want the heroin or not?"

The line was silent. Caleb waited, winking confidently at his partners. The heroin had a street value of close to a million dollars. It was a lot of money for one night's work, and Alex knew it. Caleb rubbed at the scar on his face. The barn would be the spot where Sonny died. Didn't matter what Alex liked. It had been decided twenty years ago when Caleb learned he could never trust his brother.

Alex said, "Fine. What's the address?"

I'll text it to you. The house is boarded up, so go to the barn out back."

Trying to regain some face, Alex said, "If we don't like the look of it, we're going home."

"You do that, and we'll have a real war," Caleb threatened.

The line went dead.

Hysko asked, "How did it go?"

"They'll be there," Caleb said as he dialed Sonny, who picked up on the first ring.

"Hello."

"Change of plans. We've got company at the warehouse next door, so I need to move the location of our meeting."

"You got another place?"

"Do you remember Uncle Jim's farm?"

Sonny chuckled. "Yes, but doesn't someone else live there now?"

"No, the place is empty. Do you think you can still find it?"

"Yep. See you soon." Sonny disconnected.

Caleb gave the woods one more look and pointed at a large stand of trees. "Hey, look. I think I see the Loch Ness monster."

"There's no such thing," Larry said.

"Let me get this straight. You think Bigfoot is real, but the Loch Ness monster isn't."

Larry nodded his head up and down. "The dinosaurs are all dead, but an unknown hominid is very plausible."

"You're an idiot," Caleb said. "Let's go."

The three men climbed on their chrome machines after strapping on their helmets. Caleb gunned his throttle, and the engine roared like a lion. The back tire spun freely, then caught on the loose dirt, propelling the bike forward. Gravel shot out, pelting the tall weeds at the rear of the lot. Hysko and Larry chased after him.

When they were gone, Aces stomped angrily out of the woods.

Chapter 42

The three men sat uncomfortably in Rick's pickup truck as it raced down the country road. They barely fit, but they needed a vehicle that could be driven off-road. Though Jake wished Rick had cleaned it first. It smelled like cut grass, armpit, and stale fast food. Driving in his usual aggressive manner, Rick crossed the double yellow line to pass a slower moving vehicle and was almost hit by a car coming in the opposite direction. Jake cringed in the middle of the bench seat, but Bobby seemed unfazed in his spot by the window.

Jake scratched the rash on his face. "Sorry I was late, but I had a call from Mary."

Bobby looked at him sideways. "You didn't tell her anything, did you?"

"No. I'm not stupid."

Rick said, "Don't worry, it's only seven. We'll be there in ten minutes. Plenty of time to find our hiding spot."

"We better hope we get there first." Bobby squinted against the sun hanging low on the horizon.

"We will." Rick stomped on the accelerator, pushing the truck above ninety miles an hour. Jake was thrust back into the seat.

"Don't kill us," Bobby yelled.

"Shut up," Rick said.

"I will when you stop driving like an asshole."

Rick shook his head. "Well, at least I'm not fat."

"I can lose weight, but you'll always be a dick, Rick."

"Right? You lose weight, that'll be the day. You've always been a fat ass."

"I wasn't fat in high school."

"Yes, you were!" Rick mocked.

"No, I was big-boned. You can ask my mom."

Rick laughed. "She's not here. Jake, wasn't Bobby always fat?"

"Don't ask me. I'm Switzerland," Jake said, shaking his head.

"No." Rick elbowed him. "You need to pick a side. Besides, claiming to be Switzerland is Tom's old line, not yours."

"I know, but it seemed fitting to use it tonight."

"Damn right." Bobby pumped his fist. "I wish Tom was here."

"Me too." Rick eased up on the accelerator, and the truck dropped back to seventy miles per hour.

It was obvious that Tom's absence would always be felt when the three of them were together. For several miles, they drove in silence as Rick drummed his fingers on the steering wheel. After a moment of reminiscing, Jake mentally ran through their plan to execute Caleb, looking for places where it could go wrong. Unfortunately, there were too many to count.

Bobby must have been reading his mind. "I still think we should've rented a warehouse to practice for tonight. It worked in *Ocean's Eleven*."

"Oh, yeah. Who would you be?" Rick asked.

Bobby smiled. "Brad Pitt."

"I look more like Brad Pitt," Rick said. "You could be Casey Affleck."

"Which one was Casey Affleck?" Bobby asked.

"He was one of the dumb ones that had the remote-controlled car," Jake said. "And if Bobby is going to be Casey Affleck, then Rick should be Scott Caan."

"James Caan's son, I'll take that. God rest his soul," Rick said.

"James Caan is alive. It's Marlon Brando that is dead, you asshole," Bobby said.

"Fuck you. I know that Brando is dead. I thought James Caan was dead too."

Bobby said. "No. He was just in that movie with Will Ferrell."

"Dwarf?" Rick asked.

Jake snorted. "That's not it."

"I think you're right. Just a second, let me google it." Bobby pulled out his phone.

Jake said, "Stop it. That bugs me."

"What bugs you, little people?" Rick asked.

"No. That any asshole with a smartphone can be smart. When we were kids, you had to read books to be smart— lots and lots of books like *Encyclopedia Brown*. Now he was smart," Jake said.

Rick nodded. "Do you remember that case where he ruined his nemesis's alibi because he didn't have a tan on his wrist?"

Jake smiled. "Exactly. I think that's why I wanted to be a detective, so I could be like *Encyclopedia Brown.*"

Bobby tapped his phone. "*Elf* was the name of that movie with Will Ferrell. Wow, and that guy from *Game of Thrones* was in it too."

Jake frowned as he elbowed his friends. They needed to stop screwing around and concentrate. "Okay, we ALL need to be smart and focus on the job at hand, or we'll end up dead too."

Shrugging, Rick said, "I'm focused. All we need to do is wait until after Caleb kills the other gang, and then we kill him."

"I don't like this. It's way too complicated." Jake rubbed his irritated chin. "I wish I'd been able to kill him earlier."

"You what!" Bobby and Rick shouted simultaneously.

Damn! Jake hadn't meant to tell them, but it had slipped out with his frustration. So he told them the stories of his two botched attempts, and how Aces almost caught him. Jake left out the part about Caleb sleeping with Sonny's old lady, but he couldn't say why.

Bobby shook his head. "I can't believe you'd try to kill him without us."

"Sorry."

"You could have asked for our help," Bobby said. "We might have pulled it off together."

"Maybe," Jake said, not really believing it.

"I would have done the same thing, Jake. You've got to take your chances in life." Rick punched his thigh.

"I'm glad it didn't work out," Bobby said. "Because Caleb doesn't deserve an easy death. Those Middle Eastern countries have it right. They whip murderers before they hang them."

Truthfully, Jake was afraid of what he'd do once they got a hold of Caleb. He'd need to maintain a tight grip on his emotions, or he'd beat Caleb to a bloody pulp. As much for himself as his friends, Jake said, "We'll see what we have time for, but an eye for an eye should be enough."

Rick said, "Really?"

"Yeah."

"Are you sure you can do it? Or do you want me to kill him?" Rick asked.

Bobby laughed. "You? Jake is the only one of us who has killed a man. You got this, right, Jake?"

Jake's empty stomach churned with anger, frustration, and fear. But mostly, rage. It was past time for that son of a bitch to pay, especially if Caleb planned on going after Mary and the kids next. He said, "Don't worry. I got this."

"Fine, but I want to hit him a few times," Rick said as he sped around another slow-moving vehicle.

The driver laid on the horn, and Rick rolled down his window to flip him off. Bobby shook his head but had a smile on his face. Jake wasn't amused though he was pleased that Rick's antics would get them to the barn quickly. They should have been in position a half-hour ago.

Chapter 43

The dying sun pulled all traces of color from the sky as it dipped behind the barn. Caleb parked in front of the wooden structure and stood watching as Larry and Hysko glided to a stop beside him. He retrieved the messenger bag from the side storage box while the pair pulled out SIG MPX's and extended their stocks.

Caleb surveyed the yard, but nothing looked out of the ordinary. The feeling of being watched hadn't followed him. Good— because getting his revenge at this barn would provide closure on that horrible part of his life.

The barn door creaked loudly as Caleb pulled it open. Hysko and Larry followed Caleb inside the pitch-black space. An oil lamp hung on a nail from a nearby post. Caleb dug a lighter out of his pocket, struck the flint, and an orange flame licked the end of the damp cloth. The lamp lit up a small circle inside the barn. Caleb crossed the aisle-way and lit two more, but the far corners were still hidden in shadow.

Motorcycles rumbled up the long driveway, and Larry jogged to the open door. "It's the Outsiders. There's four of them."

"Four! Damn it, there was only supposed to be three." Caleb shouted, "Get into position."

Larry ran back, and they formed a triangle with Caleb at its point.

"I have a bad feeling about this," Hysko whispered.

Caleb growled, "We've got nothing to worry about— Alex doesn't have the balls to try anything."

"I hope you're right," Hysko said as engines sputtered off.

Caleb held the bag of drugs tightly with one hand. With the other, he pulled out his gun and rested it on his thigh. "Wait until they're all inside. I'll distract them with the drugs, and you two start shooting. Got it?"

"Yes," both men agreed.

Gravel crunched under boots as the Outsiders walked to the barn. They stopped at the door, standing four across. Alex took one step forward; the flickering lamplight exposed his craggy features.

"Alex, my old friend! I hope you didn't have trouble finding the place."

"Caleb! We were never friends."

Alex raised a gun and fired.

The bullet whizzed by Caleb's ear, missing by inches. He momentarily froze before diving for cover. What was happening? This wasn't the plan. Caleb was supposed to double-cross Alex, not the other way around.

The Outsiders lifted semi-automatic weapons and sprayed the room with lead. Larry and Hysko reacted quickly, returning fire. The sound was deafening in the enclosed space, worse than the grand finale on the Fourth of July. Shots missed their targets on both sides; however, enough found their mark. Two Outsiders toppled over, and Hysko was struck in the chest. He stumbled backward as his gun clattered to the old wood floor. However, Caleb managed to hit Alex.

The last Outsider dove for safety in the growing darkness outside. Caleb shot at him repeatedly until his gun's slide locked open, but he missed with every shot. Caleb's hand shook like a leaf as he released the used clip and slapped home a new one. Blood pounded in his ears as he scanned the destruction inside the room.

The smell of gunpowder and death filled the barn. Caleb took slow steadying breaths to bring himself back to the moment as he tried to figure out where it all went wrong. The fact was he didn't know. Things were really bad, but they could recover. There were two of them and one Outsider still alive. They just had to be smart.

Larry's mouth gaped open as he stared at the hole in Hysko's chest. Muttering obscenities in a sing-song pattern, he rocked back and forth on his heels. "No. Fuck no. Hysko's dead. This can't be fucking happening. It can't. Hysko's dead! No fucking way. Can't be happening."

"Shut the hell up and pull it together!" Caleb screamed.

Larry's jaw snapped shut. "Ok."

Alex tried scooting his butt towards the door, but his pumping legs got him nowhere. Moaning, he limply raised his gun. Caleb ran up and punted it out of his hand like a football. It bounced off a wall with a hollow thud. Menacingly, he stood over Alex. "What the hell?"

"Fuck off. You were going to double-cross us."

"No, I wasn't."

"You're a liar." Alex spat up clotted blood. A bubble formed in the corner of his mouth.

"Was it just the four of you?"

"No, there's a few guys down the road," Alex said, not meeting Caleb's stare. It was an obvious fabrication.

"Look who is lying now." Caleb kicked Alex in the ribs. He screamed, twisting his body around Caleb's heavy boot.

"Good. I'll finish off that last guy," Larry yelled as he ran to the barn door, his silhouette framed by the lamplight.

"No! Don't!"

A single shot rang out, and the back of Larry's head exploded. Bits of skull, brain, and blood rained down on the wood floor, followed by Larry's limp body a second later.

"Shit!" Caleb screamed.

He involuntarily started towards the door himself but stopped when a gun boomed from the yard, and bullets sang through the room. Hot steel chased him as he crashed headfirst into a stall. Seconds passed before a motorcycle roared to life outside. With a throaty growl, it tore down the driveway as the driver mashed through all the gears. Cursing, Caleb remained in the smelly horse stall. Sweat stung his eyes, and his knees and elbows throbbed from diving for his life. It would do no good to give chase. He'd never catch the backstabber. Besides, he needed time to prepare for Sonny and Aces.

Could he kill Aces and Sonny by himself? He had to, but he'd have to use this fiasco to his advantage. While Sonny and Aces were assessing the destruction, Caleb could kill both of them. It would be tricky, but he had no other choice. He'd painted himself into a corner underestimating Alex.

Caleb watched the Outsider's president pull himself across the floor with his hands; his useless feet dragged behind him. He futilely tried to reach Hysko's abandoned weapon, but Caleb leaped from the stall and stepped on his hand. He pulled out his backup revolver and put all six rounds into Alex's back.

Blood splattered on his face and arms. He felt a dull satisfaction, but not as much as he wanted to feel for this minor victory. He wiped at the droplets, leaving small smears across his cheek. With his smoking gun still in his hand, he stepped back to study the room. Guns, shell casings, blood, and old hay scattered the floor. Larry and the two Outsiders lay next to each other like children told to take a nap. Hysko's body lay just inside the ring of lamplight; his eyes stared up to the loft.

Caleb squatted down next to Hysko and shook his head to clear away the tears. "Sorry, my friend, you didn't deserve this. You were true to me to the end."

Standing up slowly, Caleb saw movement out of the corner of the barn. His breath caught in his chest. A shadow descended on him. Caleb tried to jump sideways but was too slow.

No!

Something hard struck him on the side of the head, and he toppled to the ground.

Jake stepped into the lamplight with a long pipe in his hand.

Chapter 44

Jake dropped the pipe. It rang like a bell as it clattered to a stop next to Caleb's prone body. He ran to the barn door and was happy to find the yard empty. Bobby handed him several lengths of old rope, which Jake used to tie Caleb's hands behind his back. Smiling, Jake pulled the knots tight until the skin underneath was bone-white. Staring at him with disgust, he flipped Caleb over roughly. A bump the size of a golf ball grew on his temple from where Jake had hit him, and blood dripped from his nose.

Crouching over the limp body, Rick said, "I think you killed him."

"No, he's still breathing." Jake pointed to his chest, rising and falling, before looking over the total destruction in the barn. "But it's a wonder anyone survived— good thing we hid in the loft."

A cut on Bobby's cheek oozed blood. Using the palm of his hand, he rubbed at the wound. "I think something grazed me."

Jake said, "It must have been a bullet."

Bobby wiped his hand on his pants. "Then tonight must be my lucky night."

"No thanks to this dickbag." Rick kicked Caleb.

The biker didn't stir, so Jake searched him. He found two spare clips and a wallet on his person. Not that there was any doubt, but Caleb Clarke's ID matched the unconscious man bound before them. Jake tossed the wallet down beside the open courier bag with several bricks of heroin visible inside. They dragged Caleb to a horse stall and sat him up. Jake slapped him hard in the face; Caleb moaned, but he didn't wake, so Jake smacked him again.

Caleb's eyes fluttered open.

Slowly, his pupils narrowed, and he took in his surroundings. His eyes stopped on the men in front of him, who he recognized instantly. Caleb tried to bring his hands up but quickly found he couldn't. He struggled frantically against his restraints, but the knots held tight.

"What the hell is going on?" Caleb shouted.

"What do you think is going on?" Jake laughed. "Your past has finally caught up with you."

"Fuck off!"

Jake wound up and punched him in the jaw, nearly falling over from the effort but stayed upright. However, Caleb toppled over sideways, his head bouncing on the floor. Jake's heart raced, the adrenalin getting the better of him. His hand throbbed, and he shook it to regain some feeling. The sting felt good, like the first drink of alcohol. He hated to admit how much he liked the feeling.

"I didn't think you wanted to hit him," Bobby said.

"I changed my mind."

"Good, it's my turn." Bobby stomped over to Caleb as he struggled to sit back up and kicked him square in the ass. Caleb gave a high-pitched grunt. Before he could right himself, Bobby kicked him again. Caleb clamped his jaw, so he didn't scream a second time.

"Stop," he said. "If you untie me, I'll let you live— that's a promise."

"You're in no position to dictate terms," Jake said.

"Do you remember who I am?"

Rolling his eyes, Jake said, "Yes. You're the person who killed my best friend, and now it's your turn to die."

Caleb sneered. "Kill me, and you'll be dead within twenty-four hours. The club will hunt you down like dogs."

Jake shook his head. "I don't think so."

"Why not?" Caleb finally succeeded in sitting up. "Wait . . . What the fuck is going on here?"

"Think about it, you piece of shit."

Jake could see the gears turning inside his head. He half-expected to see tendrils of smoke coming from his ears. It didn't take long for Caleb's shoulders to slump after he put the pieces together.

"Sonny figured it out, didn't he?"

Jake chuckled. "Got that right, asshole."

Sweat dripped down Caleb's face. He tried to blink it away. "I can double what the club is going to pay you, and there's heroin in that bag, a million dollars' worth. Take that too."

"We aren't doing this for money," Jake replied flatly. "We're doing it for free. We're doing it for Tom."

Caleb spat a mouth full of blood onto the ground. "Your friend was a rat. He got what he deserved."

"And so will you!" Rick caught Caleb with a beautiful backhand; his head rocked to the side before flopping back it to center. Then Rick smacked him with a forehand, turning his head into a giant tennis ball.

Jake nudged Rick aside as he pulled back for another backhand. "Enough."

With all the gunfire from earlier, there was no guarantee one of the distant neighbors hadn't called the police. As much as he would like to, they couldn't spend all night torturing him. Jake pulled his gun out from his jacket. It felt cold and heavy in his hand as he aimed it at Caleb's head. The room shrunk around him; only Caleb and the barrel of the gun remained.

Caleb's eyes went wide with fear. He stuttered, "I . . . I . . . I didn't kill your friend."

Jake shared a tired look with Bobby and Rick. "You're a terrible liar, Caleb."

"I . . . I'm not lying. It was Sonny."

A tendril of doubt tickled Jake's brain, but he swiftly pushed it away. Caleb had been wearing Tom's watch. He was the killer; Noles had said as much. The truth was Caleb would say anything to walk out of this barn— Jake couldn't let him mess with his head.

"I don't believe you." He turned to Rick and Bobby. "Last chance to hit him, then I'm putting a bullet in his head."

Bobby stepped forward and punched Caleb, putting all his weight into it. His nose made a sickening wet crack like pulling apart a raw chicken wing. Blood gushed out from Caleb's nostrils, soaking his mouth, chin, and shirt. Bobby rubbed his hand, a shit-eating grin on his face. Jake turned to Rick, who shook his head.

Good, it was finally time to kill this asshole. Jake raised the gun again and took careful aim at Caleb's heart. The sights fixed on his target.

Caleb stared back, eyes pleading as he licked his lips. He said, "Fine. I killed your friend, but you'll never guess why."

Chapter 45

"I know why," Jake said. "Because you're a piece of shit."

"Maybe I am, but there's another reason." Caleb rubbed at his nose with his shoulder, smearing blood across his face. "And you know it'll eat at you if you don't hear me out."

Jake lowered the Glock. "You have one minute, and if you try anything stupid, I'll put a bullet in your kneecap."

Caleb nodded his head as he made a show of stretching his shoulders. The strain from having his hands tied behind his back was evident, but Jake didn't care. Why massage a pig when it was about to be slaughtered? Bobby and Rick stood menacingly to either side of Caleb for insurance. He was not going anywhere.

Caleb swallowed; his Adam's apple danced in his throat. "The reason I killed your friend was because Sonny wanted him dead. I was just following orders."

"Tom was a family man. He had nothing to do with you guys," Bobby exclaimed.

"Yeah!" Jake said, "Why would Sonny order a hit on Tom?"

"I don't know. All I know was that I was told where to find him on that Sunday morning. Do I look like a guy that would get up early to go to church in the country?"

"No, but you look like the type of guy to pass out in a rundown bar on a Saturday night and have to drive home the next day," Jake muttered.

"Just shoot him. He's trying to save his neck," Rick shouted.

Caleb pleaded. "I'm not. I swear."

"Fine. I'll get the truth out of you." Rick ran to the back of the barn.

Jake and Bobby watched, unsure of Rick's next move since he was off the script. On a tool bench covered in grime, he grabbed a pair of horseshoe tongs; the handles were over two-foot long. He walked back towards Caleb, dragging them along the floor. The tool left a long scar in the dust and hay.

Beads of sweat shone on Caleb's forehead. He tried to scoot away, but his back was already to the wall. Rick nodded at Bobby, who lunged for Caleb and put him in a headlock. The tongs opened with a loud screech. Rick gripped Caleb's nose and twisted. Caleb screamed in pain as his nose was turned to hamburger.

"Please stop. I'll tell you anything," Caleb pleaded. The words were nasally and almost unintelligible.

Bobby released him from the headlock. Rick stepped back and let the tongs drop to the floor with a clatter. The rusty iron left an orange-brown residue on his hands.

Jake said, "Just tell us the truth."

"The God's honest truth is your friend, Tom, was waiting for me in the road. He must have found out about the hit somehow. We got into it, and I shot him. I had to. It was Sonny's orders."

Jake raised his gun and centered the sights on Caleb's head. "You're still lying."

"Fine. Don't believe me." Caleb licked his lips and blinked the sweat from his eyes. "But I can tell you where to find your friend's watch."

The Glock dropped an inch. Jake said, "You didn't trash it?"

Caleb pushed himself up the wall to stand solidly on both feet. Blood still dripped from what remained of his nose. "No. It's right here in the barn."

"Fuck you."

"It's true. It's on Larry's wrist."

"Which one is Larry?" Jake scanned the dead bodies.

"He's the one by the door with the back of his head missing."

Jake walked over to the tall man whose arms splayed out to both sides. His right arm was empty except for a bad tattoo of a spider, but on his left wrist was Tom's watch. He couldn't believe his eyes—it was really Tom's watch. Setting the Glock at his feet, Jake squatted down next to the dead body. He fumbled with the clasp as Bobby and Rick shifted their attention from Caleb to Jake.

Bobby's mouth hung open. "It can't be."

"No fucking way." Rick took two steps forward to get a closer look.

Jake wiped the blood from the glass face off on his pants and held it up. "It's true. It's Tom's watch."

Using the distraction, Caleb pushed off the wall and launched himself across the room. Bobby threw up his hands as Caleb slammed into him, spinning him around like a top. Caleb stumbled towards the open barn door with his arms still tied behind his back. He picked up speed as he ran past Rick.

Jake dropped the watch and scrambled for his pistol. He'd die before he let Caleb escape. Judging the distance, Jake knew he'd get run over before he could pull off a shot. So instead, at the last second, Jake pivoted and stuck his leg out, tripping Caleb. He sailed through the air, bouncing twice before landing on his face in the gravel outside. The air escaped his lungs like a punctured balloon.

Casually, Jake walked over to Caleb, who writhed like a turtle stuck on his back. Jake flipped him over as Caleb fought to catch his breath. Enough messing around; it was time to kill Caleb. Jake aimed the Glock.

"This is for you, Tom," Jake said.

A cool breeze blew across Jake's face, whispering in his ear. Jake could have sworn he'd heard the words, *Thank you.* He looked around, but no one was in the yard with him. Rick and Bobby waited in the doorway with puzzled faces. If he had any remaining doubts, they were gone with the wind.

Jake said, "You're welcome."

Caleb's left eye twitched uncontrollably. He stuttered, "P . . . please. L . . . let me go. I'll disappear. And every dime I make, I'll send it to your friend's family. Please just don't kill me— I'm not ready to die."

Jake shook his head in disgust. "You douche bag, Tom had a wife and kids and a good life. He wasn't ready to die either, not that you cared."

"Please!"

Jake pulled the trigger.

Caleb's head rocked back, and a red hole formed in the middle of his forehead. His lifeless body slumped to the earth. Jake pulled the trigger again. A second bullet entered his skull, ensuring Caleb was dead. The job was done. Tom could finally rest.

Jake plodded back to the barn and handed his gun to Rick. "Can you hang onto this one for me?"

"Sure." Rick took it with a smile.

"Thanks." Jake pulled out the pistol Sonny had provided. He gripped it several times to get his prints on it before setting it down next to Caleb's body. "Joke will be on Sonny when the bullets don't match this gun."

Walking back into the barn, he retrieved the watch and held it up to the lamplight, examining it closely. It was definitely Tom's watch; recovering it was the icing on the cake of this eventful night. He slipped it into his pocket for safekeeping.

Bobby put a hand on Jake's shoulder. "How are you feeling?"
"I feel surprisingly good."

"Do you believe that shit about Sonny putting a hit on Tom?" Bobby asked.

"No. I don't."

Bobby said, "The asshole almost got away when he distracted us with the watch."

"No thanks to you, fat boy." Rick snorted.

"You didn't do anything to stop him either," Bobby said, shifting his weight from foot to foot.

Rick walked to the center of the barn, stopping over the messenger bag. "Fuck off."

Bobby leaned against one of the horse stalls. "Whatever. Jake, you should probably call the cleaning crew."

Jake pulled the phone from his back pocket. "Right. We should get the hell out of here. I could really use a drink."

"Me too," Bobby agreed.

Something metallic clicked behind them. Both men froze. They turned to find Rick pointing the gun at Jake's head, the messenger bag over his shoulder.

"About that . . . I'm going to need you to put the phone away."

Chapter 46

"What the fuck are you doing?" Bobby yelled at Rick.

Rick shifted his aim to Bobby. "Isn't it obvious? I'm taking the drugs."

"You can't be serious," Jake said.

"Dead serious. Landscaping sucks— I had to declare bankruptcy last week. The bank is going to take all my equipment. I'm completely screwed."

Bobby's hands clenched into fists. "And your solution is to screw us too?"

"No, it isn't like that. I just need a little seed money for a clean start outside of Michigan. You heard how much this stuff is worth." Rick patted the bag.

"Rick, don't be stupid," Jake pleaded, the phone still in his hand.

"I'll be fine." Rick pointed to all the dead bodies. "The Devil's Hand has bigger things to worry about than me."

"You're crazy. They'll search the ends of the earth for you," Jake said with a sigh. "You're stealing a million dollars' worth of drugs from them."

Rick laughed. "Ends of the earth? You overestimate them; they're a local club. I'll go to LA or New York, someplace they have no influence. I can sell the drugs and get a new identity, but the less you know about my plan, the better."

Bobby moved towards Rick. "They'll hold us responsible."

Rick jabbed the gun in Bobby's direction. "No. They won't. You're a friend of the club, remember."

"You're dumber than a bucket of piss. It doesn't work that way," Bobby shouted.

Jake slipped the phone back in his pocket and brought his hands up in front of him. The fingers splayed wide. "Rick, think about it. The Devil's Hand has a reputation to uphold. They will hunt you down and kill you."

"I'll have to take that chance."

Jake said, "Why don't you put the gun down, and we can forget this ever happened. I've got a little money saved up. You can have it."

Momentarily distracted by Jake's offer, Rick lowered the gun, and Bobby inched closer. He was only five feet from Rick now.

Rick shook his head. "Sorry. Your little bit of money isn't going to cut it. Not for what I want to do."

"What do you have planned, Rick?"

"I told you, the less you know, the better."

The determined look in Rick's eyes also told Jake that Rick couldn't be reasoned with, but Bobby missed the memo. Rick noticed Bobby was only four feet away and jumped back with the gun raised. "Back off, Bobby!"

"No." Bobby took another step forward.

"I mean it," Rick growled. "I'll shoot you."

"You won't shoot me."

"Try me."

A chill ran up Jake's spine. Shit! Loyal Bobby wouldn't stand for their friend's betrayal, while Rick had painted himself in a corner with his bad choices. Neither one of his friends could back down, and the slightest move by either man would end in more death and destruction.

Before Jake could devise a way to end this stalemate, Bobby leaped, grabbing for the barrel with both hands. Rick pulled the trigger. The bullet hit Bobby in the chest. Both men froze as blood oozed from his shirt. He stumbled back and then crashed to the floor. Weakly, he tried to get to his hands and knees but fell down with a heavy thud.

Jake watched in horror. No. It couldn't be. Had the whole world gone insane? He shouted, "You shot Bobby!"

"He made me do it," Rick cried. "I begged him to stop."

The blood thrummed in Jake's ears. "No, you didn't."

"I'm begging you, Jake. Don't make me shoot you too."

"You're a selfish bastard!"

"Maybe. Now get out of my way," Rick said as he eased towards the exit.

Jake moved to block his path. "No!"

A bullet whizzed within inches of Jake's face. Reflexively, he jumped away, almost tripping over a dead body. Tendrils of smoke wafted from the barrel of the gun. Looking like he'd aged twenty years in the last five minutes, Rick scanned the room and shook his head before resting his gaze on Bobby. A small pool of blood grew under his shoulder.

Rick asked, "Is he ... Is Bobby dead?"

"You better hope not."

"Or what? You'll hunt me down and kill me too?"

"I wouldn't do that to a friend."

Rick shook his head. "You think you're better than me, don't you?"

"No."

"You're lying."

"Fuck you."

"Ask yourself who you did this for," Rick said. "Because it wasn't for Tom."

"Then who did I do it for?"

Smiling, Rick said, "You know who."

The implication made Jake's blood boil. He said, "Maybe, I will kill you."

"We'll see. Tell Bobby I'm sorry. You need to call that number and get him help."

Rick sprinted out the door, and Jake ran to Bobby, putting a finger to his neck. The pulse felt strong, so with some effort, Jake flipped Bobby on his back. The wound looked bad. Blood soaked Bobby's shirt. Jake was no doctor, but he thought the bullet had missed his heart, though it could've nicked an artery.

Outside, Rick's truck turned over and dropped into gear. It roared around the barn. Metal crunched on metal as the truck clipped a motorcycle before it raced down the driveway. Jake pulled out the burner phone and hit the speed dial for the first number. It rang and rang and then went to a generic voicemail recording. Fuck! Jake ground the end button down, nearly breaking it. He wanted to throw the stupid phone at the wall but didn't. Instead, he turned his attention back to Bobby— the pattern of blood had grown larger. Jake pressed his hand to the wound, and Bobby squirmed under the pressure.

"Come on, Big Man, I need you to hang in there."

Bobby groaned; his eyes fluttered open. His unfocused gaze settled on Jake, reminding him of Leroy Jones. Bobby mumbled, "It hurts a lot."

"I know. I'm sorry."

"Did you call Sonny?"

"He didn't answer. I think I should call 911."

Bobby grimaced. "Look at this mess. We'll go to jail. Try Sonny again."

Still holding Bobby's wound, Jake cursed himself and Rick. He cursed Sonny, but most of all, he cursed Caleb. Everyone was to blame for this mess they were in, except for Tom. And Mary. What the hell did Rick know? Manipulating the phone with one hand, Jake tried to call Sonny again. He didn't answer.

Screw it. Jake would serve a life sentence before he'd let Bobby die. His finger tapped the nine button on the burner phone when he heard the roar of motorcycles cutting through the night air, followed by tires hitting the gravel driveway. Crap! Had the rival gang come back to finish Caleb off? Or was it the Devil's Hand? Did it matter? Jake and Bobby were in trouble either way.

Jake got a hand underneath each of Bobby's armpits. "This is going to suck, but I've got to get you somewhere safe."

Grunting and straining, Jake pulled Bobby towards the back of the barn. His screams momentarily drowned out the roar of the motorcycles while blood spurted from the hole in his chest. For his efforts, Jake only succeeded in moving Bobby two feet. They were screwed.

Multiple engines shut off, and footfalls converged on the entrance to the barn. Jake grabbed a nearby semi-automatic from the floor and jumped in front of Bobby. A quick look told him the clip was empty, so Jake might as well have been holding a rubber chicken, but he didn't have time to find a loaded weapon before a deep voice called out from the darkness.

"Drop the gun, dumbass."

Chapter 47

Jake dropped the useless gun and held up his hands as Aces flowed into the barn like an avalanche. Two members of the Devil's Hand followed him in, walking side by side; their shoulders scraped the doorway.

Aces whistled. "Holy fuck! They're all dead— the gang's problems are solved."

Sonny paused outside the door, a solemn look on his face. He knelt down next to Caleb and laid a hand over his brother's heart. Sonny's lips moved as if he was saying a prayer. It was more than Caleb deserved. Afterward, Sonny moved to the edge of the yard, probably to compose himself.

Jake squatted down and reapplied the pressure to Bobby's wound. "You might have a new problem."

"What the hell happened to him?" Aces asked.

"He got shot."

Aces came to stand over Jake while the other two men fanned out to the corners of the room. "That looks bad. We told you guys to stay out of the way."

Jake frowned. "We did."

"Obviously not."

"This happened after the massacre."

Aces kneeled down to examine Bobby's wound closer. "Did Caleb shoot him?"

Jake sighed. "No. Our friend Rick shot him."

"Not much of a friend."

Blood soaked through Bobby's shirt and stained Jake's hands. "You got that right."

Sonny made his way into the barn. Any trace of grief was gone from his face. He analyzed the devastation like a mathematician attacking a calculus problem before he settled his sights on Bobby and raised an eyebrow. Jake gave him an abbreviated summary of the night's events, finishing with a plea for medical aid.

Shaking his head, Sonny said, "You should've listened to me."

Jake tried to bite his tongue, but it freed itself from his teeth. "Screw you."

Aces's eyes narrowed on Jake. He stood up and flexed his massive muscles capable of ripping a phone book in half, but Sonny held up his hand. Aces reluctantly heeled as a fresh set of tires crunched on the gravel outside. Everyone looked at one another and then at the door. Aces took a position in front of Sonny. The skinnier of the two members slipped into the darkness of the barnyard, hugging the side of the building.

Sonny, Aces, and the remaining member readied themselves, their semi-automatic weapons pointed at the entrance. A cold sweat broke out on Jake's forehead. He felt totally helpless as he applied pressure to Bobby's wound. Car doors opened and slammed closed. No one in the barn said a word— the only sound was the buzz of flies hovering over the dead.

Without warning, the skinny guy stuck his head back inside the door. He was lucky he didn't get his head blown off before he shouted, "It's our guys."

Three more members of the Devil's Hand joined the party, one of whom was almost as big as Aces. He stomped into the room like he was auditioning to be the front half of a Clydesdale. He was followed by a handsome guy in a cowboy hat and a young guy with a shaved head. The new people took in the scene with surprising coolness as if it was something that they saw every day. Maybe they did, Jake thought.

"Damn!" The young guy said, "I can't believe Hysko was a traitor. He brought me into the club."

All the members mumbled similar admonishments as Bobby's moans grew more intense. Jake cleared his throat loudly. "Are you going to get help for Bobby, or do I need to call 911?"

Aces pointed his gun at Jake. "Do you want to die?"

"No. And I don't want Bobby to die either, so fucking do something for him!"

Everyone in the room turned to Sonny, waiting for his direction. He nodded his head and turned to the young guy and the Clydesdale. "Get Bobby in the van and take him to the club's doctor, then come straight back here. We'll need the van to haul this mess over to the landfill."

Aces said, "Some gasoline and a match would be a whole lot easier."

"With Caleb's name on the deed, there'd be an arson investigation," Sonny said.

"I know," Aces said. "But Jesus Christ, Mary, and Joseph. What a bloody mess."

Bobby groaned. Exasperated, Jake shouted, "Can we get this moving?"

Sonny agreed. "Hurry up, men! Bobby's a friend of the club."

The members eyed the ground sheepishly while Aces pushed the younger guy aside. He and the other big man got about their task, and Jake happily moved out of the way. Aces grabbed Bobby under the arms, and Sal gripped his feet. Bobby screamed in pain when they hoisted him up, but they ignored his cries as they shuffled him out of the barn.

Jake went to follow, but Sonny stepped in his way. "You're staying here."

"What? No, I'm not!"

"Yes. Yes, you are."

"No. I need to go with Bobby."

Sonny shook his head. "And I said you're staying here."

All the guns in the room were leveled at Jake's head, so he did as he was told only because anything else might delay Bobby's departure. Maybe Jake should've been worried about his own skin, but he wasn't. He was quickly running out of friends, and he couldn't afford to lose another one.

The van's sliding door crashed shut, and the vehicle drove away, the tires kicking up gravel. Aces returned to stand in the doorway. Sonny gave him a slight nod. "I'm going to need a minute alone with Jake."

Aces paused and then shouted, "You heard the man. Everyone out!"

The Devil's Hand members filed past Aces, and he slammed the door closed behind them. The sound echoed through the small space. Afterward, an eerie silence filled the room broken only by the buzzing flies. The stench of blood and death crawled up Jake's nose, and he suppressed a shudder. Jake wiped his hands on his pants and turned his attention to Sonny. The sights, smells, or sounds didn't seem to bother him.

"So, what's going on? Why did I have to stay?" Jake asked.

Sonny smiled devilishly. "Because I have one question for you."

Chapter 48

"What's your question?" Jake asked. He feared Sonny wanted to know if Jake wanted to be shot in the head or the heart.

"Don't rush me. I'll get to that in a minute."

Sonny circled Jake like a hungry tiger with the Glock at his thigh. He stepped over a contorted body, and the fat black flies buzzed in protest. Jake wondered why Sonny hadn't delegated this task, but he knew the answer. Sonny would take pleasure in toying with Jake before he killed him. And he would kill him. What choice had Jake given him after losing a million dollars' worth of the club's drugs?

Taking the conversation in a different direction, Sonny said, "I'm glad you were the one who ended Caleb's miserable life, Jake."

"You are?" Jake scanned the room, assuming Sonny was putting him at ease before he executed him.

Several guns lay scattered amongst the corpses. If Jake could find one with ammunition, he might be able to kill Sonny, but there were four men outside to deal with afterward. There was no way Jake would make it out of here alive.

"Yes." Sonny stopped his pacing.

"Why me?"

"Isn't it obvious? We're two sides to the same coin."

"Fuck you. We're nothing alike," Jake growled.

Sonny laughed. "I guess not, because I like you. I liked you that first night behind the bar. Most guys would've run with their tail between their legs, but not you, Jake. You faced five guys and didn't back down."

"Some people would call that stupid."

"Not me."

Jake was feeling a little better about his situation, but not much. "So, what happens now?"

Sonny shrugged. "What do you want to happen?"

"You could let me walk out of here."

Holstering his gun, Sonny said, "I have a better idea. Why don't you stay and join the Devil's Hand? A former cop would be a real asset to the club. Come on. What do you say?"

Jake spotted the iron tongs they'd used on Caleb's nose. It was the only weapon in the room that wouldn't draw the attention of the men outside. He moved closer to them as he said, "Have you heard the tale of the fox and the scorpion?"

"Maybe— but go ahead and tell it anyway." Sonny pulled out a cigarette and lit it.

Jake leaned against a support post; the iron tongs were near his feet. "Ok, there is this scorpion, and he asks a fox to help him across this river because the scorpion can't swim. The fox is a nice guy who wants to help, but he's worried. So, the fox asks the scorpion if he'll sting him when they're crossing the river, and the scorpion tells the fox, 'No way!'

"The scorpion explains that if he stings the fox, then they would both die, and the scorpion is not an idiot. The fox considers the scorpion's plea and agrees to help him. So, the fox lets the scorpion climb on his back, and he starts to swim. But halfway across the river, the scorpion stings the fox in the neck.

"As the poison paralyzes the fox, and they start to drown, the fox screams, 'Why? Why did you sting me? Now— we both will die.'"

"The scorpion replies, 'What did you expect? I'm a scorpion.'"

Sonny slapped his thigh and laughed. Jake joined in half-heartedly while he inched closer to the tongs. When the laughter died down, Sonny's smile turned into a frown. Neither man spoke while the flies buzzed around the dead.

Finally, Sonny asked, "So I take it from your little tale that you won't be joining the club."

Jake nodded his head. "There's not a snowball's chance in Hell."

"I thought you would say that," Sonny said, exhaling a long plume of smoke. "Which is why the boys are collecting a little evidence outside to tie you to Caleb's murder."

Jake chuckled. "Fat chance. The gun that's next to Caleb— the one you gave me. It's not the one I used to kill Caleb."

"Bullshit!"

"It's the truth."

"Then where's the one that killed Caleb?"

"Rick stole it along with your heroin."

Sonny growled, "That's fine, but I bet your clothes have Caleb's blood on them."

"Probably. But good luck getting them off me while I'm alive."

Sonny pointed a finger at Jake's hand, where the skin had split after punching Caleb. A drop of blood trickled off Jake's knuckles and fell to the floor. Sonny smiled victoriously.

"I won't have to kill you— not yet. Because I bet your sweat and blood are on Caleb's clothes too. That should be enough evidence to convict you on first-degree murder."

Filled with rage, Jake balled his hands into fists. He was totally screwed. Why had Jake been so focused on ballistics and fingerprints that he forgot about DNA evidence? How stupid!

Sonny laughed. "I'm no detective, but I do like to watch *Forensic Files.*"

"You're a motherfucker."

"No, I'm a scorpion. Remember?"

"Exactly. You pretend to be different, but you're no better than the rest of the crooks. What now? Are you going to blackmail me into joining your club?"

Smiling, Sonny took a step closer to Jake. "Maybe."

Jake's stomach twisted like a snake. He had been made a fool despite his best efforts, but he wouldn't become a pawn in Sonny's game. The time for talk was over; he needed to act now before he got stung.

Jake threw a quick jab. It landed on Sonny's hairy chin, knocking him back. Pumped with adrenalin, he followed with a hook that caught Sonny on the temple. The blow stunned him. Jake bent over and scooped up the long iron tongs, but Sonny recovered too quickly. He shifted sideways and pulled out his Glock. Jake swung the tongs like a cleanup batter, and Sonny tried to duck out of the way. The heavy tool struck Sonny's shoulder, and he cried out in pain. The pistol flew into the air, but the tongs slipped out of Jake's sweaty hands as well.

Both weapons clattered to the floor.

Sonny lunged for a nearby semi-automatic, and Jake grabbed a large shiny revolver. Both men turned and aimed. Sonny sneered. "Go ahead. Pull the trigger."

Jake shook his head. "Don't tempt me."

"I dare you. My men will tear you apart if you kill me."

"I know. I'm not afraid to die."

"Good. Me either," Sonny said.

"Then before we meet our maker, tell me, did you order Caleb to murder Tom?"

"No," Sonny answered without a pause.

Jake said, "That's funny because Caleb said that you did."

"Why would there be a hit out on your friend?"

Sonny met Jake's stare. His body language revealed no signs of deception, but that was typical for a career criminal.

"I don't know," Jake said. "You tell me."

"There wasn't a hit on Tom. Caleb was an impulsive asshole who picked a fight with your friend after sleeping off a drunken stupor, and things got out of control. Sorry, but Tom had bad luck."

Jake frowned. "So Caleb was lying?"

"Yes. He'd say anything to save his own skin."

"I could say the same thing about you." Jake pulled the trigger.

The hammer hit the firing pin, but nothing happened. Sonny laughed heartily, the muzzle of his semi-automatic aimed at Jake's head. The seconds ticked by, and Jake's heart pounded in his chest like a bass drum. He was a dead man.

Sonny lowered the weapon to his side. "I like you, Jake. So like I said, I'm not going to kill you."

"Thanks," Jake said. "But I bet your gun is empty too."

Sonny aimed the semi-automatic back in Jake's direction. He tapped the trigger, and a bullet whizzed by Jake's head, missing him by inches. It slammed into the wall behind him with a hollow thud. He said, "However, I don't like you enough to forget about the two kilos of smack."

Jake's chin dropped to his chest. "I can't pay you back."

"That's why you're going to owe me."

"Owe you?" Jake looked up. Of course, it was just as he suspected, Sonny would blackmail him. "Let me guess. You're going to make me join your club?"

"No, I won't force you to do that if your heart's not in it," Sonny said with a grin. "But you are going to owe me a favor."

"What favor?"

"I haven't decided yet."

"I won't kill for you again." Jake stabbed a finger at Sonny.

Sonny slapped Jake's hand away, the shit-eating grin still pasted on his face. "No, you'll do what I want, how I want. And when I want, or I'll turn Caleb's body over to the police."

"You wouldn't."

"I would, and I hear they are not too nice to ex-cops in prison."

Sonny had Jake over a barrel, and he knew it. What other choice did he have but to agree for now? Jake could always double-cross Sonny later. He asked, "Only one favor?"

"Yes."

"And then I get to destroy the evidence?"

"You have my word."

Jake believed Sonny, probably because he'd kept his word to Caleb in the face of death. "Fine. One favor."

"I knew you would see it my way."

"Whatever, are we done now?"

"Almost. I'm going to need the full name of your friend who stole my drugs."

Jake didn't give it a second thought. Rick didn't deserve his protection. "Richard Stahl, Jr."

Sonny closed his eyes and nodded. "Stahl. Got it. Any idea where the dick ran off to?"

"Nope."

"Then, I guess we're done here," Sonny said indifferently as he headed for the exit.

Jake held up a hand. "Wait! The van's not back yet. Are you going to take me to Bobby?"

Sonny shook his head. "You're not cute enough to be my backwarmer."

"You can't be serious," Jake shouted.

"I'm dead serious." Sonny pushed open the heavy barn doors and walked outside. "Only Devil's Hand MCs are riding with me tonight, so it looks like your bitch ass is walking."

"Fucker."

Looking over his shoulder, Sonny said, "That's me, and I wouldn't be here when the sanitation crew arrives, or you may wind up in a barrel of acid too."

Sonny disappeared into the darkness. Jake stood there dumbfounded as motorcycles roared to life in the yard. The sound of engines revving momentarily drowned out the buzzing flies until they sped off into the night. Jake tried to process everything that had happened tonight but couldn't— it was sensory overload. As near as he could tell, Jake had won the battle but was on his way to losing the war.

Eventually, the rot of death pushed him out of his trance, and Jake exited the barn. The watch bounced in his pocket, which brought him a spark of hope. The watch was a symbol for all that he'd accomplished for Tom and Tom's family tonight. Now they could heal without a future reckoning with a mad-man. They could close the book on this bad chapter in their life— unless Sonny had been lying.

With that thought, Jake put one foot in front of the other and began his long journey home.

Chapter 49

The sun shined brightly through Jake's windshield, making him sweat. He couldn't sit in his car any longer, not with the windows up and the engine off, so he might as well get it over with. And what was the big deal? Sure, he'd stayed in Michigan and not told Mary. Yes, he'd avenged Tom's death after she'd told him it would be against Tom's wishes. Then there was what happened to Bobby! Yes, Jake had nothing to worry about— except that Mary may never speak to him again.

Furthermore, he still had his doubts with the roles of Detective Noles and Sonny played in Tom's death. But that's all they were— doubts because real cases never wrapped up cleanly. This wasn't TV.

Nor did he feel like he'd seen the last of Dolan. Tom's boss had an unhealthy obsession with Mary. The creep. She was young enough to be his daughter.

Jake opened the car door, but before he could get out, his phone rang. It was Sam. He should pick it up, but now that he'd finally found his nerve, he decided he'd call her back later. Nothing could be more important than the conversation he was about to have with Mary. Sam was probably only checking on him; it had been a week since they'd last talked.

Jake exited his vehicle and walked around Hunter's new bike lying in the driveway. Its chrome wheels sparkled in the daylight. Hesitantly, he stepped onto the porch and rang the doorbell. The sound echoed through the house. He waited, but no one came, so he knocked loudly on the door. This time, he heard footsteps. The lock flipped, and the interior door opened slowly. Emma's face appeared in the crack.

"Uncle Jake?"

"Hi, Emma."

She opened the door wider. "Were you out here long?"

"Not too long. I rang the bell first."

"Sorry. It's been acting up, ringing when no one is there."

"Weird. Must be a loose wire," Jake said.

"Yeah, so we've been ignoring it. Do you want to come in?"

"No. I'll stay out here. Is your mom home?"

She hesitated, staring at him a little too long. "Yep. Hang on."

The look scared him. He could be reading too much into it, but it all but confirmed for Jake that Emma knew their big secret. However, unless she outright asked him, Jake would keep his promise to Mary. As her mother, she should know what's best. Besides, even if Emma was his biological daughter, Jake could never replace her father.

The screen door slammed shut, and Emma disappeared in a blur of blonde hair and knobby knees. Jake turned and leaned against the porch railing. It offered some support as he studied the suburban landscape in its manicured perfection. Yet, it appeared fragile too, like it could fall apart in a heartbeat— Tom had proven that. Luckily, Jake's mind didn't have enough time to go to a dark place because the door opened behind him.

"Jake?"

Mary's eyes narrowed on him while the sunlight danced in her naturally blonde hair. She wore an old t-shirt and yoga pants along with a frown on her beautiful face.

Jake said, "Hope you don't mind that I stopped by unannounced, but I wanted to check on you after your break-in."

She came outside on bare feet. "Oh! We're fine. The house was turned upside down, but we couldn't find anything missing."

"That's odd." Jake shrugged, not knowing what to make of that information.

"I know. It makes no sense."

"Do you want me to have a look around?"

"No. There's nothing to see. Everything is put back together, so you should've called before coming back to Michigan to check on us."

She opened her arms to him, and Jake surrendered to her embrace. It was a good sign, but he needed to tell her the truth without any more delay. So much had happened since he'd been here last, not the least of which was murder.

He stepped back and studied his feet. "I never left."

Her frown returned. "What?"

"Sorry. I had unfinished business here."

"But I thought you were out of vacation time?"

He rolled his eyes sheepishly and forced a smile. "I was, so I quit. I hated that job anyway."

"Jake— we talked about this."

Still not meeting her eyes, he said, "I know."

She flopped down on the swing. "So, what are you going to do now?"

He sat down on the swing next to her. "Maybe I'll walk the earth and get into adventures, like Caine from *Kung Fu*."

"You're such an ass." She slapped him on the leg. "You should get a job as a cop again. You were happy doing that."

"I can't, not in Chicago. My father-in-law, the judge, has made sure I'll never work in that town again."

"Well, you did break his nose."

Jake cracked his knuckles. "And I'd do it again."

"Maybe you could get a job in security or as a private investigator."

"I guess. Yeah. Maybe I'll have a look into that on Monday."

Jake knew what her next question would be, and he wasn't disappointed. Mary elbowed him in the stomach while giving him the side-eye. "Fine. Now tell me, what was so important that you had to lose your job over it? I hope it wasn't your investigation into Tom's death."

Squirming under her gaze, he scooted away from her. "How have the kids been? The break-in must've been rough on them."

"The girls seem to be fine," she said with a sigh. "But Hunter got scared; he climbed into my bed last night."

"That sucks. Did you ever go through Tom's stuff?"

"After the break-in, I kind of had to, our bedroom seemed to be hit the hardest. So I put all of Tom's stuff in bags, but it's still sitting in the corner of our room waiting to go to Goodwill."

"Do you want me to take care of it?"

Looking frustrated, she shook her head. "I can do it, Jake. Now quit stalling and answer the question. What did you have to take care of?"

He opened his mouth but found his tongue was tied, so he dug in the front pocket of his jeans. The answer to her question was caught in a crease of the denim, but he slowly worked the object loose. When she saw it, she gasped, and her hands went to her chest.

Jake held out Tom's watch. "I think this belongs to you."

Chapter 50

A tear spilled down Mary's cheek, followed by another. She brushed them away quickly. "Where did you find it?"

"It doesn't matter." Warily, he held it out to her; the sunlight reflected off the watch's face. "Here. Take it."

"I can't believe you found it. You must've searched every pawn shop in the state."

At that moment, he considered lying but thought better of it. Mary deserved the truth. "I didn't find it in a pawn shop."

"Where did you find it?" Mary bit her lip, not reaching for the watch.

"I took it from him."

"Who?"

A golf ball-sized lump formed in the back of his throat, but he pushed the word past it. "Caleb."

"How . . . ? How did you get it back from him?"

"Maybe it's best if you don't know."

"Jake!" She grabbed his arm and squeezed it. "You need to tell me how you got that watch from Caleb."

He'd rehearsed his explanation a hundred times in the car, but he couldn't recall a single line of it now. She grew impatient, and her grip grew tighter. When he was sure her nails would pierce his skin, the simple truth spilled from Jake's lips.

"I did it."

"Did what?"

"I killed him. I killed Caleb."

Mary dropped Jake's arm and brought her hand to her neck. "Please tell me you're lying."

"I can't. I did it."

She inched away from him. "Jake . . . "

"Sorry. Do you hate me?"

She didn't answer. Instead, she eased herself up and moved to the railing. Leaning heavily on it, she stared out into the yard as he had done moments ago. The silence was terrible, and it seemed to drag on forever. The acid in his stomach felt like it would eat through all his organs.

He stood up. "I'll go."

"Sit back down, Jake." She turned to him, her face drained of emotion. "I don't hate you. I could never hate you, but— "

He remained standing but dropped the watch back in his pocket. "But?"

"I don't know what to think, Jake. You just told me you killed a man."

"I had no other choice."

"Really?"

"Yes. I learned Caleb had plans to tie up loose ends. He was going to kill you, me, and the kids after he took control of the Devil's Hand."

Mary hung onto the rail for support. "Are you serious?"

"Dead serious."

"Fuck me. Why didn't you tell me that in the first place?"

Jake ran his fingers through his hair. "I don't know. This is my first time confessing to murder."

Mary was silent for a moment, and then she nodded her head once. Her jaw jutted out like a veteran boxer's. "Well, good. I'm glad you did it. I wish I could've done it myself— but aren't you scared you'll be arrested for murder?"

"No. I'm too smart for that."

"Are you sure? That's what everyone says right before they're caught. And you can be . . . a little impulsive, my friend."

A little impulsive was an understatement. For that reason, Jake decided to delay telling Mary about Sonny's blackmail plot. Hadn't he already laid enough at her feet for one day?

"Don't worry. I've got it covered."

"Good, because I can't take on any more. I love you, Jake, but the kids need to be my top priority right now."

"I wouldn't have it any other way." He placed a hand on her shoulder, pushing his guilty omissions to the side. "I owed it to Tom to protect his family, so with this Caleb business behind us, we can all move forward. I will find a new job, focus on my relationship with Sam, and work on improving myself. I swear."

"I hope so, Jake, because you could do so much more with your life. If you don't make some changes, you could wind up like Rick."

"Oh! Rick!" Jake knuckled his forehead. "I forgot to tell you that Rick shot Bobby and stole a bunch of drugs from that motorcycle gang after I killed Caleb."

"Oh, my God? Is Bobby all right?"

"Yes. The bullet fractured his collar bone. It was touch and go for a while, but he's fine now."

"Ok. Then you need to tell me everything that happened."

Jake wiped his sweaty hands on his shirt and told her the fateful story from last night. He moved quickly over the killing and told her the details of finding Tom's watch, Rick's treachery, Bobby's valor, and Jake's long walk home.

When he was done, she eyed him suspiciously. "Is there anything else you're not telling me?"

"Nope. That's everything."

She smiled. It reached all the way up to her weary eyes. "Damn. I can't say I'm surprised about Rick, and I'm glad that Bobby is all right. I'll have to visit him when he's feeling better."

"He'll like that, especially if you bring a pizza."

"Pepperoni and sausage?"

Jake laughed. "With extra cheese."

"Got it." She leaned over and kissed him on the cheek. "Thanks for all that you've done for us, Jake. You could've been hurt too or killed."

His cheek felt warm where her lips had touched. "You're welcome. I'd do anything for you and the kids."

Nodding, she said, "I know. You're one of the last people I can count on in this fucked up world."

"I feel the same way about you," he said with a grin.

"And it might make me a bad person, but I'm happy Caleb is dead. I think I'll sleep peacefully tonight for the first time in a long time."

"Good. It was worth it." Jake smiled.

"Yes. But I hope this time won't mess with your head like Leroy Jones."

"Stop. I told you. Don't worry about me." He retrieved the watch from his pocket. "Here. This is yours."

She held up her hand. "I want Hunter to have it. It's his birthright. And you should be the one to give it to him."

"Are you sure?"

"Yes. Give me a minute, and I'll send him out." Mary gave Jake another hug. "Call me when you get to Chicago to let me know you got home safe."

"I will." He hugged her back.

"And please don't do anything else dumb. I can't lose anyone else that I love."

Jake stupidly promised, "I won't."

REVENGE

ABOUT THE AUTHOR

Henry Scott is the author of numerous short stories and novels since he began writing in 2015, though he's been an avid reader since the age of five. He lives in metro-Detroit with his family, two lovable golden retrievers, two cats, and a turtle. Fans can see plenty of pictures of them on his Instagram, @henry_scott_. He enjoys coffee, deep-dish pizza, true-crime TV shows, bonfires on cool nights, and his Triumph motorcycle.

Please visit his website and join his newsletter to learn about upcoming releases and the latest news.

www.henryscottauthor.com

Made in United States
North Haven, CT
29 May 2023

37122858R00124